O.B.E.

OUT-OF-BODY EXPERIENCE

O.B.E.

OUT-OF-BODY EXPERIENCE

A JOURNEY INTO PURE CONSCIOUSNESS...

MARQUIS WHITE

Enigma Productions LLC

Enigma Productions LLC

P.O. Box 80795
Rochester, MI 48308

Cover design by Enigma Productions
Drawing by John White

For information address:
Enigma Productions
P.O. Box 80795
Rochester, MI 48308
email: maw@enigmaw.com
WWW.ENIGMAW.COM

First Edition: 2007

10 9 8 7 6 5 4 3 2 1

Manufactured in the United States of America

Printed on acid free paper ∞

LCCN: 2007901746
ISBN: 978-0-9794321-6-3

To all those who've helped...
Ma, for all the love and providing the perfect sanctuary,
Tino, for your guidance and protection throughout the years,
Moe, for showing me the world in a new light,
Dad, for being open and honest,
Adam, for being far more than just a friend,
Victor, for helping me to stay on the path,
Gary, for providing aid when needed,
And especially Pam, without you this book would not have made it!

And, of course, Brittany, for being who you are and becoming one with me!
Because BMW's last forever...

Astral /'astrel, aas-/ **1:** consisting of, belonging to, or being a supersensible substance supposed to be next above the tangible world in refinement **2:** an astral body or spirit, counterpart of the physical human body accompanying but not usually separated from it in life and surviving its death —

Projection /pre'jekshen, prō'-/ **1:** the act of externalizing: as **(a):** the spontaneous localization of a sensory impression or memory image — **(b):** the attribution to other people and to objects of one's own ideas, feelings, or attitudes —

"The Way that can be walked is not the true way. The Name that can be spoken is not the true name." - Lao Tzu, Tao Te Ching

Within darkness there is comfort. Within emptiness there is peace. Is there emptiness in fulfillment? Can there be vision where there is no light? If truth lay all around us then why is it so many cannot see it? What is it that blinds us to the truth? So many search for the answers but few find them. This leads one to the question, are there answers out there? If so why can't we see or hear them? What if the answers were heard all the time and seen everywhere? What if that answer was no answer? Would anyone get it?

Chapter 1

At first there was darkness...

"Hello... Confused...? Don't be... We're just going to do a few exercises. First and foremost, relax. Get comfortable. You might want to keep your eyes closed. Try to sit upright if you can. Keep the spine erect... Ready?" a calm voice said.

Light Tibetan bells rang vibrantly in what sounded to be an enclosed room. The sound of these bells was both piercing and soothing to the ear.

"I want you to see if you can feel your inner body. Can you feel the life inside of you? It might be easier to start with your hands or feet. Don't think about it... just feel. It might only be warmth or even a tingling sensation. Take your time... Now, see if you can feel the rest of your body. Feel your arms, legs, chest, and your abdomen. Let the feeling run through you like a wave... Now, I want you to open your eyes,"

The young man, in his early twenties, sitting in the patient's chair, opened his eyes. He almost forgot he was in a doctor's office. His name was Alan, a quiet individual with dark features, average height for a male, a slim build, and a disdain for society's standards. He took notice to everything around him, plaques on the wall, pictures of the Doc's family, and so on, and then turned his attention to Doc, waiting to see what he would say next.

Doc, a middle-aged Caucasian man with a calm and pleasant demeanor, sat and studied Alan with a great deal of intrigue. He had been seeing Alan since his teenage years and viewed him as sort of a test subject for. Though Alan never knew what for.

Alan let out a deep yawn as he stretched, and was forced to smile at the doctor. These visits were truly helpful for him and they were usually the only time Alan would feel at ease. His body felt deeply relaxed and soothed, as if someone put a heating pad on every muscle within him.

"Well? How do you feel?" Doc asked.

"I feel... relaxed. Kind of weird, like... I don't know. It's different though. Feels good."

"Well, different is good. It lets you know there is progress of some kind... Are you still having trouble with your parents?"

The thought of his parents took away some of Alan's relaxation. "Eh, kind of. They think I'm wasting my life away. And by hounding me they feel I'll get the *big picture*."

"And what do you think the *big picture* is?" Doc asked in his usual friendly tone.

"You know, to be honest with you, I don't know. It's like they want me to be like them and do exactly what they did. And you definitely know I hate even thinking about going down that path."

"What is it, do you feel, you *must* do in life?"

"I don't know. I've got no clue what I want to do. I kind of just want to live... What do you think I'd be good at?"

"I didn't ask what you'd be good at," Doc said kindly. "I asked what you feel you *must* do. In other words, what drives you, or any of us for that matter?" Doc got out of his chair and walked to his bookshelf while Alan contemplated Doc's last question. He grabbed a medium sized black book from the top and glanced at it with a smile.

"Doc, to be honest with you I don't know what I want to do. I'm almost to the point where I feel as if I don't want to do anything just to prove to people that they can live without the need to *do something*. Do you know what I mean?" Alan asked feeling a little lost.

"I do. Probably more than you think I do," Doc said feeling the bond between them. "Do you think your anger or frustrations with the people around you have anything to do with your inability to find the answer to this dilemma?"

"I don't really feel angry with anybody in particular. I'm just tired of dealing with all of the stupidity. I wish that I could be free of all the pressure so I could be clear enough to make good decisions in life. I mean, I guess I want to make something of myself. I just really don't know what to make myself into."

Doc nodded his head as he watched Alan be tortured by his frustrations. "Well, here's the thing. You could spend the rest of your life searching for that answer. But the real question is: does what you do in life make you who you are?" Doc looked at Alan waiting to see his reaction.

Alan thought about the question and leaned back in the chair. "What makes us who we are?" Alan asked.

"Plenty of things could make you who you are. There are lots of parts to your *self*, if you understand what I am saying. But I guess, more importantly, what part of us is the real self? ...Or, maybe, there is no real self and nothing makes you who you are."

"Then what am I?"

Doc shrugged his shoulders and handed Alan the book he was holding titled *Astral Projection and the Nature of Reality*, by John Magnus.

Alan looked strangely at the book. "What's this for?"

"It has some pretty good exercises for clearing your mind of conditioned thinking patterns. I think you'll like it."

"What else should I do?" Alan asked paying little mind to the book.

"Why don't you go ahead and contemplate on what we talked about. Try not to think of an answer. Let it come to you," Doc said.

Alan flipped through the pages of the book. The material was on out-of-body experiences, it was a *how to* guide.

"And uh, try some of these meditations before bed. You might find the side affects interesting," Doc said with a little smile on his face.

Alan stood up feeling relaxed with the silly *I'm stoned and in bliss* look still on his face. He handed Doc a check signed by his parents and sighed.

"What's the matter?" Doc asked.

"Nothing…" Alan said while looking at the check. "No offense to you at all but I feel as if my parents could let me do something more with that money."

"I guess, if you never had it than you really never lost it, right?"

Alan nodded and sarcastically smiled. With a sigh of acceptance Alan walked out of the office getting back into the meditative frame of mind. Even the attractive receptionist behind the front desk didn't grab his attention, whereas normally he would check her out when walking out of his sessions. As usual, she didn't pay any attention to him either.

Alan came strolling out of the building feeling refreshed. He could almost hear the song *A Beautiful Morning* by the Rascals playing in the air as he walked across the street and into the small park. The sun shined on his face, the birds chirped his favorite song, and the squirrels played in the background. He felt very peaceful; something that rarely came in his day-to-day life. He almost always felt pressured by the expectations of the world around him and there were many pressures coming in. But there were two pressures that laid the biggest impact, women and money, both of which he didn't have.

He took a look at the mothers playing with their children on the swing sets nearby. At first he appreciated the beauty of love transferred between a mother and child and smiled. He watched the laughter from the toddler as he enjoyed the care and attention given by his mother. However, Alan's smile turned into a slight frown as the father came walking into the scene. Alan wasn't so much jealous as he was bothered by the fact that he was alone. Looking around at the random couples throughout the park, Alan was reminded once again of how badly he wanted to be with someone, he hadn't had a girlfriend in years. Aside from the occasional fling he remained in solitude.

With his hardest effort, Alan tried to shun out his thoughts about loneliness and sat down on a nearby bench. He turned his attention away from the couples and stared at the birds playing in a nearby water fountain.

This is more like it, he thought. *The trees are blowing in the wind, the birds are singing. What else do I need?*

But, just when Alan thought he was free and clear of his desires, a couple of attractive girls came strolling passed him. His head turned towards them like a tiger watching a prey. They both wore short skirts with low cut tops revealing their curvaceous physique. Alan couldn't help it. He didn't want to stare them down like a hawk but something within did it automatically, as if he had no say in the matter.

Damn it!

Alan turned his attention elsewhere. Unfortunately, there was simply more of the same in nearly every direction. Ironically, he was bothered by the presence of other people yet his frustrations were due to his loneliness. He couldn't take it anymore. The mental torture urged him to move on about his day.

Just as he stepped out of the park and into the street, the noise from the surrounding small city filtered into his consciousness. He took notice to this *pollution* and cringed. His bliss had faded away and the repetitive, predominantly negative thought patterns came back into action within his mind. The noise felt like a virus infecting his body.

Almost as if it was attracted, a young kid in a BMW nearly hit Alan as he crossed the street.

"Are you crazy?" Alan yelled.

The kid in the BMW returned gestures with the honk of his horn as Alan hopped onto the sidewalk.

The nerve of some people, Alan thought.

He thought of smashing the guy's windows with a rock and then smashing the guy. But, of course, he did neither. Seconds later Alan came crashing into a girl who was in a hurry.

"Oh I'm sorry. That was—"

"Look at where you're going prick," the girl said while walking away.

Alan put his hands up as if to say, "What do you want me to do". Of course, the girl's back was turned to him.

Is everyone in this town blind?

The wonderful effects of the therapy sessions were now long gone and Alan was back to normal.

The downtown of this quaint little city was a fairly busy place with an upscale edge to it. The trophy wives shopped for expensive, overpriced clothing and other knickknacks while their husbands worked for the money they spent. The teenyboppers walked freely through town goofing off and occasionally stopping into a coffee shop to spend some of their parent's money. Alan came strolling around the corner and walked through the main strip observing the people as he passed them by. It was one of his favorite pastimes.

Let's see what schmucks are roaming the town today.

He stood next to a group of young suburban would-be gangsters who reeked of marijuana.

Their eyes drooped and their speech was drawn out. "Dude I've got a dime bag in my truck. Let's smoke that now so my parents don't smell it on me later."

I don't think that'll make a difference, Alan thought. The overbearing smell forced him to keep walking.

Just down the street was an older conservative couple, both with scowls on their faces, arguing about something. The husband spoke furiously to his wife. "I'm not having an out of wedlock baby in my house!"

"We can't have her get an abortion. It's unholy!" She screamed back.

"I am a man of God. There is no way…"

Alan shut his ears off to the conversation and continued on with a faster stride. He stood at the corner watching everyone with a disgusted look on his face.

What do any of you know? If reality jumped up and bit you in the ass you'd look for someone to sue.

His cell phone rang just as he was dwelling on the ignorance of those surrounding him. Alan picked up the phone and a sarcastic smile appeared on his face. It was his friend Kyle. They'd been pals for years. They were thick as thieves in high school but as years pressed on their paths seemed to be splitting into different directions.

"What's up Kyle?" Alan said with little sincerity in his voice.

"What up player play? Whatchyou doin today?" His friend said on the phone.

Alan chuckled at the obviously fake dialect. "What's the scoop my brother?"

"Not much my brother from another mother," he switched to regular suburban dialect, "What are you up to dude? Oh wait a minute, wait a minute, you are, hold on a second, I'm getting a signal from an outside source, you aaarrrrrrrrrrrre," Kyle sneaked up behind Alan, "DOWNTOWN!"

Alan jolted around and shook his head at the prankster. "Jesus Christ. You scared the shit out of me," he said laughing.

Kyle poked his finger into Alan's chest. "You want to know how I knew you'd be down here? Cause ya-don't-go-anywhere else."

"You're here too."

"I know, I know, it's pathetic. And we're always asking why we don't get laid. Here's our answer," Kyle threw his hand up and looked around.

"There are chicks everywhere down here," Alan said.

"But we never talk to them."

"Well knock 'em dead Tyson. There's some prime 14-year-old meat down there," Alan said with a hint of sarcasm.

"Hey, there's nothing wrong with a little premature—" Kyle cut himself short when he noticed a mom and daughter walking behind them. The mom gave him the evil eyes knowing what he was about to say.

Alan noticed a group of girls down the street yapping away. "There you go. Right there, go *spit some game*."

"Forget about game I'ma spit the truth, I won't stop ti'll I get them in their birthday suit."

Alan shook his head once again at Kyle. "You need help."

"That's why I'm in school, my friend."

"How is conformity going for you anyway?"

"Ah it's alright. They haven't replaced my current chip with the 9-5 one yet so I've got some time to have a little fun. Your parents still naggin ya about starting up college?"

Alan had been pressured to go to college ever since he got out of high school; however, the thought of going put a knot in the pit of his stomach.

"Of course. It's the 'thing' to do so I should be doing it," Alan looked down as he thought about the pressure of *doing something with his life*.

Kyle walked on with an outer cockiness. "What's so wrong with school?"

"Nothing if you want to go. And I'm definitely not going because I *should*. It's not written into nature you know," Alan's tone grew a little more serious.

"But I think it's one of the Ten Commandments."

"Good cause I'm not Christian," Alan replied in a joking manner.

Kyle got into the preaching mood and stuck his chest out. "Ahh, but the commandments apply to everyone."

Alan laughed. "Except Catholic Priests near a group of alter boys."

Kyle laughed at the joke in a sort of fake over dramatic tone. "Except Catholic priests near a group of alter boys."

They came to a corner and looked around. Neither of them had anywhere to go. Kyle's mind was on the young flesh walking about while Alan was thinking about more serious matters.

This is stupid. I'm supposed to amount to something so I can become a part of this? Alan thought as he looked around.

Kyle saw the look in Alan's eyes. "You ok? You look like somethin's begging to pop out of that little brain of yours."

The frustration was popping out of Alan's eyes. "Our whole lives we've been told that if we do not make something of ourselves in society we won't amount to anything."

"Right... Where's the confusion?"

"If all my worth is in the eyes of others than I really don't see the point in living."

"It's just natural man. Get over it."

"No. It's far from natural. They drill this crap into our heads subliminally and it becomes a dominant driving force for people to either stress themselves out to make ends meet or do nothing and sulk in their misery... I've got to get out of here."

Kyle looked at Alan and shook his head at him. He became bored with standing on the corner and listening to his friend complain. "So what's your plan for today?"

"I don't know. I'm trying to avoid going home."

Kyle's response was automatic. "Let's get some java."

Alan shrugged his shoulders and they walked on.

Chapter 2

There was a coffee shop on almost every corner in this downtown. The *Java Lounge* was particularly popular with the youth and was well crowded. As they walked in Alan headed for the back while Kyle went to the counter. The place was filled with people studying, doing homework, yapping away on the cell phone, and talking to friends but somehow it remained relatively quiet. Alan sat down to relax a bit and happened to catch the conversation from the guy on the phone next to him.

"Yeah, I got back last week… no… no he's just sitting there doing nothing. I mean if you're that old and you don't have a job or you're not going to school…" the dude on the cell phone rambled.

Alan sighed as that statement seemed to hit home. He actually looked around paranoid as if someone were to know that this guy's words applied to him.

The guy continued, "Yeah I know, it's pathetic… he can't even get a girlfriend…"

That was enough of the degrading conversation. Alan got up to relocate to a new area. He looked around for a new spot but saw his friend over at the counter and decided to stand in line with him. But then, something else caught his eye on the way over there. There was a Brittany Spears clone sitting down across the room. Two more *hot chicks* sat next to her with some drinks and immediately began complaining. Though this was the type of person Alan saw as the epitome of the downfall of the human race, but he couldn't help but stare at them. The color combination of tan skin, pink undertones in the clothing, and sparkly jewelry automatically attracted Alan, and he didn't know why.

"Hey! Dude!" Kyle grabbed Alan's attention.

Alan turned to Kyle still mesmerized by the yapping mannequins. Kyle handed Alan a drink while watching him stare at the girls across the room. He then took notice to the book Alan was holding.

"What's that crap? Your shrink give you that?" Kyle asked sarcastically.

Alan barely paid him attention. He looked at the book for a second but quickly returned his attention to the girls sitting down. "Yeah he did."

"Is it about all that out of body stuff?"

"Yeah," Alan said. He looked at the book for a second and gave it some thought. "To be honest I don't know if I believe it's possible. I mean how do you know you're not just dreaming when it happens?"

"Dude, it's *all* in your head. There's this guy Carlos Castaneda. The guy claims he went to all sorts of alien worlds or something but the dude was on peyote the whole time," Kyle said not really knowing what he was talking about.

"He's had me do these meditations at night and they work as far as calming me down and relaxing me. But he says the meditations in here can have *different effects*, whatever those are."

Kyle's sarcasm was in open season. "You ever uh, leave your body?"

"I've had weird stuff happen like waking up paralyzed and having funky dreams. But to be honest I've never been through anything convincing enough to call substantial evidence."

"So could someone like, do something to your body while you're out? If you know what I mean."

Alan was able to shrug off Kyle's condescending joke, besides, his attention was on far more interesting matters. When Kyle realized Alan wasn't feeding his comedic ego he became frustrated.

"Just go talk to them!" Kyle scolded.

A shiver of nervousness flew down Alan's spine. "Come with me."

"I can't, I'm dating someone."

"You're lying your ass off!"

Alan needed a wingman. He was afraid he couldn't pilot his own plane without one. However, he wanted desperately to talk to these girls and the possibility of going in alone was growing.

"Go talk to them or I will," Kyle said calling Alan's bluff.

Alan knew him too well. He knew that Kyle was not the type to go in alone either.

"Ok. Do it."

"Ok, maybe I'm not dating anyone, but dude come on. Make the day interesting," he watched as Alan seriously contemplated going over there. "Come-on, you know you want to."

Alan thought about it for a moment and gathered his strength. "Alright I'll go, since this is so important to *you*."

He loosened his shoulders a bit a headed over to the table of *hot chicks*. Their mindless chatter grew louder as he approached and so did his nervousness. When he looked back at Kyle he thought about aborting the mission but when he turned back it was too late, the girls made eye contact. Alan couldn't help but freeze up. He was trapped and choking desperately, his plane was falling. All he could think about was why the hell he walked over to the table in the first place; he could have gone perfectly about his day without the embarrassment. But the personal slamming would have to come later; he had a mission to complete.

"Hey what's up? Do you guys mind if I uh, sit-t down?" Alan stuttered.

They girls look at each other and giggled. "Why?" said the over-tanned leader of the pack.

Alan thought hard about that one word, "why". The smile on his face faded as he saw them return to the mindless chatter between one another and completely ignore him. Kyle clinched his teeth at the sight of his friend plummeting to his doom. Angry and feeling extremely foolish, Alan stormed out of the shop.

"Bitches," he mumbled to himself as he slammed open the front door.

He bumped into someone walking by and spilled his drink in the process. The individual kept going while mumbling. "Excuse me".

Alan's mood jumped from bad to shitty as he tried to wipe off the beverage. He picked up his drink and shoved it into the trashcan.

Kyle walked out of the store and hung his head. He knew he should have been there with his friend but it was too amusing watching it from safety. While he was trying to hide his laughter he went over to the curb and lit a cigarette. "Didn't see it going that way."

Alan stood defeated and sulking in the embarrassment. "Neither did I, that's funny."

"Aaahhh they weren't your type anyway. You're deep, you know. You need someone like you."

"I'm no different from them. They just think they're queens of England because they've been getting attention their whole lives," Alan said with frustration while wiping off of his clothes.

"So why are you attracted to them?" Kyle asked with a little smirk on his face.

"I think it's because I've been subconsciously programmed to be."

Kyle gave Alan *the look* knowing he was a red-blooded male. "No dude, it's cause you're like the rest of us. You want a nice piece of you know what, no matter how dumb or stuck up it is."

"Maybe it's time to find something else in life."

"What are you talking about?"

"I mean if I slept with them I'd still feel just as empty. It's all bullshit," Alan felt a little sour now. All this talk about girls kept reminding him how hard of a time he had with them.

"What happened to that one girl you were talking to last week?"

"We talked once and the conversation seemed ok but… she's a party girl, you know," Alan avoided saying what he wanted to.

"So?"

He just didn't want to be with her. Though he wanted to hook up with a *hot chick* he needed more than a hot body.

"You know… she goes to clubs, gets wasted all the time, that sort of thing. I don't mix well in that crowd," Alan said knowing that this was Kyle's main skill.

"Give it a shot. It's not all that bad."

Ever since reaching the age of eighteen Kyle partied hard and left drunk. He would go anywhere he was invited, drink anything passed in front of him, and slept with just about anything that walked his way.

Alan shook his head. "I'm getting the hell out of here anyway."

Kyle laughed at that statement, he'd heard that before and found the idea silly. "Where are you going, Alan?"

"Anywhere but here. I can't stand this place anymore."

Alan truly felt that by moving away he would start fresh and be free of his problems.

"What makes you think it's gonna get better anywhere else?"

Alan thought about his idea becoming reality. The thought of him being in a place where no one knew who he was sent enthusiasm down his spine. "Because somewhere else I'll be starting all over."

There was a moment of silence as Kyle took a few final puffs from his cigarette. "You know, maybe you just need to accept what you have to do?"

"I need more though. There has got to be more out there."

"The whole world has got problems. I'm sure it's going to take a lot more than changing your address get passed yours," the tone in Kyle's voice grew more serious, something that rarely happened.

He looked down upon Alan for not doing the "right thing" and going to school. Kyle always said that people should follow in the footsteps of others to help build a better society, what he really meant was everything seemed fine the way it was and that trying to change things was a fool's job.

"What does it take to be free from problems? You know, since you know it all," Alan asked defensively.

Kyle, who was used to the conversation turning this way, tried to lighten up the mood. "My friend, that's a question that will never be answered."

"Well if there's a question to be asked there's an answer to be given."

The answer for "what it takes to be free" was one Alan would spend his life searching for if he had to.

"Maybe you could leave your body and never come back," Kyle sarcastically said.

Alan joked back with his friend. "Maybe."

Though when he thought about it the idea didn't seem all that bad.

Chapter 3

Alan came strolling down his subdivision late afternoon after hanging out with Kyle. Kyle had invited him to a party, but Alan was too wrapped up in his thoughts to enjoy going out anywhere. He figured he'd spend most of the time thinking about talking to somebody but never actually doing it. The usual outcome was Alan going home alone while Kyle went home with some girl he'd just met. Though, for some reason, Alan always went out to the parties in hopes of meeting someone different.

He lived in a cookie cutter neighborhood with cookie cutter neighbors. Today, of all days, seemed to be filled intense negativity. He looked all around him taking notice to the cars and lawns of the houses.

Everything looks the same… How do people live like this…? These people are the epitome of the drones of society… Hell, everybody's becoming a drone… You all give each other fake smiles and fake waves in the morning and then ridiculed and judged one another with your families in the evening… You're all fake…! I can't believe people work their entire lives to live like this… What the hell good is money if you hate your life…?

He complained mentally about his neighbors until finally reaching his driveway. He stood, stared, and hesitated until finally deciding to go in. The first thing Alan did when walking into his home was listen for noise. He always hoped to the high heavens that no one was home. Unfortunately, the television along with some chatter was immediately noticeable. He cringed and wished he hadn't walked through that door.

"Hello!" his mother yelled from another room.

"Hello," Alan reluctantly answered.

Across the house came the voice of his father. "Yeah hey! Come in here!"

He walked into the kitchen and saw his Mom cooking and his Dad watching a football game on TV in the living room. This was the usual at his house. They were both working parents but his father felt as if it were a woman's job to do womanly things like cooking and cleaning. Of course there were the manly things his mother would never have to do like cutting the grass or change a tire. Alan had grown his contempt for society, mostly, by watching his parents.

Alan looked at his dad and started analyzing his life. He frowned upon him while he watched the routine football game and occasionally flipped to the other fifty sports channels to check scores. *My God, this is sad... You're running in the rat race to sit down and watch T.V. No wonder your marriage is shallow... Everybody seems shallow... I don't think anybody appreciates anything anymore.* He looked at his mom cooking. *Poor ma, you're worn out and tired all the time... You've become a zombie... Waking up at six in the morning everyday to do the same damn thing for the same damn people in the same damn office.*

He walked over to the back window and stared outside, letting out a sigh in the process. *My God. We live so unnaturally.*

"Did your psychiatrist put you in a trance or do you normally stand in the middle of the room and zone out?" His mom asked in a joking tone.

Alan turned around a little startled. He almost forgot she was there. "I've just got a lot on my mind."

His mom raised her eyebrows while getting into interrogation mode. "Where were you today?"

"Oh you know. I was out," Alan said trying to avoid answering the question.

"No shit," his dad halfway responded while watching TV.

Knowing the answer to her next question she asked anyway. "Did you find a job?"

Alan immediately rolled his eyes. "Mom, come on. Not right now."

"What do you mean not right now? Did you at least enroll in class?" His mom asked.

"I checked it out," Alan responded with an attitude in a way only a child would say to their parent.

"Did you at least check out the community college?" She knew exactly what he did; however, she still felt the need to question him.

Alan sighed at the question. "I don't know what to look for."

"Take a math class or something. It's not *that* hard." his dad threw in a comment from the couch. He wasn't really involved in the conversation. He was more or less just shooting out words and letting them bounce off the walls in hope that someone would hear his opinion.

"Yeah, not for you," Alan said halfway under his breath.

Alan grabbed his stuff and tried to make way out of the room and the conversation. His dad simply stayed on the couch never looking Alan in the eye. He was too interested in the game.

"Hey, I went to school and finished."

"And you hate your life," Alan muttered.

His dad turned around as he caught some of that statement. "What was that?"

"You guys, I don't want to be stuck doing what you're doing, ok? If I go to school I want to make sure it's for what I want to do."

At that moment he thought to himself all the actions he could have taken to avoid talking to his parents. He almost wished he had gone to the party Kyle was going to.

His mother tried to talk to her son directly. She knew what it felt like to be talked *at* and not *to*, something her husband did well. "You don't have all the time in the world you know? Before you know it you're 30. And then you'll—"

Alan cut her off, "You'll be saying the same thing when you're 60."

"Alright smart-ass, keep it up."

His mom turned back to cooking. She was frustrated with her husband for not paying any real attention to her son when she felt he needed their guidance the most.

"You're going to have to do something with your life. You can't just sit around here hoping for something to come your way."

His mother's words made Alan feel tiny. One of the worst things he felt was that he was not good enough just as he was in the eyes of his parents. This was the part in the argument where Alan began poking at his parents. He started to think about ways he could offend them. "That's true, but I don't want to be miserable my whole life just so I can be a tool and say I did the respectable thing and went to school."

"It's not about the *respectable thing*. It's about making sure that you are prepared for the future," his dad shouted.

"No, what you mean to say is, it *shouldn't* be about the *respectable thing*. School is just like every other corporation in this country. It's there to take money from people who don't have it so some fat cat and his cronies can sit back and enjoy a brandy while driving their 911 Porsche to work."

Alan's dad finally turned from the television and looked to his wife for some support. "Where does he get this shit from?"

"I'm just trying to make sure that I'm going in the right direction and from what I can see a majority of the population is in the wrong direction."

"How can you see the *majority* of the population? You haven't been alive that long," his dad said.

Alan knew he was frustrating his father and it felt like sweet revenge.

"Look outside this little box we call home. Everyone is constantly competing to have a better lawn, a better car, more money, the right religion. It drives us crazy. And no offense but you guys are sailing on the same ship."

His dad looked at Mom wondering what his son was talking about.

"What does this have to do with you getting a job or going to school?" His mother asked.

"It has everything to do with it. I don't want to spend the rest of my life being fake! I want to live my life being true to myself."

His dad turned around, back to the game on TV. "You need to lay off the video games. Let me know when you join us in the real world."

Alan's mom thought about what her son was saying. Something inside of her sympathized and even understood what he was talking about.

Alan realized he now had the perfect chance to escape and avoid any further ridicule. So he slowly backed up and made his way upstairs.

His mom yelled from the kitchen, "Are you eating?"

"I'll grab some food later," Alan yelled back.

His dad, needing to get in one last jab, tossed in a comment, "You know without a job there would be no dinner!"

Alan went in his room slammed the bedroom door!

Alan's room wasn't that far off from the average twenty year-old's room. He had posters of his favorite movies up on the walls. Quite a few CD's and their cases lay on the dresser and floor. And of course no young males room would be complete without the video game system. But these things were becoming less interesting for Alan. Ever since making the choice not to go to college the pressures of society became a little heavier. His mind had been torturing him with thoughts and feelings of not being adequate enough to make it in life.

The most recent adoption to his room was the *Tao Te Ching,* a book about finding the answers and truth of the universe in nothing. The book sparked an inner quest within Alan and motivated him to stand up for what he felt to be true; you don't need to think, look like, or become anything other than what you are. And every answer could be found within the essence of the Tao, nothing. The simplicity of its pages was like music to his ears as he read them night after night. However, even with the knowledge and wisdom of the book he still felt a void within.

Alan picked up the *Tao Te Ching* and thought about its message. *If the universe is perfect as it is, why are so many struggling to find happiness? If all of this is true, than how can such obvious truths be so evasive to the masses?*

The lack of an answer was frustrating. So Alan sat in a chair and picked up one of the many magazines sprawled out on his desk. The headline read:

The 10 worst breakups in Hollywood history!

How can people read this crap? he wondered.

The attention that such *superficial filth* received was disgusting. This was one of the many magazines that circulated through his home and he hated it when his parents put junk like that in his room.

He crumbled up the magazine and chucked it into the trashcan. It was just another symbol of how society was going down the tubes and he was fed up with the bullshit around him.

"Is there nothing real on this planet?" he said out loud.

He walked over to his bed and looked at the book Doc gave him. After analyzing the book with skepticism he decided to open it up to a random page:

Behind the scenes lies a non-physical energy field that we call the astral. This field has no form, taste, or sound. It does not conform to how we believe a proper world should act. It is simply

neutral non-physical energy. There is nothing in it, except the ability to create anything.

An interesting concept, he thought. He read through a few more sections of the book out of curiosity. Some of the meditations that Doc recommended to him were in there.

Was he trying to get me to leave my body? Alan wondered.

The author noted that we are all *very* capable of traveling beyond the physical body and into a world free of rigid structures; in other words a non-solid, non-physical reality. This universe, as it said in the book, is in front of us all the time, the only thing stopping us from seeing this other dimension is our level of consciousness.

"Everything has a level of consciousness." This was something Alan had known for years and it instantly hooked him when he read it in the book.

Alan became deeply entrenched in the book's pages for hours. Chapter after chapter he was entangled by the ideas and the possibilities proclaimed within the book. The concept of leaving *this pathetic world behind* was so amazing to Alan that his doubts and skepticism turned into desire and wishful thinking. The author spoke of astral worlds and higher dimensions. And the way to access these dimensions was to raise our level of consciousness. Perhaps the most interesting concept of all, to Alan, was the possibility of creating your own world through your thoughts.

That is what I'm talking about!

Long into the night, Alan let out a slight yawn and blinked his eyes a few times. His ability to stay focused was fading. Realizing that he'd been reading for way longer than he expected he checked the clock on his dresser. It was three in the morning! He grabbed a bookmark from the shelf and placed it in the book.

Throughout his room were colorful lights that dramatically changed the atmosphere of the room. He turned on a dimly lit blue light and settled in for the night, though the mental stimulation of the book was still racing through his mind. The concepts and information he found not only fascinating, but also, now plausible. Even scientists knew that the world is made of energy, everything down to the smallest subatomic particle. Was it so far-fetched to believe that this energy operated on levels beyond our physical sight and reach?

Alan began trying some of the exercises he found easiest. First he started with his hands. The book said to relax and see if you could feel anything within the body; this was one Doc had him do all the time, though he never experienced any out-of-body state. The most that ever came out of Doc's meditations was Alan slowing his thoughts down and eventually falling asleep. This time, Alan was motivated and really gave it a try.

I feel everything around me but that's it.

But then, it came, a tingling sensation; it was strange, unlike anything he'd ever felt before. It was a faint feeling but it was there. As the feeling became more present Alan wondered if he wasn't just making it all up… and the mental noise of thinking began blocking out the feeling. But he was too determined to let it go. He tried again only this time with his feet… The sensation returned, this time to both his hands and his feet. He focused on both areas and the feeling intensified. It ran up his legs and arms eventually traveled throughout his entire body. The feeling was incredibly relaxing, like a deep inner body massage.

Why haven't I felt this before?

Like the book said to do, he imagined as if his body were like a rubber band. He tried to feel his *energy body* separate from his physical one. The effects of this were strange. He could feel his body rock back and forth, side to side like a wavering piñata, but his physical body wasn't moving at all. He expected something else to happen after this but as time passed on not much else happened. So, he decided to move on to a new technique. This time he imagined as if he were walking around his home. He imagined feeling the texture of the objects he came into contact with. He imagined running water over his hands in his mental sink. And then, as if tapping into a deeper source, the vividness of his imagination kicked in. Small minute details began to filter in on their own like the feeling of the cold tile in his bathroom pressed against his feet, and the feeling of warm air coming through the ventilation system. Then, he had an idea. Alan wondered what it would be like to look into the mental mirror of his mental bathroom. He lifted his head up and looked forward. The reflection was fuzzy at first but seconds later the image focused. Alan soon forgot that he was visualizing. Everything seemed so real and vivid. He leaned in closer, making sure to feel the sink beneath his hands, and studied the mental reflection of his face. Strangely, as he gazed at the mirror, the reflection smiled at him! Alan quickly opened his physical eyes in shock.

I didn't do that!

After a moment of excitement he calmed down and closed his eyes again. He ran through the exercise of feeling his energy body waver like before only this time he felt his energy body *separate* from his physical! It was as if he were walking away but still in the same spot. Before getting too wrapped in the new sensation he imagined walking through his home again. He ran through the same routine of feeling and touching as he strolled through his mental house.

But, after about fifteen minutes of mental travel, random thoughts began filtering in into his mind. *Wouldn't it be sweet to fly...? I wish I could leave my body and never come back... I should sneak into my neighbor's house and catch her naked...*

Before long his mental house became other locations and his feelings were lost into a sea of thoughts. Other scenarios then mixed into his meditation, like previous incidents throughout the day and so on. He was drifting off into unconsciousness.

Alan tried to fight the sleep off a few times but eventually gave in to the desire to lose consciousness. Before dosing off completely he took notice to how good it felt to fall asleep.

The urge is so strong. I wonder why that is?

Moments later he was out like a light.

Chapter 4

After a period of unconsciousness Alan subconsciously found himself in the woods. He wasn't in control of his actions; he was more or less following a track led by his instincts. He was dreaming!

The area was foggy and he was having a hard time seeing ahead. The abnormal height of all the trees stood out as one of the more predominant aspects about the forest. They seemed to have no end from Alan's point of view. All around him were noises of frogs, crickets, and other things that go bump in the night.

His subconscious was overlaid with an overlaid eerie unknown feeling. Alan's thoughts were fearful that he'd run into something hidden in the fog. But the fog, however, did not slow him down. He swam through it as if he were drawn to something ahead. That's when a feeling from outside Alan's subconscious began tugging at him. Something was drawing *him* in!

His inner urges lead him to a steep hill where, up at the top, there was a mysterious man hidden by shadows. The moon outlined his shadowy figure as he stood there waiting for Alan to approach him. This was it; this was what Alan was looking for in this creepy forest.

He hesitantly continued walking up the hill to find out just who this mystery man was. Alan's gait slowed when he heard a freaky noise filter in around him. Curiously he looked around to see if the noise was coming from something nearby. But it wasn't! Eerily, the closer he drew to the man at the top of the hill the louder the noise became. It soon became apparent what the noise was, thousands of voices ranting away, but there were too many of them speaking at once to make out what any of them were saying.

Alan stared at the person ahead wondering if the noise was coming from him. The man's dark hair, strong cheekbones, and olive skin tone resemble that of a Native American's, that and the nineteenth century Native American outfit. The guy looked like he came right out of a tee-pee. Alan found himself uncontrollably moving closer to the to the Native American and was now within arms reach.

Mysteriously, the voices slowed down just as the man spoke. "Al—n wa—p," said the Native American.

His words were hard to make out over the other voices but seconds later the voices came to an end. Alan and the Native American stared each other in the eyes.

"Who are you?" Alan asked.

"You are lost. Open your eyes!" The Native American said.

Alan stood still feeling clearer than he'd ever felt before. Normally there would be an endless succession of streaming thoughts running through his mind, but not now. He felt so...conscious. The dream was turning into reality. Alan was becoming fully conscious within the dream, realizing at the same time that he was dreaming. The Native American put his hand on Alan's forehead. This had an effect on him unlike anything Alan had ever felt.

An odd vibration ran vigorously through his body. The feeling was harmless but it was strong enough to scare the *shit* out of him! Alan stared at his hands wondering what the hell was happening to him. When he looked back up the Native American was no longer there, Alan was there! Alan was staring at himself!

The fear quickly snapped him back to his room. He opened his eyes startled, but did not move.

What a screwed up dream.

Something else was strange now. Alan had the urge to roll over but couldn't. He couldn't move at all. He was paralyzed! That freakish vibration feeling returned accompanied with a strange buzzing noise. The feeling rushed through his body and the noise traveled with it. Suddenly three hard knocks at the door snapped him out of the trance. Control of his body returned and he instantly sat up. The first thing he did was check out his body. Everything seemed normal.

"Yeah!" he answered expecting it to be his parents.

He waited for an answer but...nothing.

"Who is it?" he said with a frustrated tone.

No reply. He got up and slowly and cracked open the door. No one. Calmly but quickly, Alan grabbed a bat from his closet and approached the door. He opened it all the way very slowly and entered the hallway waiting for some intruder to jump out from the shadows. There was no one out there. He checked across the hall. It too was safe. He checked down the stairs. Safe. He ran down to the basement and turned on a light, bat ready to swing. Nothing!

Stooped and still groggy Alan walked back upstairs and stood in the open living room. He stared out of the large window looking into his backyard. Everything seemed normal. The moon outlined his silhouette in the darkness, as he stood attracted to it.

Once again a knocking noise was heard at a door. Alan looked around... somehow he was mysteriously back in his bedroom. It was like he just woke up from a dream but he wasn't dreaming... was he? This time he charged to investigate. He opened the door, no bat this time, and searched the hallway. There was an odd figure across from his room. Someone was balled up in the shadows off in the corner of the hallway. A rush of fear trickled through his body. Alan approached the person with caution. He stuck his hand out to wake the person on the ground. It was him! The person on the ground was Alan!

The being lying on the ground lifted his head up sharply looked at his counterpart. "What!"

Alan backed up into the bathroom, as he was jolted with a rush of fear. When he turned around he found himself looking in the mirror once more. The reflection was once again smiling; the real Alan was not. The vibrations returned stronger than ever this time and the closer he got to the mirror the louder that buzzing noise grew. He put his hand to the mirror and the reflection did the same. Their hands met at the surface and melded into each other like they were touching water. Alan put up his other hand and leaned in out of sheer curiosity. The reflection and Alan met at nose point. Their faces came together as if they were both passing through the surface at the same time, but no one came out of the other end.

Alan opened his eyes once inside what should have been the mirror, but he was back in his bedroom! The buzzing noise now sounded like a UFO hovering above and in full gear! But there was nothing above or around him. The noise was coming from within and the pulsating vibration grew even heavier. Soon, both the noise and the vibration began to flow in unison.

In one fluid motion Alan sat up, putting an end to the vibrations and the buzzing. He took a second and sucked in everything that just happened.

What is going on?

However, something was still wrong. He had that strange feeling once again, though this one wasn't all that bad. He felt clearer, lighter, and free, kind of like he did in the forest. But something else was different. The random thoughts in his head had cleared once again but the feeling of freedom was new, like he dropped all body weight. There was also no fear, no emotion. Alan felt strangely omnipotent but in the most graceful way. He felt as if there wasn't a thing in the world that could harm him.

The sound of ducks quacking took his attention outside the window. He'd never heard anything so clearly. The depth and range of the sound was so clear and crisp. Alan wondered what he ate before bed because he'd never felt so great. He felt like he took a bath in the fountain of purity.

When he got up to close the window he immediately noticed his movements were different. He didn't feel the constraints of his muscles and skin. There was no strain to move around. Everything about his movements was light and effortless. The only thing that kept him from investigating the situation further was his ability to make contact with objects. He felt his hands grabbing the bed and pushing off of it. But there was something different about that too. His contact with the objects around him, the floor, the bed and so on, were much more intimate. It was like he was connecting with objects on a level deeper than any sense perception could ever pick up. To put it simply, he felt like he was becoming everything he touched!

Am I dreaming again?

When he continued to the window he noticed he was floating. Now there was no question about what was happening.

But how? he wondered. *How could I have gotten out? I didn't see my body.*

When Alan turned around he stood like a statue looking towards his bed. It wasn't panic on his face, but rather confused disorientation. Lying on his bed was *his* physical body. The feeling running through him was so wondrous and beyond comprehension that he took it for fear at first. Although it was the best feeling of fear he'd ever felt.

He moved in closer to get a good look. His body looked so material, so frail and imperfect, so…useless. Strangely, at that moment he realized that all of human pride and possessiveness, all the fighting to protect and gain, were the most futile of actions.

What's it all for? We're living for the wrong things, he thought with an inner smile. If he had eyes he would have cried from joy at that moment.

But then it hit him hard. He was standing above his living, breathing body. This was who he thought he was his entire life. How could *he* be standing over *himself?* The question was so perplexing it forced him to back up from the feelings of disillusionment. He backed up right through his own door not realizing what happened until he was in the hallway. Now things were interesting. If he could go through walls what else could he do?

Before heading down the stairs he felt the need to check on his parents. He didn't know if he'd see them again. At this point anything could have been happening to him and on top of that he didn't know if he ever *wanted* to return. As he approached the door he stuck his hand through first to test it out. The feeling was amazing! It was like he was communicating with the wood and every other particle. It may have been an inanimate object but there was life in that door. There was life in the carpet, the banister, the air, everything! Once again if he had tears he would have shed them at that moment. His whole being was filled with an overwhelming sense of joy and appreciation. He was totally free. He peeked through the doorway and watched his parents snoring in their sleep for a few seconds. Now, it was time to play.

Alan wafted down the stairs and through the front door. He was stunned. The outside world was even more incredible. Everything breathed so much life. From the clouds above to the moon and beyond, the universe was all one living, breathing system. The trees, grass and lake in the distance all seemed to *communicate* with each other. Alan slowly began to understand what was being "said". Alan felt like a humble cell in gigantic body. If there were ever an answer to the universe it was definitely out here in front of him.

The sound of the wind blowing crisply flew by and this gave Alan an idea. One of Alan's long time dreams was to be able to fly and now, more than ever, seemed like the time to do it. He opened his arms as if asking to be taken into the skies, and without effort, there he went.

At first he only flew to the roof of his own home but his desires would soon be unleashed. Taking a glance at the moon Alan began laughing hysterically. There wasn't a thing he couldn't do nor a place he couldn't go. He checked out the next rooftop and thought for a second. *How fast can I go?*

He backed up like a bullet in a barrel and shot forward, jumping from one roof to the next. His landings were feather light but his movements were swift and quick. Roof after roof he tested his ability to jump as far and as high as he wanted to. After reaching the last roof Alan soared into the air like an eagle. He twirled around like a stunt plane doing tricks. Loop after loop Alan was having the time of his life. That's when he captured a glance of the ground below him. Suddenly a fear of falling entered his psyche and he slowly headed for the ground. The fear seemed to debilitate his abilities to go beyond what he would consider normal.

As he watched the sky fall away, he felt disappointed. He wanted to stay up there. The cleanest landing strip available was a street to his left. Alan dived down and returned to the safe looking surface. Once again the landing was feather soft. He was so discouraged as he looked up, wanting to be back into the sky. It was so much fun and it was all cut short.

In the distance was the sound of a motor. He looked behind him to find a truck headed straight for him.

I could move but why? I'm invincible out here… right?

Alan walked toward the vehicle testing to see what would happen. His bravery thickened and he stuck out his *chest* as he waited for impact. Three seconds before it hit Alan shut his eyes and cringed… the truck passed right through him. Alan peeked out from his arms checking to see what happened. He was fine, just as he thought he would be.

Now it was time for more exploration. Alan looked into the sky once again and floated upwards slowly. He made sure not to look at the ground as that might have brought him down again. The higher he ascended, the faster he went. Once he was higher than he'd ever been he looked down towards the surface. It looked so tiny down there.

Where would I like to go?

Alan spread those wings again and propelled into motion. He kept his speed along fifty miles an hour, something he was use to, but soon his curiosity kicked in and he began speeding up at an alarming rate. His speed jumped from fifty to five hundred in three seconds. He reached the speed of sound and did not stop there. One thousand, five thousand, fifteen thousand miles an hour he traveled with ease!

When he stopped he was obviously no longer at home. Beneath him was the color green, and not the dull green of farmland, but the rich vibrant green of a rainforest! The time of day had also changed.

This is nuts!

Alan swooped down for a closer look. The first thing he noticed was how different the animal and plant-life was. It was fascinating just to see the amount of color that was present in a rain forest. Everything was so vibrant and alive. This was in great contrast to the sight he was used to, dull suburban life. But as fascinating as it all was, Alan quickly pulled back up before the fear got to him again and he was stuck in the Amazon.

Hmmm.

He was thinking of just where he wanted to go. Realizing now that his potential was limitless, Alan looked to the stars and got excited. He put his gears into warp drive and zapped into *outer space*!

Chapter 5

Alan traveled nearly the speed of light and it was quickly becoming overwhelming. Everything around him was a blur, if that can even describe it. He realized that, in this form, he could probably go as fast as he wanted and the sheer capability of his potential frightened him to a halt. When he stopped he witnessed one of he most amazing sites he'd ever seen, the planet *Jupiter*! Its size was beyond anything he'd ever fathomed and the surface was even more awe-inspiring. He could see endless miles of gaseous clouds swirling within the atmosphere; they covered the entire planet. Lightning tangents ran amuck throughout what looked to be massive hurricanes. The sizes of the storms were larger than *Earth*! It was truly amazing.

Alan looked around and was obviously nowhere near his home planet. This realization prompted the fear that he might never return home. He now regretted never paying attention in astronomy. Those years of boring planetary alignment would have paid off right about now. But when he looked around at the rest of space he wondered at its magnificence. Its infinite depth and countless stars were enough to look at for a lifetime, but for right now they were helping to calm him down. He flew out to get a better view of the sun. It looked small from here. The sun had never looked small. That's when Alan realized how cool it was to actually be able to look at the sun. Then he wondered where else he could go.

What if I could find planets with alien life on them?

Alan looked out and found what looked to be the North Star. Like a slingshot Alan backed up as if to gain momentum. When he fired forward he instantly entered light speed, everything around him was a blur. Stars and planets looked like strings of spaghetti as he passed them by. And then he did it; he traveled faster than the speed of light! At first he found himself in total blackness. No planets. No stars. Nothing. Then, a white light cracked through the space in front of him. It opened up the space around him like a paper bag being ripped apart. Soon Alan was engulfed in a brilliant white light and everything stopped moving, or better put; Alan realized that there was nowhere to move to! Everything was light. There was no apparent source either.

Something soon caught his eye, something that wasn't there before. There was a crack in the light and it wasn't three-dimensional. This was no object.

Is it space? he wondered.

He reached his hand out to touch it. Instead of finding an opening he found a surface of some kind. It was strange. The texture felt familiar, kind of like metal. He pushed at the surface revealing it to be a door. It was large and copper colored. Strangely enough it wasn't the light revealing the appearance it was the absence of light. He gave it one more strong push and opened the large door completely. It sounded like it hadn't been oiled in decades. The light from behind him seeped into the room like a cloud of smoke.

Beyond this doorway was a room built out of blue marble about the size of a large auditorium with a dome ceiling and Roman pillars to support it. The swirls of black embedded in the marble moved around like waves in an ocean. The ceiling above was like a movie screen. At first it looked like the depths of space but then the stars came together forming odd formations of different shapes and sizes.

To the far right were ten aisles of bookshelves several stories high; they extended further than any eye could ever see. Around the edges of the room were more large copper colored doors with people coming in and out. Directly opposite of the bookshelves was the largest of the doors. It was two stories high and made of gold. No one came out of this door but a couple of people went through it. When this door opened a heavenly light nearly blinded everyone. In the middle of the room, which was two steps lower than the rest, were four rectangular glass cases each filled with beaming luminous balls of light.

Hundreds of people walked around the room, people not only of different ethnic backgrounds and races but people of different time periods! All were dressed in different eras of clothing, from the Stone Age and Biblical times to the Renaissance period and modern day businessman. Some looked as astonished as Alan while others seemed to be used to the surroundings and mingled about in total comfort. For the uninitiated there were dozens of monk-like individuals walking around greeting those who looked lost. They were dressed in white robes and moved very gracefully. One of the monk" like tour guides was giving a lost looking group of Chinese businessmen a tour around the place. He and Alan made eye contact for about two seconds, but in that short amount of time it was as if they spoke an entire conversation. Almost as if Alan sent a signal out and this guy picked it up and connected with him. As the guy turned his head Alan continued on.

He stepped further into the blue room aware of every step he took. He was mainly interested in the center of the room. As he stepped closer he gazed uncontrollably at the light within the cases. There was something so powerful about them. He could feel an odd subconscious urge drawing him towards them. Directly in the center of the room was a golden triangle embedded on the floor. It was within the center of this triangle, directly center of all four pillars, that Alan felt the need to stand. As he stepped onto the center of this triangle a surge of power rushed through his astral body. He felt as if the power of creation was within his hands. When both feet were on the triangle everything around him turned dim but the pillars of light, Alan and the triangle beneath his feet were illuminated like light bulbs. The feeling of power and control were so overwhelming he was left to cry with a smile on his face. The feeling was so great and so intense everything around him became a blur to his awareness.

His astral body began to change its shape. The room began to lose its solidity and color. He took a look at the ceiling and watched as the swirls of light changed into a reflection of space. There were millions of stars and planets, asteroids, and meteorites. A shooting star whizzed across and faded away. In some odd and unexplainable way Alan was able to view, what we consider, the entire *universe*! He watched dumbfounded. If the sites he witnessed earlier were not enough, he was truly awe-inspired now.

"First time here eh?" a voice said from behind.

The light from the pillars faded away, his body and the room return to *normal*. Alan turned around to find a young oriental looking guy in his early thirties with dark features, dressed in white robes with a Chinese symbol on it, standing behind him. He was the "monk" tour guide who he'd had made eye contact with.

At first Alan couldn't speak. It took a moment for him to come back from that feeling of orgasmic bliss, but slowly the silly smile faded away from his face. As Alan came back to normal he realized it was a person speaking to him and that the proper thing to do was respond.

"Where am I?" Alan said still feeling omnipotent.

"I like to call it home but most call it the Akashic Library," the man said.

Alan looked around the place expecting to understand the meaning of the name but fell short. "I don't uh…"

"To explain this place wouldn't do it justice. Let me show you around," the man in the robe raised his arm and extended it outward.

Alan took a look at some of the people walking around. He saw a couple of Buddhist monks walking along bowing their heads at the people they greeted. His eyes then traveled to a group of Shamanistic Aborigines sitting down meditating. Everyone and everything was so wonderful to Alan. The man in the white robes noticed Alan looking at these men.

"Those are the ones who frequent this place," said the man in the white robes.

Alan noticed a guy straight out of the thirties staring at the ceiling and everyone around him just like he had done. The man placed his hands around one of the pillars and dropped to the floor while holding on. He too had that silly smile on his face just as Alan did when he stepped on the triangle.

"He's a little more like you," the man in the white robe said.

"Who are you?" Alan asked while checking out the man's attire.

"For you my name is Wu Ming," he said with a friendly smile on his face.

"What is it for everyone else?"

"The word means nameless as does this symbol," Wu pointed to the symbol on his back. "I am a guide for those still lost in conceptualized living."

Alan sarcastically asked, "Why does everyone think I'm lost?"

They walked over to the endless bookshelves. Alan looked down the aisles and found himself squinting his eyes. The endless length of the shelves was almost frustrating to his understanding.

How is anyone supposed to get to the last book?

Wu Ming looked up, down and across the shelves. "These shelves hold information to anything and everything you'd ever want to know; information about the pasts and information about the futures. There's information about every existence, every possibility and every thought to go along with it. There is an endless source of information here."

Alan thought about the plural added to the terms past and future as if there were more than one. "Pasts?"

Wu smiled, now understanding that Alan was from an era where people lived only in the concepts of their minds. "My friend we all live in a universe of endless possibilities. For every possible scenario there is, was and could be, someone and something has lived through it."

Wu took Alan over to the center of the room. The man who was holding on to the glass pillar stepped onto the golden triangle. First came the smile on his face then, like Alan, his body lit up like Alan's did, only this guy turned into a gaseous form of light and evaporated. Alan's jaw dropped as he witnessed this unusual phenomenon. Wu smiled at Alan like a parent would do to a child in a toy store. Wu pointed to one of the glass cases taking Alan's attention away from the center.

"Did that happen to me?" Alan asked.

"Almost," Wu Ming replied. "You see this? This is the beginning. This is consciousness in the purest form you can see it. This is the origin of all things."

"What are you calling consciousness?" Alan asked

"Consciousness is what manifests everything in the universe. It's the intelligence that provides the miracle of birth. It's what allows particles to bond and stay connected. And, of course, it is those particles too. Consciousness, in the way that I use the word, is creation," Wu pointed up to the ceiling, "Let me show you."

He walked Alan over to the center of the triangle and they both stepped on it. Like before, the light from the glass pillars illuminated everything. That feeling of absolute power rushed through Alan's body again and their bodies fuzzed away into particles of light.

Wu Ming looked over at the hypnotized Alan. "Just try to relax. The feeling will stabilize in a few moments."

The ceiling above sort of melted around them and became the endless depth of space. Stars, comets, and planets flew by like a sort of three dimensional computer simulation. And just as Wu said it would the feelings within Alan were stabilizing. When Alan snapped out of his trance, the first thing he noticed was that he had no body. They were both points of consciousness floating about. Alan could feel the presence of Wu Ming rather than see it. That's when the thought occurred to Alan, *What am I?*

"Am I, and by *I*, I mean all of me, consciousness?" Alan asked.

"Be careful not to get too wrapped up in words. What I am calling consciousness is the awareness that lies within everything and everyone. Some might call it the origin or source of creation. Pure energy is my favorite term," Wu Ming said.

"But what am I?" Asked a confused Alan.

"You are the awareness," Wu Ming replied. "You are the same as everything else. You are simply aware of yourself. You could be called a self aware point of consciousness."

The planets around them morphed into subatomic particles. Those particles morphed into atoms and those atoms morphed into molecules, which in turn morphed into cells.

"You, like the cells in your physical body, are part of a self sustaining system. The system I am referring to is existence, the world of manifestation."

"What other systems are there?" Alan asked.

"Oh, there are countless other systems but the origin of these systems is the unmanifested, non-existence. What you might call the true origin of all things. It really isn't a system because... it really isn't anything at all. But since we are using words to communicate we will call it the system beyond all systems."

The cells morphed into a human body and that human body faded away into nothing. Out of nothing came a tiny ball of really dense matter. It swirled around like a ball of hot liquid and finally ignited. The particles of the explosion shot everywhere. Those particles morphed into galaxies of hot gasses and those gasses morphed into stars and planets. One planet in particular was the product of the next morphing sequence. Alan was looking at Earth as a planet of hot gasses. Those gasses cooled down in most areas forming one large ocean with volcanoes sporadically placed throughout the planet, both above and below the water. They dove beneath the great ocean of earth and arrived at an under water volcano spewing its lava. That lava morphed into landmasses and those masses separated into the masses of present day continents.

"What about the creator. Is there no God?"

Alan was brought up Christian but over the years his faith diminished. What was left was a bunch of questions and a hint of fear still embedded within him from the early teachings of organized religion.

"God is a word as is consciousness. The humans of your time are trapped in words. They are trapped in their thoughts and controlled by the emotions their thoughts produce. By definition, God means the creator."

"Humans create all the time."

"That's because you are another form of consciousness. It could be said that you are an extension of God or whatever word you choose to say," the words of Wu Ming were starting to click in Alan. "In fact every second you create with your thoughts and concepts. Humans are *stuck* in a state of constant creation. They can't stop."

The continents swirled into a busy city street as the people sheepishly traveled about in their daily lives.

"Reality for most humans is what they are doing and above that what they and other people think about what they are doing. They constantly do more and more never truly finding satisfaction but believing that satisfaction will come from their actions."

"But..." Alan wasn't sure what to say.

"The average human, aside from sleep, will spend less than fifteen hours in their life without a thought running through their head. You are constantly bombarded with signals, interpretations, and judgments unable to stop or see passed them."

"Why can't we see passed them?"

"Because you believe that you are your thoughts, feelings, emotions, and actions."

The image changed from busy city streets to random images of people interacting, suffering, getting angry, and so on.

"That belief keeps you stuck in the creation of thoughts. You hardly get a pause in the constant stream of thinking but when you do, you feel great. Unfortunately that usually only comes after you've gotten what you wanted and only for a very short period. Rarely do you feel satisfied for any other reason."

Alan felt the need to defend his species. "We can get out though. There are some of us that aren't stuck... right?"

The thought that everyone on the planet was blind to the truth scared Alan. It gave him a feeling of hopelessness.

"There are a few and the numbers are growing. But are they growing fast enough to save themselves is the question."

The images turned into the warfare and the violence that plagues earth. The scenes changed rapidly from one act of violence to another throughout the ages. Hitler, Stalin, Amin, Osama, Bush, one after the other, leaders and dictators, including the Prime Ministers and Presidents of the free countries, were shown in acts of action and reaction; one act of ignorance creating another in an endless cycle. The images then changed to people getting wasted in bars and at parties, prostitutes walking the streets selling their bodies for money, people worshiping devilish cult leaders and blindly following the ideals behind them, religious leaders preaching control and domination, the holy wars, the civil wars, kids homeless on the street starving, begging for food, doctors in hospitals treating the sick, mass famine and disease, THE INSANITY, THE TORTURE!

The images around them faded into darkness and left Alan speechless. Even without a body he felt so heavy, so burdened by his own species' ignorance.

"Humans are so stuck in identification with their minds that they're always afraid of what's outside of it, what they can't control. It's driving you insane," Wu said.

Instead of a blissful trance he was feeling drenched in negativity. He was so distraught he barely paid attention to Wu's last comment.

"What?"

"It's why you suffer the way you do. Humans are so afraid of losing the things that make up their identities that you're constantly fighting to keep them. Of course what they are really doing is fighting to keep the concepts alive in their minds."

These words hit Alan at his core. "Isn't that who we are? Our identity?" He felt everything had been stripped away from him, everything that ever truly mattered.

"Your identity is something that belongs to you in some respects but something that belongs to you can be lost and anything that can be lost isn't who you are," Wu chuckled at his own words, "Otherwise *you'd* be searching for *yourself*."

But how could we lose ourselves? Are we not ourselves all the time, even when we think we are not? Alan thought.

There was still a little inspiration left within him. The thought that he wasn't his mind discouraged him at first but the realization that he was more gave him hope. *If people are more then what they identify with then there is the possibility that they can, not only see passed, but also live passed what they fear the most, and what humans fear most is losing themselves.*

A small trickle of light formed beneath them. Then came the formation of the pillars and triangle followed by the rest of the blue room. They wafted down from the ceiling as tiny balls of light and burst into particles, which then formed into their bodies. Alan walked away from the center. He was still fascinated by what just happened. He checked out his body and wondered about the laws that governed the current world he was in.

"I don't get it. One second I'm flying around my neighborhood the next I'm floating in space and now I'm in here, in this sort of intergalactic waiting room. Where exactly am I?" Alan asked.

"You're here."

"...Ok. Where is that?"

"I'll say it's a world between the form and the formless. Matter isn't as rigid out here and is drastically affected by your level of consciousness. You could say this place is a gateway."

"To what?" Alan asked.

"Well you can't really call it anything because it can be anything you want. Everything can change from one thing to the next in an instant."

"How did I get out here?"

"Because you came, it's that simple… the ones that make it this far are usually the ones awake enough to see passed what their mind tells them. You seem like you're searching for the truth to your reality."

"Have I found it?"

"My friend the truth has always been in front of you no matter where you were. The *search* for truth is just another way of getting lost in the concept of it."

Alan simply nodded his head. Wu placed a gentle hand on his back and they walked over to one of the large iron doors. Wu opened it up with a foreshadowing smile. Through the door was Alan's neighborhood just the way he left it. Alan looked at Wu a little disappointed.

"So. Do you want to go home?" Wu Ming asked Alan. Wu could tell Alan was anxious to explore but as kind of disclaimer he offered him the chance to return home.

"Kind of tired of home. Where else can I go?"

A night in shinning armor opened a door three doors down. Alan gazed upon the soldier with the oddest expression. The night removed his helmet and walked into the room bewildered.

Wu looked at Alan and smiled. "Anywhere you want."

"What else is up there?" Alan pointed to the ceiling above the triangle.

"I don't know if you're ready for that."

Alan actually took slight offense to that, he wasn't afraid of anything… he thought. He walked over to the pillars and looked up into the dome of infinite possibilities.

"Why not?" he said like a boy wanting to be a man.

"Well the choice is yours. But it is easy to get lost up there."

"Lost? Like the human race lost?" Alan asked. Wu Ming didn't answer. "Well, like you said, I was aware enough to make it this far. Why wouldn't I make it back?"

Wu Ming remained silent. Alan was waiting for him to give his approval but it never came. Alan would have to make the choice on his own.

"I'll do it," he said with a cocky smile on his face.

Alan walked over to the center and turned to face Wu Ming. The lights filtered in as usual followed by the feelings of creative power.

"Can you feel that? It feels great."

"I feel it all the time. No matter where I am."

"What is it?"

"That's for you to find out," Wu said with a saucy smirk on his face.

Alan's body began to separate into tiny pieces. "What's happening?"

"Would you like some advise?" Wu asked ignoring Alan's question.

Alan nodded wondering why the hell he didn't say anything before he hopped onto the triangle.

"Be aware of your thoughts. It's easy to get lost in them."

You already said that, Alan thought. "I'll be ok out here… right?" he asked before disappearing.

Alan was fading into the light. As Wu spoke Alan had a hard time hearing him.

"You've always been ok. Just accept whatever co…"

Alan heard nothing else from him. Before long everything around Alan was lost in a sea of light.

Chapter 6

A brilliant flash of colors exploded all at once! Alan felt as if he was at a disco ball. At a snail's pace the colors intertwined together forming a dark shade of blue. The blue materialized into a vast body of water filled with vegetation, small fish, and creatures much larger than Alan! He looked around as a formless point of consciousness. It felt weird looking around and not having a body, almost like a security camera watching the world around it. Then, seconds later, Alan's thoughts of a body caused a massive pressure buildup in the water. The pressure carried Alan to the top and rocketed him out of the water and into the sky. Particles from all directions formed together around him. First the outline was drawn and then came the water to fill in the mass. Seconds later he had not only his body back but also the clothes he was wearing when he first went to sleep. The satisfaction of having his body was cut short when gravity came into effect and pulled him down into the water. Alan belly flopped on the lake below like a pancake, but he quickly resurfaced.

"What the hell is going on?" he said, a little slaphappy.

He was in the dead center of a large lake. All around the lake were mountains and forests. He thought about flying out of the water but was unable to do so. His earthly limitations had returned for some reason. Luckily, about a good mile away was the shore, so Alan sucked it up and started swimming.

Finally he reached the edge. As he took a look up he noticed the mountains formed a perfect circle around him.

That's strange? he thought.

The next move was obviously to venture off into the woods. He looked above at the treetops and closed his eyes. Unfortunately, just as he suspected, things returned to normal... sort of. Alan was sorely disappointed that he couldn't fly anymore. He thought he'd be able to come out here and create and do what he wanted.

Where's the refund?

Just when his mind was kicking in full throttle something caught his eye. About forty feet ahead there was a black bulge at the bottom of a tree. As he drew nearer he was surprised to find that that bulge was a foot. The foot belonged to a gorgeous young girl, about his age, lying down passed out against a tree.

She's beautiful... What the hell is she doing out here...? I didn't create her... Of course I didn't create these woods either.

At first he looked at her with curiosity. It seemed so weird to be next to another human out in these woods. She had a very innocent look to her but mature in the same respect, maybe it was in the clothes or haircut. She was about five-six with long black, well-groomed hair, fair colored skin, though tanned, and the eyes of a feline. She was wearing a vest with a black turtleneck and black slacks, winter stuff. Alan took notice to how warm the temperature was and came to the realization that she must be like him, lost and confused.

Alan leaned in closer to see if she was breathing but pulled back a little to admire her beauty once more. He could not have imagined a more attractive girl. Her outfit looked modern so it let him know she'd relate to him at least on some level, if she woke up that is. As useless as it was out here he checked her pockets for an ID.

Untimely for Alan, the girl began to feel something rocking her. She slowly opened one eye and all she could see and feel was a male fooling around *within* her clothes.

She knocked him aside the head and yelled at the top of her lungs. "Get away! HELP! Somebody help me!"

She sprung to her feet and took off with cat like reflexes.

Alan was really embarrassed at this point. "No, no don't worry. I wasn't trying to..." he cut himself short seeing how useless it was yelling for her to come back. He thought about it and realized that he'd be feeling the same way if he were she. Alan chased her down trying hard to get her attention. "I was just trying to see if you were alive!"

"Why were you in my pants creep?" she yelled while running.

The only clear path was in front and it leads up the mountain. The girl staggered as she climbed up the rocky slope with the heels she had on. Alan kept his distance but he could have easily caught up to her.

"Just stop. Please let me explain," he pleaded.

She continued to climb. The path up was mostly rock, making it hard for her to get some footing. Finally, she reached a flat bed and pulled herself up. The girl shivered with fear when she found that it dead-ended. Her only escape route was another steep climb up, one she had become too tired to make. She stopped and looked back like a cornered animal prepared to sink her claws into Alan.

"I'll kick your nuts if you come near me!"

"I just want to know what your name is?"

"Stay away!" She yelled.

She looked to the ground searching for any sort of weapon and picked up a loose rock. With her hardest throw she lugged it at him. Her hardest throw wasn't that hard; he caught the rock with one hand.

"Would you relax?" he begged.

"Where am I?" she demanded.

"Honestly I have no clue. I'm a little surprised to find you here. I thought—"

She cut him off, "Why did you bring me here?"

Alan was thrown back by that last comment. Not only did this chick think he was molesting her she thought he brought her out here too.

"Whoa, whoa, slow down turbo. I found you lying down."

The fire in her eyes told Alan she would maul him like a lion if he came any closer.

"Hey look around you. Doesn't it strike you as odd that there is no one else around?"

"We're in a forest. Perfect place to take someone to rape them and then stuff 'em in a body bag."

"Yeah but... ok that's a good point. Look I don't know who you are or where *we* are, but I think we'd have a much easier time if we traveled together."

"What? Did someone kidnap us both and decide to just drop us off?" she said with sarcasm.

Alan began to laugh. *How does this girl not know?* Alan squinted his eyes and looked at her slightly confused. "No, you've got the wrong idea... Do you know what's happening to you? I mean, don't you remember how you got out here?"

She thought for a second, *That's strange. I can't think of anything.* She looked him in the eyes for a second as she gathered her thoughts. Somewhere in there was a memory of something recent. But she couldn't find anything. "I can't remember the last thing that happened to me. I can barely even remember two days ago."

"So is it safe to say I didn't kidnap you?" He wanted desperately for her to calm down.

"How did you get out here?"

Alan hesitated on telling her his experience. He got the feeling it might be a bit much for her to handle right now.

"Honestly I don't really know either."

The thoughts of the situation brought tears to her eyes. She tried to be strong and hide it but the vulnerability was too much. Her mouth began to tremble. Her eyes began to soak up. She cupped her hands around her face and sobbed out by the gallons. Alan was a sucker for girls in need of comfort. He walked a little closer to cheer her up and she immediately backed away.

"Hey come on. It's ok. We'll be fine," he said in his most comforting voice.

"How do you know? You don't know what's going on either," her words were saturated with fear.

"At least we're ok. There's obviously been no harm to you... We'll find a way back, I promise."

He wanted desperately to tell her about the Akashic Library and flying around. After all it was how he got here. Her point of entry must have been similar if not the same.

"Were you able to fly at one point?

As if she didn't hear his words correctly she continued crying. "What are you talking about?"

"What was the last thing you remember doing?"

"I don't know," she thought hard, "I remember falling asleep."

"You didn't fly around and pass through walls?"

He cringed, as he was afraid he'd come off as a weirdo and she'd run again.

Tears still fell but the intensity of her fear wore down. What he said threw her off. "What are you talking about?"

It was obvious to Alan that this was not the time to talk about his experience. He'd have to wait for the opportune moment.

Above them was a steep but climbable mountainside. He looked up with the motivation to get moving. "You think you can climb that?"

Aside from the previous odd questions something about the sincerity in his voice made her feel more comfortable with Alan. She accepted the fact they were the only two individuals around and she believed they should stick together. So she looked up at mountainside figuring the climb was doable and nodded.

"Yeah. I think I can make it."

She kept her distance but followed him as he made his way upward. For a second she dreaded climbing the mountain but there wasn't anywhere else to go. So, she reluctantly continued on while trying to piece together the situation in her head.

It took them a while but they finally reached the top. Alan was amazed at the level of energy still within his arms and legs; it was as if he could do it forever. He pulled himself up, flipped over the edge and relaxed for a second. He wasn't really tired; he was more or less feeling the sensation of energy flowing within his body.

"Hey!" She yelled.

He almost forgot about her. He reached over and pulled her up and she crawled over to the other side. That's when a great rush of exhilaration sped through her body. She couldn't believe what she was seeing. Alan watched as she rose to her feet with her jaw dropped.

"What is it?" he asked her.

Alan, still not wanting to rise to his feet because of the height, crawled over to the other side. He too felt great elation throughout his body. They were looking down the deep, deep slope of a volcano. That's why it looked like the mountains were in a circle. At the bottom of this slope were miles of trees expanding as far as they could see, and in all directions.

"How the hell—"

"Did we get up here?" he said finishing her sentence.

It was of great mystery to the both of them. But as scary and insecure as the situation was it was one of the most beautiful sights they'd ever seen. They were both tantalized by the view.

"What is your name?" he randomly asked.

She was a bit thrown off by the timing of the question but she answered. "Amy".

"My name's Alan. Nice to meet you," he said with a touch of playful sarcasm.

"How are we going to get down from here?" she asked.

"I have no idea."

Alan did have an idea but he was afraid to tell her. He looked over the edge again to reassure himself that there was no other way down.

I guess I could do it. She'd never believe me if I explained it to her anyway.

He rose to his feet and thought hard about the decision. She walked around frustrated and thinking to herself. *How the hell am I ever going to get home?*

Alan gathered the inner strength and decided to go through with it. He turned around sharply and stared her in the eyes. She saw something boiling within him and she didn't like it. Something in his eyes was different, something that reminded her of a killer with grim determination. She feared that she had made a bad decision in trusting this stranger. Now he had her at the top of a mountain with nowhere else to run.

"I need you to trust me," he said in a very insecure tone.

Alan charged at her with vigor and she screamed at the top of her lungs while attempting to move out of the way, but he jumped and grabbed her before she could do anything. They flew over the cliff and down thousands upon thousands of feet to the bottom!

Chapter 7

After rolling, tumbling, and flipping all the way down the slope they landed in the canopy of the trees below. Amy got stuck in the branches above while Alan managed to slip through and smack into the surface. The thump was loud and hard. Other than some disorientation and the shit scared out of him he was relatively ok.

"Amy!" he yelled.

Alan looked above trying to see through the branches. Amy held on tightly high above. She looked down and saw at least three stories beneath her.

"Just let go!" Alan yelled.

"I'm not letting go are you crazy?" She peeked over to reconfirm how high she was.

"Amy! If we just fell a thousand feet from the top of a volcano and we're ok, what is another fifty going to hurt?"

She thought about it for a second. He was right! *How the hell did we do that?* She looked up towards the top of the volcano. It seemed like miles away. This eased her grip on the branch and she thought about jumping… until she looked down again. *What if it were a miracle? I might not be so lucky if I jump from here,* she thought.

"Amy, come on. Trust me."

"Last time I trusted you, you tackled me off the cliff of a volcano," she yelled.

"I had to. You wouldn't have come down." Alan thought about ways to get her down. *Perhaps I can shake the tree.* Then he looked at it. It was way too big. But then he had a better idea. He was indeed a clever little boy. With a smile on his face he turned around and started walking. "I'm going to get help," he yelled.

This scared her. She did not want to be left alone out here. She didn't even know where *here* was.

As Alan walked along he heard a loud thump behind him and that smile on his face grew even bigger. *I knew it would work.*

He ran back to get her while she remained on the ground motionless.

Oh shit. What if I was wrong? What if only I—

A sigh of relief came as he saw her body trembling. He put his hand on her back and looked closer to her face. She was terrified, but coherent.

"You ok?" he asked.

"What the hell is going on?" she demanded know.

They were finally up and moving through what seemed to be an endless forest. Amazement of the fact that they just fell from a mile above and survived seemed to fade a little. What did increase, however, was Amy's comfort around Alan. She was now near full confidence that he wasn't a rapist or killer. He still remained in her creepy guy category though. He was talking about passing through walls and traveling through space. He spoke of a mystical blue room with an endless amount of books and a golden triangle that created anything you wanted.

You've played too many video games and watched one too many sci-fi movies, she thought.

She let him ramble on but she wasn't buying any of it. The miracle that just happened was perfectly explainable to her, though *she* could not explain it.

"So what is your theory about what's going on?" she asked with a sarcastic edge.

"I have a couple, but when I think about them they don't make sense," Alan said. She looked at him waiting for him to explain. "Ok, either this is a really intense dream or we're..." Alan hesitated to say it and her frustration intensified, "...we're dead."

The look on Amy's face changed from frustration to anger. *This is total bullshit!* she thought. "Obviously we aren't dead or we wouldn't be walking around right now and obviously we aren't dreaming because this is way too real and way too long for any dream," But there was something in her that thought it was possible. So there was only one way to feel secure in her theory, "How old are you again?" she became defensive.

This chick isn't buying anything. She's shaking her head and sighing at nearly everything I say. And she asks me how old I am? "What's so crazy about it? I mean look at where we are."

"Yeah, ok space-boy."

Alan's kindness was fading. "How do you suppose we got up in that volcano?"

"Maybe you flew us up there," she said with a sarcastic smile.

His initial reaction was to get upset but when he saw her smiling he relaxed a bit. He had a real sweet spot for a gorgeous smile. "You don't have to believe me if you don't want. But when you explain how we magically got into the middle of the worlds largest volcano and then rolled down it without a scratch, let me know."

She knew what happened was much more than a miracle. It was impossible. But still, the idea he proposed was out of the question... for her. "So right now we're not in our bodies is that what you're saying?"

"I don't know. We seem pretty solid," he grabbed his arm and poked it. The nerves in his arm seemed to be there, though he did feel lighter than normal. "I was able to fly around and walk through walls when I first got out but now it's different."

Amy shook her head again. *This guy is nuts... Of all the people I end up with it's some lunatic who feels we're not in our bodies even though we're walking in our bodies... Of course I don't have any scratches from the fall,* she thought with a great deal of hesitation. "What makes you think you *left your body?*" she asked with sarcasm.

"I saw it."

She looked at him like he was a dweeb from a Star Trek convention.

"I'm serious," he said in defense. She nodded her head sarcastically agreeing. "I'm serious!"

"So uh, why don't you fly off right now and show me what you're talking about."

"I told you I can't do it now for some reason. Before I felt weightless and clear if that makes any sense. But now I feel heavy and confused. Maybe that's why."

This is starting to irritate me, she thought. "Maybe, when you get your powers back, you can wisp us away, but for right now lets just look for help."

"Do you *not* realize what's going on? I mean, how more obvious can it be?"

She gave him a blank reaction. "My grandma believed in all that 'out-of-body' stuff but she was senile. The mind is a powerful tool and can make things seem like they are happening... but they aren't. This is obviously Earth and we are obviously in our bodies."

"We're like, in a different world. Another universe. This isn't Earth," Alan said pleading his case.

She checked out the surroundings. It seemed like Earth to her and he knew it.

"It may look like it but... Amy you can't think I'm crazy."

Actually I do wacko, she thought. "Honestly stop," she couldn't even speak to him with a straight face now. "I don't know where you came from or what you're into, but stop. Listen to yourself. We're in like Montana or something. We've had some strange coincidences I'll give you that, but space travel and out-of-body experiences are passed my realm sweetie."

He found the remark condescending and was offended by it. *Next time you need help I'm leaving your ass behind.*

With little else to say he shook his head and continued forward in silence.

They realized they'd been walking for hours and everything looked the same. Amy was not enjoying the experience whatsoever while Alan on the other hand was still fascinated. He knew that this universe had more up its sleeve and that it would only be a matter of time before something came their way.

"God. Does this place ever end?" she said while stomping her foot on the ground.

Alan was not so hopeless. He recently noticed the trees had started to thin out in this direction. "You know they say a little patience pays off," Alan said.

I'll give you some patience you—

Suddenly, Amy squinted her eyes and looked ahead. "Wait a minute!" She saw something. It was in the near distance and was provocative enough to slow her down and stop her thoughts.

Alan looked at her wondering what it was she saw. "What is—" before he could finish, she took off running. "Amy wait!"

She must have found a reservoir of adrenaline because she was running like a marathon man on steroids. She leaped over bushes and fallen branches until finally reaching... the end of the forest. Alan was excited too but ran at a much slower pace. He'd seen it all before. Both of their excitement faded, however, when they laid their eyes to... a wide-open barren field of grass.

He ran out laughing. This was hilarious to him but she did not find any humor in the situation. But this was not the biggest surprise. Her knees caved in when she turned around. The forest and the volcano were gone, evaporated, vanished into thin air, or so it seemed.

"No. It can't be. Wha… where?" She began crying uncontrollably while Alan had tears of joy flowing from his eyes.

"This is what I'm talking about. None of this makes any sense!" Alan yelled with a smile.

"What the *hell* is going on? How can you be enjoying this?"

In all directions was an infinite landscape of rolling hills and grass. There were a couple of trees here and there, and what looked like a few bushes in the distance but not much else.

"This is nuts! I'm not so crazy now am I?" he said vindictively.

Her fear was now more of a disturbed confusion. "How can this be? Where did all of it go?"

Alan bent down to feel the grass beneath him. It was as solid as ever. "Wherever we are, it's not at home," he said laughing.

"How can you laugh at this?"

Amy threw a fit. She tossed her arms in the air. She tugged at her hair. She covered her face with her hands in disbelief. She worked herself up so badly she had a panic attack.

"Don't you feel so great? Don't you feel free?" Alan said.

Alan didn't notice her behind him. She sat on the ground in an attempt to catch her breath. This girl was freaking out!

Alan had his face in the air enjoying the sunshine. He felt so free, so alive. The weather was perfect, the scenery was incredible and there was no one to bother him, no pressure anywhere.

"What if we never go back home?" she asked.

"Who cares? We can do whatever we want out here."

"I care! I don't want to be stuck out here. I have a life at home."

Tears began pouring out of her eyes once again. She was shaking with fear. The thoughts of *what if*, *how could* and *this can't be* were coming at her full throttle. She looked up at Alan as he opened his arms like a bird. He closed his eyes and felt the wind blow by. It was so bewildering to her how he could be enjoying the moment.

It took him a few seconds but he finally opened his eyes and saw Amy bawling her eyes out. Guilt crept in for enjoying himself while she was having a near heart attack, so Alan lost the smile and tried to comfort her.

"Hey, it's alright," he said to her like a baby. He was not very good at this.

"No it's not!" She did not take to his comfort very well. She knew he was enjoying himself and that upset her.

"At least there are two of us out here. And we really don't have anything to worry about."

He placed his hand on her shoulder and she threw it off. "First I don't know you and second we are in the middle of *nowhere* with *no* food and *no* water."

"Somehow I get the feeling we won't need either of those... Just, calm down. We'll figure out how to get you home. It may take a little time but we'll figure something out."

She knew he had no clue where they were or what they were going to do. His attempts at being valiant were actually pissing her off even more. "Home! The forest just disappeared and there are no people anywhere, ANYWHERE!"

"Let's just keep moving. Eventually we have to find something. If anything it'll change again... I think."

He kept constant eye contact with her trying hard to bring her to his level. With little choice she gave in and calmed a little. After helping her to her feet he tried giving her a hug but she wasn't going for it. This girl was independent. She didn't need any help. This was what she believed anyway.

Alan extended his arm forward and began moving forward on their uncertain journey. As self sufficient and as strong as she wanted to be, she had to admit to herself that Alan's touch was comforting. He rubbed her back to let her know things were ok, and this time she didn't throw his hand off.

Chapter 8

It was soon apparent that there were three stars in the center of the sky. Funny enough they formed the shape of a triangle. However, after dealing with vanishing mountains and forest ranges this was easy to adjust to.

With the exception of disappearing landmasses and three stars above everything else seemed normal about the place. The two travelers aimlessly walked over hill after hill hoping to run into some form of intelligent life. Amy began to wish the area would magically change in front of her again so that at least she would be entertained. Even Alan was getting tired of the rolling hills.

Though the situation was confusing and somewhat upsetting there was something very peaceful out in this open land. There was no disturbance. No telephone lines or factories, no pollutants in the air or man made structures. Knowing that everything was pure and untouched gave the land a sense of purity. And though she did not want to admit it, Amy had felt a sense of serenity out here.

As they traveled there was at first an odd and awkward silence between them.

What is up with this girl? You'd think that being the only person on the planet would open up some conversation... She is pretty though... I wonder if she knows I'm checking her out... The last thing I need is her freaking out again.

Alan was attracted to her but her focus was not on him. Her mind was driving her nuts with thoughts of fear and uncertainty. Everything she had been brought up to believe in made absolutely no sense in this foreign land. Even worse, she had no control over the situation and this was something she wasn't used to.

"Hey, think of it this way, at least there's no bills to pay," Alan said trying to lighten her up. "We could even start our own system of government," he pressed on.

But she would only smile and give a fake giggle.

Even in this world people are insincere.

Alan kept glancing at her when he thought she wasn't looking. She was, however, catching all of his looks. She was actually trying to avoid conversation with him.

What the hell does he want...? I'm not in the mood for flirting... God...! Even out here guys are pigs... How the hell am I going to get home...? Shit, what am I saying...? I don't even know if this is real... What if he was right and we're dead... No, there's no way... He's just out of his mind... Uuhhgg...! Why did this have to happen...? Her mind was non-stop, until she looked up at the stars above. *That's so amazing! How is this possible?*

The lack of an explanation brought about a gap in her thinking. It took a pause in her thoughts for her to realize she was alienating the only person she knew in this strange universe. She looked at him while his head was turned. This was the first time she looked at him as a person, as someone real and not just a step in her path home.

He's not bad looking. Not really my type though.

She was used to guys who grew up in the more traditional fashion. Guys who went to school, got excellent grades, had perfect teeth, and were going to make at least a hundred thousand a year when they left nothing smaller than a Big-Ten university. Alan was quite the opposite and she knew it. He was the guy her mother frowned upon. He was one of those boys who skated on the edge, whose grades were average or below. A guy who looked into the sky for answers and didn't care about the rules of the game society laid for him.

"So, what did you do before you came out this way?

He turned to her surprised. "Who me? I'm sorry, was it me you were speaking to miss?" he said sarcastically.

She laughed it off as she realized was being a bit cold to him. "I'm sorry. This is all so overwhelming. I want to believe that this is all a dream but you're right, it's too real."

Alan laughed. "The funny thing is I never believed in any of this either. I guess it takes experience to really find out eh…"

He's not as weird as I first thought, she realized as he was speaking. *He is actually pretty interesting.*

"I know what you mean. I never would have thought…" she started saying.

I guess she's not really a bitch. Probably all just a self-defense mechanism she thinks she needs to get through life, Alan thought as he looked into her eyes.

"Maybe we both created each other in our heads," Alan joked. This time she genuinely laughed.

Time seemed to be non-existent in this foreign land, what could have been considered hours seemed much shorter as the two travelers began getting heavy into conversation. They tried to keep an eye out for something new to show up but the bland landscaping became dull to their minds. The boredom nudging at their skulls forced them to keep up pointless chatter.

"…My parents always wanted me to go to school to be an accountant or something but I've always wanted to do something else," he said.

"Like what?" she asked with genuine interest.

"I think I've always wanted to help people get through their problems. I want to show people that they don't have to live like rats in a maze, looking for a little cheese like my parents."

"So you want to be a psychiatrist? That takes school."

The sound of the word school made him cringe. "No, not a psychiatrist. Most of them seem like rats too. In fact, everyone seems like a rat somewhere in the maze of life trying to find the ultimate prize, but somehow they never find it."

"That's just a part of life."

"But there's got to be something else, underneath all of the searching. Maybe most of us just don't see it because we're looking in the wrong direction. If *most* people are lost that means someone has to know what's going on. I think that if I could reach that point myself maybe I could show others how to become free."

"You say free like we're in prison."

He gave a funny grin. "Maybe we are."

All this philosophy was too much for her. "You analyze things too much. That image of life, it's real. And that struggle to reach that 'golden cheese' is the point of living. It keeps us moving so we're not vegetables wasting our lives, doing nothing."

"But wait a minute, if we didn't search for that *answer to everything*, if we didn't spend most of our lives looking for something that doesn't exist—"

She cut him off abruptly, "How do you know that it doesn't exist? It's different for everybody."

"But no one has found it. No one ever finds *it* because there is no *it*."

This conversation was infuriating for her. What he was saying went against the way she was brought up. "There's no way for you to know that."

"Yes there is. Every time something ends there has to be something after it. Every time you get what you want you feel satisfied but soon after there is just another craving."

"Exactly! It keeps us moving through life," she said feeling triumphant. "Life is about chasing down your dreams and being satisfied by them. Bums sit around begging their whole life because they're lazy. They'll make absolutely nothing out of themselves and sit and complain about it because they're to pathetic to do something about it."

"But don't you see what that means? Our chasing has nothing to do with what we're after. Life, for most, is all about the thrill of *chasing*, which means it's all an illusion. We're always trying to satisfy that craving. It doesn't really matter what we're after... It's the root of all addictions is what it is."

"That's the real world buddy."

Alan threw his arms in air. The "real world" was a term he's heard since the day he understood the English language. His dad would use it in statements to signify Alan's apparent lack of understanding about the social world around him. "What the hell is the real world? If this isn't real than what is real?" he said. "I still feel the same as when I did back in my body... actually, I feel better."

"What do you mean?"

"Doesn't this feel real to you? I mean just what is real?"

"The real world is life. Going to work, starting a family and...stuff."

"So you're telling me that if you don't have a *social* life than you aren't real?"

She paused for a second and rethought her concept of *the real world* and now wasn't so confident she knew what it was. She was fully conscious, fully aware, and fully capable of making decisions, just like in "real" life.

"Maybe reality is where you are, not just what you do."

"Yeah but this could all be just a dream... I think."

"Even if this were some elaborate dream, we can still touch, feel, think, and interact," he rubbed the ground to further elaborate his point. "Everything you do is translated through your awareness so it doesn't matter if we're in some dream world or a physical one."

"No everything you do is translated through your brain. Without it we wouldn't exist," she said in a snappy tone.

"No, no. The brain works for the body. Without you, the individual, the observer, nothing would exist. There would be no thoughts to interpret, or a need for a body. The universe doesn't need a brain to operate. It functions perfectly because it is conscio—" he stopped in mid speech.

"What?" she asked curiously.

Alan's attention focused ahead. Amy wondered why he stopped talking until she looked too. They both saw it, about quarter of a mile away. It was hard to distinguish but then it became clear. It was a highway they were looking at! And a highway meant civilization. Alan took off running for it as if his life depended on it.

"Hey! Wait up!" Amy yelled. She looked at the road feeling intensely hopeful. *Finally, a sign of hope!*

Alan approached the road with great expectations of a sign of some sort. He was disappointed to find only a rail and painted lines. This did mean one thing though; in some way this universe was a reflection of theirs; either that or it was a strong coincidence that an alien race used yellow paint for their highways.

Amy caught up to him and smacked him on the shoulder for leaving her. "Which way do we go?"

"Does it matter?" Alan said smiling.

Alan sprinted to the right in a split decision.

"Would you slow down?"

"It's not like I'm gonna lose you," he yelled back.

"You don't know that!"

Chapter 9

Their run changed to a fast walk. They weren't out of breath, just mentally tired of looking with no results. In fact they could run for hours and possibly never stop; this fact hadn't occurred to them though. They were frustrated and tired of looking for a change in the road. But, like the other landscapes, this highway stretched out forever. Alan and Amy were both seeing a pattern.

Amy stopped jogging and put her hands on her hips. "There's nothing out here, this is useless," she said, extremely frustrated.

He stopped a few feet ahead and rolled his eyes. "You were the one all worried about going home now you want to give up?"

"We haven't found anything at all. No road signs, cars or anything. This is useless! And besides it doesn't seem to matter how fast or how far we go because *shit* keeps disappearing in front of us!"

"There has to be something out here," Alan started walking again.

"Would you stop for a second?" Amy got pissed at him now.

Alan stopped, put his hands on his hips and then turned to face her. "What would you suggest we do?"

"I don't know, but this road goes nowhere."

"Damn it!" His anger wasn't towards her; it was towards the present situation. "There has to be something we can do," he yelled into the sky as if talking to the gods, "Something!"

"Like you said, it's our thoughts that have the biggest effect out here," she reminded him.

"I'm *thinking* I'd like to get the hell out of here. Find some civilization or something!"

She thought about his words earlier. "Weren't you telling me that craving for an illusion is insane?"

"Yeah but—" he was stumped. These were his words she was using.

She looked him dead in the eye, waiting for him to finish his sentence. This forced him to take a second and realize that she was right. After taking two deep breaths to relax he began pondering.

"I was able to fly when I first got out of my body but now it's like I've entered into a different world... again. I don't get it."

"Maybe we're on a different level of *consciousness* or whatever," she was being sarcastic but Alan really thought about it. She watched him formulate a theory. "What? What real difference would that make anyway?" she asked.

"Wait a minute now. You might have a point. What if our level of consciousness had an effect on what happened to us and not just us but our surroundings too?"

Amy raised her shoulders. She figured it was as good a guess as any.

"We should meditate for a little bit?"

She instantly frowned upon the idea. Meditation was not her "thing". She thought meditation was for people of the Orient and those who followed the culture. She was definitely not from the orient and definitely not about to follow the culture. "I'm not into all of that yoga stuff," her remark was filled with cynicism.

"You don't have to be into *yoga* to meditate. Let's just try to clear our heads. Just take a second and breathe. That's all you have to do."

There was a moment of silence between them. Amy's eyes rolled back as she sighed at his "silly" meditation. This was what she thought about getting into the "meditative" mood. Alan gave her a look of discontent and grabbed her hand. She rolled her eyes again but eventually gave in.

"Ok," she said with dissatisfaction. "What do we do?"

They sat down in the middle of the road and closed their eyes. Alan grabbed her other hand in an attempt to guide her. She had no clue where to start first so she followed his actions. He sat upright and closed his eyes and so did she.

"First," he said in his most calm and relaxed voice. "Relax. Breathe in and out... Pay attention to your breathing... Feel the air flow through your body."

The wind picked up a little bit taking Amy's attention with it. Amy opened her eyes and looked around but Alan pulled her attention back.

"Keep trying. Don't give up," he said with his eyes closed.

They both relaxed. This time she put forth some actual effort. As the minutes passed by Amy began to forget she was in the middle of a highway. The wind blowing by actually helped her to ease her mind on the situation.

This stuff might actually be working, she thought. But like the average human it only took a second before her mind began to question what she was doing. *This is so silly... I feel ridiculous... This doesn't work... What am I doing? We could be putting our minds together figuring something else out... We're wasting our time!*

After a few more moments of heavy breathing she caved in. She stood up shaking her head. "This isn't working out. I can't stop thinking about getting out of here."

"Son of a bitch," Alan mumbled. He lost his patience with her impatience.

At that moment a faint whistling sound became present. They instantly both looked down the road. Things looked a bit different in that direction now. There were road signs, strange looking fences on both sides of the road and in the far distance… an odd-looking vehicle was hauling ass towards them! This was unlike any vehicle they'd ever seen. It resembled a pickup truck but with no wheels. It was floating a good three feet off of the ground!

This is a good thing, they both thought.

Alan looked at Amy, amazed. She looked at him trying to figure out what they should do next. Alan started doing jumping jacks trying to flag down the person in the truck and Amy quickly joined in.

"Hey! Stop!" Alan yelled with a confused look on his face.

"Slow down!"

They both were yelling at the top of their lungs, even though the person would not be able to hear them. Coming to that realization, they both slowly quieted down. Alan was the first to acknowledge that the truck wasn't slowing any. Either the person in the truck was blind or Alan and Amy were not visible. It wouldn't be the first time a vehicle ran through him, after all.

They cut back on the jumping and flagging down and then finally came to a complete stop, though Amy still waved her hands and made funny facial expressions.

"Is he retarded? Can't he see us?" she asked.

The "retard" in the truck began picking up speed the closer he came to the two travelers. Amy walked to the side of the road realizing the dangers of standing in front of a moving vehicle, but Alan stood curiously in the middle, waiting. This person was either going to see him or they were going to run him over. That was until Amy pulled him by the arm off to the side of the road. The truck flew by at nearly one hundred miles an hour.

She squinted her eyes and shook her head. "Are you nuts?"

They quickly noticed that the other direction had been altered as well. Instead of a straight empty highway it had curves and a couple of blank road signs. Off to the right was a huge advertising billboard. In big white letters placed against a black background, it read:

You are here!

Alan looked at the sign curiously. "No shit."

"Alan!" Amy said excitedly.

Up the large hill to the left was a red, clay looking home. It was about the average size of a modern day colonial but the design was unlike anything they'd ever seen. Perhaps the closest style of housing were those used by the early Native Americans in the desert or Middle Easterners living between mountains. It had windows with glass on it and a couple of vehicles, much like the one that nearly ran them over, parked in what looked like the driveway. This time they ran together.

They approached the home cautiously. As they crept up the hill they were delighted to see more houses like it down the road. Though things were different from anything on Earth, there were some striking similarities. It was more like an alternate universe with some connection to the one they were from.

"Funny, this looks a little like my old neighborhood," Amy said.

Alan didn't respond back. He felt something weird here. There were emotions flowing into him that were odd and unwarranted. There was a strange sense of comfort like he knew these streets. As he looked around everything felt familiar but he knew he had never seen any of this before. "Does this look *kind of like* your old neighborhood or *is* this your old neighborhood?" he asked.

"No, this definitely *isn't* my old neighborhood," she said with a raised brow.

She was starting to feel a little weird as well. A strange overwhelming sense of child-like expectations crept into her consciousness, a feeling kids have while they are still under the guidance of their parents.

Alan was feeling tired and worn out as if years of decision making and babysitting were under his belt. Alan was not the type to baby-sit. He would only watch his cousin if he were forced and after turning into a legal adult he never did it again. He was also feeling a strange sense of protectiveness over Amy. This wasn't the valiant bravery a man would give a woman in distress, no, it was a more natural feeling, as if she belonged to him and somehow physically connected to him.

All Amy could think about was having fun. She was daydreaming about being a secret agent in the future and how cool it would be if they had a flying car to travel around in.

"Do you feel weird?" she asked.

Alan nodded with an alienated look on his face. *What is going on?* he wondered.

But then, that familiar whistling sound returned not far out in the distance, and it was getting louder. Sure enough, it was the same vehicle that nearly hit them before. Had he returned for a second try?

As this "nut job" sped up they heard the sound of a little girl playing behind them. They both instantly turned around to see *a little girl* playing in the middle of the street. When Alan turned back he saw that the truck was magically closer than it was a second ago and headed straight for them!

Amy's concern was the little girl. "Move!" She yelled to her.

The girl did not respond. As Amy ran to move her Alan was stuck in a trance-like state. He felt something with that little girl as if she was his.

Is this the child of Amy and I from the future? he wondered.

He was feeling like… a *woman*! He was also thinking about what it would be like without his baby, the little mysterious girl in the middle of the street. The instincts inside of him wanted to take action but he could not move fast enough. His movements were suspended in slow motion while everything else happened at a normal pace around him.

The truck was on his tail and not slowing down. Amy was trying to move the little girl when she saw the truck seconds away from running over all three of them! Her movements were not suspended but the girl in the street did not want to listen to her.

"Leave me alone or I'll tell mom," the girl threatened.

With only enough time to save Amy, Alan shoved her out of the way. As the truck made impact with his ass, Alan flipped over the truck like a pizza maker tossed him in the air. He watched the truck smack dead on with the little girl in the street. This was the most horrific sight he'd ever witnessed in his life. The little girl's body was tossed twenty feet away in bloody mutilation.

"Audra NO!" Alan yelled.

He suddenly became aware that he knew the girl's name. This was his child and he was her *mother*! While suspended in the air it all hit him. A flood of memories and visions of living the life of a thirty five year old woman named Sara. This is who he was. It was her red house at the end of the neighborhood and it was her child in the street. The table was turning and Sara began wondering why she was having thoughts as a young man named Alan. He was fading quickly into a state of unconsciousness, within a split mind of identification. The emotions became so strong in his body that he could not handle them. He was too confused as to why he was having the emotions in the first place.

With one last punch of energy Alan called for the one person who mattered to *him*, "Amy!"

Amy was lying on the side of the road helpless. The need for security was so strong it incapacitated her. The only thing she could do was curl up in a ball and wait. She wanted her parents and her parents only, to get her. All that she heard next was the sound of the little girl screaming and a loud thump immediately following. She knew it was her sister who was just hit.

I don't have a sister, she thought.

This increased her sense of identity as Amy, and she snapped out of whatever it was she was going through.

A strange fog mysteriously moved into the neighborhood. This was particularly strange, as there were no clouds in the sky.

Amy ran over to where Alan should have been. With the fog so thick it was hard to see anything. There was a body lying in the street but it was not Alan's, it was Sara, the woman from Alan's vision. She rose to her feet and stared strangely at Amy.

"Oh my God! Where is she?" The woman asked.

Amy was thrown off and didn't know what to say.

"God damn it! Where is your sister?" The woman demanded to know.

Amy felt a connection with this woman. This woman had total control over everything she did.

Why is this happening? Amy thought.

Amy tried her hardest to fight off the feelings and thoughts she was having. She knew they were not hers yet she felt them definitely coming from within. She followed Sara, as she looked around frantically for the little girl who was playing in the street.

"Audra! Audra! Honey, baby." Sara saw her little baby mutilated not ten feet away. "No! No! Noooo!" Sara ran to the little girl and cradled her in her arms. "Audra, get up! Get up!"

There was blood on the street and more gushing from the girl. It was the lack of life, not the gore that had the most impact on Amy. Normally Amy would have strong compassion and sympathy in such a situation as this but the feelings of loss and terror were worse than they would be if *she* were *herself.*

"What happened? Is she ok?" Amy asked.

The woman, sobbing as she held her dead daughter, yelled hysterically at the top of her lungs, "I told you not to play in the street!"

Amy was extremely confused as to why the woman talked to her like that. *Just what the hell is happening?* she thought. *Where is Alan?*

"Somebody call the police! HEELLLLP! Somebody!" Sara yelled.

Amy ran across the street to the red house at the end of the neighborhood. A confused man walked out of the home and stared at Amy. She saw in this man's eyes… her father! She was bombarded with visions of living as a young boy playing with his sister, Audra, who was just hit. Amy began to cry helplessly in front of this man.

"What happened…? Joseph! What happened?" the man demanded to know.

The name he called her only added to the identity she was becoming. She looked at her hands and saw that they were *not* hers.

These were the hands of a little boy. The more confused she became the less *she* was herself. When she looked into the man's eyes again she lost the battle. Amy was gone. Who was left was a seven-year-old boy named Joseph. He felt extremely guilty for not moving his sister out of the street in time. He couldn't speak or move or make any kind of gesture. He froze up.

I killed her. It was my fault, Joseph thought.

"Joseph what happened?" The man demanded to know.

His little face turned red and his eyes filled with water. "We were playing in the street and this car came."

"Oh no," the man's voice trembled with terror. He knew something horrible happened to his daughter. He quickly ran out of his home and searched through the fog. "Sara!" he yelled.

The first person he saw was the drunk alcoholic in daze behind the wheel of the vehicle. The man stumbled out and wobbled around a bit. Not only was he shaken up by the accident, he was also heavily intoxicated. The father ran up to the drunkard not really sure what was happening. All he knew was that this man probably hit his daughter.

"Is she...ok?" The drunken man slurred. The man knew the girl was probably dead but the booze was throwing him off.

The father grabbed him by the collar. "Get off the *fucking* road!"

He threw the drunkard to the ground and continued looking for his wife and daughter. As he saw the front of the truck his stomach plummeted. Not only was there a big dent in the front, there was tons of blood smeared everywhere! Quickly he pulled out a thin piece of metal resembling a cell phone and called the emergency line. Just a few feet away his worst fears came true. His wife was holding his dead daughter in her arms. He ran up to them and kneeled to the ground.

"Is she breathing?

Sara was still hysterical "No," she said as she cupped her hands around little Audra's face. "Wake up baby, wake up. Everything will be ok. Don't worry. Everything's going to be fine."

The father, Jeff, reached someone on the emergency line and described the situation. The drunken guy sat on the ground terrified by the reality of the situation. Joseph stood behind the front door of his home trying to feel some comfort behind the screen. All he could feel was the guilt.

I did it. I killed my sister. Oh no!

Sara remained in the street yelling at the top of her lungs holding on to her little girl. Somewhere within the confines of these identities were Amy and Alan. They were so caught up in the situation, so consumed by their thoughts that they became lost, just as it was foretold. To make matters even worse, they didn't have a clue.

Chapter 10

It was a cold and cloudy day at the cemetery. The color in the sky was sucked dry. Every plant and animal, even the headstones, were distorted as if filled with sorrow. The tall abnormally curved trees drooped down with open orifices in the shape of sagging mouths. They were as black as night and crispy as if burnt in a fire. This place was not friendly to the eyes of the living. Life all around the area seemed shriveled up and dead. The squirrels running from tree to tree were thin as bones with bags in their eyes the size of pebbles. Deranged black crows circled the area looking for prey. Their eyes glowed yellow and their talons were overgrown and razor sharp. They would occasionally swoop down and tackle the little animals running around.

All the creatures seemed to focus on the preceding funeral where a tall, thin, ghostly looking undertaker spoke in tongues as family and friends gathered around the body of little Audra. They could not see the body however. She was held in a large chalice-like device high above the ground where flames ignited from within and incinerated her body.

Everyone there was heavy with emotion. They could think of nor feel anything else but this little girl's death. Neighbors held their children tight as they were reminded of the fragile nature of the universe. Aunts and uncles hung their heads as they thought about the face of that innocent little girl. Sara wept on her husband's shoulder while Joseph clung to one of his aunts. The emotion was so thick it could have been sliced in half.

Strangely, neither Joseph nor Sara realized the truth of their identity, not even a faint memory.

Jeff and Sara held a gathering at their home after the funeral. Everyone walked down the middle of the street with his or her heads drooping. They seemed completely oblivious to the fact that the neighborhood seemed drained of life. The colors of everything were dull and stale. The houses seemed run down and drab. This was in great contrast to how it looked a few days ago.

The biggest change was that red house at the end of the street. It looked as if someone took charcoal and smeared the house with it. The roof was peeling up like dead skin. The windowsills were cracking and ready to fall off. The wood on the front porch was warped and twisted.

Inside of the home everyone gathered around pictures and items that reminded them of Audra. There wasn't a face in the place without a tear rolling down it. Strangely, every time someone walked into the house the atmosphere turned a little greyer and the structure of the home warped an extra inch each time someone began sobbing.

As Sara held on tight to her daughter's teddy bear she buried her head in her arms in an attempt to hide her face.

"Sara," Jeff said.

Sara lifted her head to the call of her husband. When she looked up one of her tears flung off of her cheek. As it collided with the wood floor it sucked the moisture out and caused the surrounding section to split and dry up. Though no one noticed anything abnormal.

Little Joseph was hiding underneath the stairs all by himself, crying in the dark. No matter what anyone said, he felt the blame for his sister's death. He couldn't help but think there would be no one to play with anymore, no one to bother him.

Someone opened the basement door and looked around. It was his aunt. She was looking for him. The second Joseph heard her coming he refrained from letting out the slightest whimper.

Go away. I don't want anyone to see me.

When she went back up the stairs she turned out the lights leaving him in total darkness. This only intensified his feelings of isolation and fear.

"Audra," he said to himself. "I'm so sorry."

There was now insecurity all around him. To feel safe he remained in the same spot for the rest of the night.

The next morning was just as gloomy. The little light shining from the sky seeped in through the window as Jeff was lying in his bed sleeping. When he rolled over he expected to hold his wife but came up empty handed. Quickly, he opened his eyes and looked around. She was not there.

He suspected she was in Audra's bedroom so he rushed in to see. She wasn't there either. He peeked into little Joseph's room thinking maybe she wanted to be next to her only child but only found Joseph sleeping soundly. The fear was increasing. He scurried down the stairs hoping to find her on the couch but all he found was an empty living room.

"Sara," he called.

He waited for a reply... nothing. He checked the kitchen and the back of the home but once again found nothing.

"Where the hell is she?"

He opened the basement door and flicked on the light.

"Sara!"

His concern grew to near anger. He moved quickly to the front window and saw both vehicles in the driveway. He looked out into the backyard and again found no one. In a panic he flew out of the front door ready to drive down the street, but much to his relief, he found her sitting on the front porch in a rocking chair. She was holding onto Audra's favorite teddy bear.

"How long have you been out here?" Jeff asked with a sigh of relief.

She simply stared at the location in the street where she last held her little girl, not once looking his way.

"Come inside honey this isn't healthy for you," he said as he turned to go back into the house.

"Our little girl, Jeff," she started bawling, "She's gone...and there's nothing we can do."

He stood there getting teary eyed himself. He tried to hold it in but found the emotion too strong. He broke down and starting crying with his wife. "I know baby."

"She was so little. We shouldn't have to go through this," she said.

Finding the pain nearly unbearable he reluctantly kneeled down to hold her hands. He didn't want to shed another tear. "We have to keep ourselves busy with other things honey. We've got to get our minds away so we can get through this," he said.

"No mother should bury her child... This can't be happening... Why? Why my little girl?"

Joseph heard noises outside of his room and woke up. As he walked out of his room he could tell the noises were coming from the front porch. So he tiptoed down the stairs while listening to the conversation of his parents outside.

"This is going to hurt for a while. But we've got to stay close and rely on each other to get through this," he reminded her.

"My daughter just died and you're telling me to get over it?"

"We've still got one child left and he needs us."

"What do you expect out of me? I can't handle this."

"We've got to pull it together for him. He's all we've got left."

Joseph was listening to the conversation through the door now. The feelings of guilt overwhelmed his stomach as those words from his father reminded him that *he* was to blame.

On the porch, Sara broke down again. She couldn't help but let out the emotion clogging her system. She fell out of the chair but Jeff grabbed her in time. All she could do was cling to him.

"God *why*? Oh my God, why? I knew they were out there. I should have been watching them. It's my fault."

Hearing this tore him up. "Oh God, please don't say that. This was not your fault."

"If they weren't playing in the street my little girl would be alive right now."

Hearing his mother say "playing in the street" put yet another knot in Joseph's stomach. The emotion was so strong his knees caved in and he dropped to the floor. He picked himself back up and staggered to the backyard. The only place he could find comfort was inside his sister's little florescent colored plastic play-set. Inside of it he could let out the tears waiting to be released.

Jeff stood up and wiped off the flood of tears from his face. He turned his head trying to avoid looking at his wife. She would only bring back a wave of emotion. He walked inside leaving Sara on the porch alone. She held tight to the bear as if it were the remnants of her daughter.

Please... Please give me back my little girl... Let me at least hold on to her one last time... How can she be gone...? This should not be... Oh god why...?

And then, there was a break in her thoughts. She noticed how good it felt. That's when a strange feeling came to her. It was weird. She felt like letting go, not of the cotton bear she was holding but letting go of the weight she was carrying. She so felt heavy, so thick and clouded.

I can't let go of this. My daughter just died, she thought.

That's when another urge came to her. She wanted to walk out into the middle of the street.

Where is this coming from? she wondered.

Her feelings of guilt increased the more she wanted to let go of the grief. She began feeling like a horrible person for thinking about *not* thinking of her daughter.

*Why am I thinking of this...? My God... I'm a horrible mother... But is it
so wrong...? Why do I want to walk over there...? That's where she was hit...
No... I can't believe it... It was too soon for her to be taken... It's too soon to
let go... Why do I want to let go...? I don't want to want to let go... I have to
walk over there... The urge is so strong...*

After a few moments she stood up and walked off of the porch.
She had to do something to ease the war within her. It was driving
her madder than she already was.

The wind blew softly across her face. This reminded her of being
in an open field. She remembered being free and not having a care in
the world.

Those were the days...

She remembered meeting Amy in the forest and then smiled.

Amy! What the hell am I thinking about?

She snapped out of her little daydream and looked around. She
was standing in the spot where *she* was hit. That's when even stranger
feelings began flowing in. There was an intense force driving her to
run away. She imagined running away from her family, running away
from her life. She was feeling that everything was superficial.
Everything she had ever done, everything she had ever witnessed, felt
like a waste of time. All she wanted to do was run.

"I can't!" she said out loud.

She felt trapped all of a sudden. She looked at the spot Audra was
hit and ran to it. She thought that if she stood in the spot where her
daughter was killed all of these *crazy* thoughts of letting go and
running away would end. As she drew closer she was reminded that
her daughter was hit not long ago and she was a mother in grief.

But then, a gust of wind came in so strong it knocked her to the
ground. Sara started feeling disconnected again. She quickly got back
up and started running. She was losing herself out here. The desire to
be free from the pain and sorrow was growing. She held on to the
teddy bear to reinforce her identity as a grieving mother. The closer
she walked to the "spot" the more secure she felt.

I'm losing my mind, she thought.

She did not want to let go of this pain. *It's way too soon. What kind of a parent is at peace when their child dies?* As she thought about it her identity started coming back.

But then, another gust of wind forced her five feet back. She felt insecure again. She felt disconnected with the sorrow. She wanted it back. She didn't feel normal without those feelings.

The clouds above grew thick and dark within seconds and a constant force of wind came swooping in, taking her even further away from the center of the road. Sara fought the force with all her might. It became a battle to hold on to her identity. Though she was fighting the wind, a part of her wanted to be taken away. She could not give in to that feeling. Everything she ever worked for was in her identity.

The closer to the spot she came the harder the wind blew. *Why is this happening? How is this happening?*

The wind seemed to be intentionally aimed at her. A force beyond her control was at work. In one last attempt to hold on, she covered her head and pressed forward with her shoulder.

"Fo—cu—sssss," a mysterious voice said.

She looked up to see where the voice was coming from and, in that instant, her guard was let down allowing the force of the wind sweep her off of her feet. A cyclone came down from the sky and suspended her in an isolated tornado. She was only feet away from the *spot*. This was now becoming a battle to regain control, no longer a battle of thoughts. She stretched her arms out, determined to reach her destination. The teddy bear flew out into the sky and she cared the least bit, her goal was to get to the center of this phenomena.

Inside of the home Jeff was looking for little Joseph. He was concerned about his well being as he had noticed how silent he'd been since the accident. Joseph came running in through the back door just as it slammed shut behind him.

"What the hell is going on outside?" Jeff asked.

"I don't know. There's a storm coming."

Jeff looked out of the back window and noticed how bad things were getting outside. He immediately thought of his wife.

"Sara."

She was in the air hovering above ground in a mysterious tornado when she saw a figure standing not ten feet away. The wind and dust covered the individual but there was definitely someone there. Her first thought was that it was Audra coming back from the dead to say goodbye, but that theory was shot down when she got a glimpse of how tall this person was. It was a man with long black hair and olive toned skin. It was the Native American, the man whom Alan had encountered once before!

Al—n. su—en—er! the Native American's calm voice spoke within Sara's head.

"What?" she asked.

The Native American walked with ease through the storm. He approached within inches of Sara and stared her dead in the eyes. *Alan! Surrender!* The voice was clear this time.

Sara felt different. *Who is Alan?* The name Alan meant something. It felt natural to be called that.

The second Jeff stepped out onto the front porch the wind slowed to a breeze dropping Sara to the ground like a rock, and she instantly crawled to the center of the street. From Jeff's perspective she looked like she was clinging to the ground where their daughter was killed.

She's lost it, he thought. He ran to the middle of the street to pick her up. "What are you doing?"

The second Jeff entered Sara's vision she began to re-identify. "Didn't you see? It all happened right here." She looked around frantically trying to see what happened to everything. "He was stopping me. He was stopping me from getting to her."

"What are you saying?"

"Something was stopping me. I could feel her."

She began thinking that the man in the dust, the Native American, was stopping her from reaching the center of the street.

It must have been him putting those thoughts in my head, she thought. *He didn't want me to reach my baby...*

"Feel who? There's nothing here. There's no one here!" Her actions were infuriating to him.

Sara frantically looked around the ground. "No. Something was holding me back. Almost like I'm in a dream and I was about to wake up."

"But you're not dreaming, this is real. What we're going through is real. You've got to face up to what's going on. Everything else is in your head."

"No, you don't understand. I felt something; she was there. Something was there waiting for me. Maybe if I tried harder."

Jeff embraced her tightly. Not only had he lost his daughter but he was losing his wife too. She paid him little attention. She looked like a nut case looking for lucky charms.

Jeff felt like he was holding a kid who didn't want to be held. "Just hold on for me, ok. Don't lose it," he said with sadness in his tone.

She stopped fighting him and held his arm. Tears began flowing from her eyes and the feelings of despair and loss returned. Her mind was back on track.

"I almost had her, I swear. I'm not crazy. You have to believe me," she begged.

Chapter 11

Sara sat alone by the fireplace just staring into the flames. Her eyes moved around frantically while she thought about what happened earlier.

Am I going crazy?

To her the timeline fit. Before the accident she was living the life of a proud parent. She knew where she grew up. She remembered the day she first met her husband. She even remembered the day before the accident…

But then she thought about it. *Do I remember what happened…? I was… I was with… I… I don't remember.* She couldn't remember anything specific. *Wait no! I do remember! I was… I was with… Amy?*

Her memory was like that of a spliced piece of film with a little extra footage mixed into the finished product, as if someone else's movie was edited into hers. She strangely remembered living as a young man named Alan. She had some of his thoughts and feelings mixed within her mind and she couldn't get rid of them. She remembered traveling with a girl named Amy as well. They were searching for something together.

Also strange was the fact that she could feel Amy's presence ever since the accident, and it scared her. All of this was torture.

She took a sip out of her coffee and slowly set it down next to a picture of the family as a whole.

This is who I am.

She picked up the picture and smiled as she remembered that day. They were all out enjoying themselves at their favorite park. She felt so comforted and secure as she remembered that moment, but the smile quickly crumbled into sobbing as she remembered that she would never have an experience like that again. The pain was so tough she put her hand to her mouth in an effort to not let out the sobbing, but it was too much. The crying had to come out. It was uncontrollable.

Suddenly, someone walked up quietly behind her and placed their hand on her shoulder. Sara shrieked as she felt the presence of that Amy girl!

Who is this person and how is she connected to the death of my daughter?

Slowly she reached back and grabbed the gentle hand with force. Much to her surprise she found her son Joseph!

"Mom," he said with a frightened look on his face.

She snapped out of it and wiped the tears off of her face. Before speaking she let a few moments pass by. She wasn't sure if she should talk. With everything that was going on she didn't know what would come out of her mouth. One of the feelings she had as Alan was attraction towards Amy. Sara was no lesbian and she wasn't into incest or child molestation, but she couldn't help what she felt.

"What is it honey?" she asked.

Joseph's little face started trembling. His cheeks turned red and his lips began to shake. What came next were the tears. Sara hated seeing her children cry but it reinforced her identity as "Sara the mother" and that felt good.

"Mom, I'm..." he couldn't finish. He tried to get the words out but couldn't manage.

"What's wrong sweetie?"

"I'm sorry momma. I didn't mean to get Audra killed," he said bawling his eyes out.

Listening to her son say this made her lose it and she started crying again. "Don't say that. It wasn't your fault," she reached out for him and he ran to the comfort of his mother's arms.

"I didn't see the car coming. I should have pulled her up. I tried but she wouldn't move."

"It's ok sweetie. This was not your fault. It was an accident," she could tell he felt alone and even worse, guilty for the death of his sister.

"Is there a way to bring her back?"

She found it hard to make the words out. "...No honey... she's gone. I wish we could though."

She warmed up her now only child while staring into the fire. This was the one person she felt that could keep her sane, as all of the drama made her feel good. It reinforced her identity.

"Don't worry, Amy. We'll be fine."

Joseph instantly looked up at his mother. "What did you call me...? Mom?"

Sara was in a daze. She was thinking about so much she didn't even realize what she said. "Huh..." she took a second but snapped out of it, "I'm sorry. I think I just need some rest. We all need a little rest."

The two of them remained sitting on the couch by the fire in silence. However hearing the name "Amy" woke something up within Joseph. The feeling would not leave his mind until he fell asleep.

Sara carried her sleepy son to his bedroom and tucked him in for the night. After taking a few moments to watch him curl up she closed the door and walked to the room across the hallway, Audra's room. Immediately tears were gushing out of her eyes.

The room was in pristine condition. Sara walked in slowly and sat on the bed. She reached out to touch Audra's favorite pillow and suddenly her head was feeling weird again. As she picked up the pillow she had the strange feeling that the daughter in her mind wasn't real. She felt as if her husband wasn't her husband either. She fought off the feelings as hard as she could. She knew the "truth". Now the waterworks really started.

Why am I thinking this…? What the hell is wrong with me…?

Immediately she felt dizzy and sick. The resistance was causing so much commotion it knocked her off balance and she felt nauseous. Her vision began to blur and everything became distorted and unstable.

Sara dropped the pillow and grabbed her head. She didn't know what to do, so she stood up and stumbled to the door. Now everything was spinning. Somehow she managed to make her way to the bathroom, although she hit just about everything along the way. She burst though the door and braced against it. Her world was upside down. The only thing she could do was hope to stay awake.

She turned the faucet on and dipped down to wash her face. This helped out. She focused her attention on the cold water and the dizziness faded, the distorted vision went back to a blur, and her thoughts returned somewhat back to normal.

I need some sleep. She splashed her face a few more times and breathed in deep. *Maybe I need some medicine.*

When she came up to reach into the medicine cabinet… she saw Alan in the reflection of the mirror! Instantly she backed into the hallway. For a second she thought she saw an intruder, but she knew it was the mirror with *her* reflection. When the fear settled she slowly stood up and approached the reflection again. The image was the same!

Alan looked at her as surprised as she looked at him, even more so when he moved. She gazed at him with uncertainty as he touched his side of the mirror. She undeniably felt connected of this young man. She had to touch his hand, through the mirror anyway. As they connected she felt the desire to let go of her identity.

"Let me out" Alan said.

"Who are you?" Sara asked.

Alan did not reply. He leaned in closer and she did the same. When she looked into his eyes she saw her own!

"No! It can't be," she said.

"You have to let go. What you feel is the truth," Alan said.

She was no longer afraid of the reflection. She was merely confused. "How can this be happening...? What is happening?" Sara asked.

"You have become lost. You will be trapped forever if you don't let go."

"I can't."

"You must. You're not real."

"But don't you see? This is my life, I can't let go of it."

But she desperately wanted to. She could feel the freedom that came with surrendering and she longed for that joyful feeling. Sara, at first reluctantly, closed her eyes and stopped resisting.

"I'm sorry Audra," she said underneath her breath.

"There is nothing to be sorry about," Alan replied.

Sara gave in to the pull and let go completely. This allowed Alan to pass through the barrier. As they pressed against the mirror Alan regained control. He filtered in through her arms and nose and then traveled down to her feet. Within seconds her body was his again. He was in awe of everything once again. Alan felt as he did when he first left his body.

"This is weird," he muttered under his breath.

The first thing he did was check below to make sure he was "all together". It wasn't weird enough that he became someone else; no, he had to be a woman. Once his manhood was *secure* he looked into the mirror. There were swirls of colors but not a solid reflection. Out of curiosity he stuck his hand in it and pulled out what looked like mercury. Alan had no recollection of what he said to Sara from the other side of the mirror. He could only remember what she said to the reflection. Her memories were his.

Playtime was over however. He had to get the hell out of this mess before he was lost in Sara's identity again. He couldn't leave without Amy though. Before taking another step he checked out the room to make sure everything was solid. When he felt secure, he moved on with the mission, *Get Amy and go!*

The wood in the floor creaked with every step. Alan knew that enough noise would draw too much attention and that would be bad. He was afraid that if he saw Jeff he would lose himself again.

Fortunately, Amy was just across the room or at least some part of her. Alan cautiously opened the door emitting a loud and annoying squeak.

"Sara! Honey, are you ok?" Jeff yelled from the other room.

Alan didn't answer. Before moving again he had to listen to see if Jeff was getting up. Sure enough he was! The bed squeaked and then came footsteps. Alan opened Joseph's door and stuck his head in.

"Amy!" he whispered forcefully. Little Joseph didn't flinch.

Alan had no time. He had to hide. The sound of heavy wind and a door slamming again and again was coming from the foyer below, and he could feel something tugging. He ran down the stairs and found the front door wide open. Ferocious winds were blowing through the house. Outside there was a terrible storm brewing. There was dust and wind blowing everywhere. With nowhere else to run he headed outside. The sky was turning a dark reddish color and lightning spewed out from the clouds. He had to get a better look.

Alan ran behind the home to see where all of this was coming from and was stunned. Far, far in the distance was the volcano! It returned, and worse, it was active! This was where the storm was coming from. The storm wasn't really moving it was growing. The smoke that billowed out from the volcano simply pushed the existing clouds further out and the once peaceful, non-active crater was now filled with red lava and shooting plumes of thick black smoke.

A thick dirt storm surrounded Alan as the winds increased. It swirled around him as if intentionally. This was familiar to Alan. He remembered this happening to him when he was Sara. He fought as hard as he could until realizing that this was probably intentional, just like last time. Also just like the last time, he saw the Native American in the mix of the dust. He was fading in and out of Alan's view.

"Who are you?" Alan yelled at the top of his lungs. The storm was so intense Alan could barely hear his own voice.

The Native American walked calmly and effortlessly through the turmoil. "F-O-C-U-S," he said in his very calm and collective voice.

Alan reached his hand out and the Native American reached back. As their hands met the Native American grabbed Alan and pulled him close. The force and will of this man frightened Alan at first. The guy had no trouble balancing in the storm. But, in the Native American's eyes was something Alan rarely saw in the eyes of any human... clarity. Alan didn't even know if this were really a human he was looking at.

"Surrender to what is. Stop fighting," the Native American said.

Though feeling overwhelmed by this man, Alan listened. Alan felt childlike in the way that he had a lot to learn from the Native American. His eyes spoke pure wisdom. The Native American waved his hands in front of Alan implying for him to shut his eyes. Without resistance Alan did so and relaxed as best he could. The amount of debris increased to the point that nothing was visible anyway.

The Native American released Alan's hands and Alan felt the wind carrying him. After a couple of seconds he became afraid that he would be carried away, so he reached out for the Native American's hands. No one was there. He opened his eyes to find himself in a violent dust storm... all alone.

He fought his hardest to get down but he was fighting the air. Very quickly he realized the futility of his actions and relaxed. That's when he noticed the stars above. The storm was relaxing. As the winds calmed down things became visible again. He was now at the top of a baron hill, alone. He looked everywhere but there were no houses.

"No! AMY!"

The only visible landmark was the volcano, and it was now twice as far away. The storm it was brewing hadn't reached this far yet.

"Damn it! NO!"

As he yelled at the top of his lungs the blurred vision and spinning returned. His mind felt heavy and ached with a throbbing pain. His pain and suffering increased the more he resisted, no matter what identity he had. He fought hard against the situation but the harder he fought the worse everything became. The emotion was so intense throughout his body it forced him to collapse just as it did with Sara. By no choice of his own he gave in. His face softened and his body became less rigid as he fell to the ground. Like much of the human race, the only respite he found was in complete unconsciousness.

Chapter 12

Joseph remained curled up in his bed till the early hours of the morning. He appeared to be sleeping soundly in his bed, but throughout the night he was bombarded with visions of a young girl begging to be released from her cage. Developing within him was the urge to find something, something hidden... within. The urge was growing and he couldn't understand why. There was also a presence calling him throughout the night. A presence he knew. The name was at the tip of his mind.

"Alan," he said under his breath. He quickly sat up and opened his eyes.

But before he could think about anything Jeff popped into the room with a worried look on his face. Joseph looked at him with equal concern. "Did you see your Mom?" Jeff asked.

Joseph took a second, not really sure why he was asking. All he knew was that his dad was afraid of something.

"Joey, listen to me! Have you seen or spoken to your mother today?"

Joseph shook his head and Jeff stormed off. He got out of bed and walked into the hall. All he could hear was his father stomping around the house and frantically yelling.

"Sara!"

Joseph heard Jeff open the front door and slam it and then walk to the back door and do the same.

"SARA!" he yelled again.

Joseph ran into his parent's bedroom and looked at their empty bed. He then immediately ran downstairs and into the backyard. He wondered if the weather had something to do with this. The storm was still brewing from afar. The wind and dust last night must have been an isolated incident but the big one was coming, it would only be a matter of time before it hit.

But then, there it was, an odd yet mesmerizing sight before Joseph's view. He could not place what it was at first but when Joseph laid eyes on the *volcano* something sparked within him. Yes, it was the origin of the storm, but the volcano meant something more. He couldn't put his finger on it but that volcano was of some great significance. He had to figure out what. His *life* depended on it.

Hours passed since Joseph woke up to the call of his *father*. A couple of *strange* vehicles were parked outside of the home and along the side of these vehicles were thin strips that emitted a bright florescent purple light... the police! Jeff stood outside talking to them while Joseph was being coddled by one of his aunts on the front porch. *No one* seemed to notice the storm, but Joseph couldn't keep his eyes off of it. It was terrifying yet he was uncontrollably drawn to it.

"Don't worry, she'll be back," his aunt said. "Everything will be ok... don't worry about a thing."

"What about the storm?" Joseph asked.

"What? Oh honey, don't you worry. Everything will be taken care of."

"No, I mean the storm. What's going to happen when it hits?"

"There's nothing wrong baby," she said talking *at* him, not to him. It was as if she didn't even see the storm.

Joseph was frightened, not just because his mom was missing but she was missing when the worst storm ever seen was coming. He looked over at the neighbors who were chatting amongst themselves. None of them seemed to notice the storm either. It was like it was oblivious to everyone. They were far more interested in the drama.

An older woman and a young couple stood on the sidewalk enthralled by the situation. "It's so sad. They just lost their little girl now the mother too. It's awful, just awful," the woman said.

Joseph couldn't help but feel isolated all over again. It seemed no one had a clue about anything, and on top of that, without the proper guidance Amy would be lost in this identity forever!

Miles away, Alan was lying in the sun staring into the bright blue sky. The gloom of the storm still hadn't reached this far. It hadn't really occurred to him to get up and find Amy. He was in a trance. The surge of emotion incapacitated him through the night and he lost his ability to move. He wasn't really conscious and he wasn't really unconscious. He was just kind of there.

The wind gently blew a few leaves by his face and he didn't glance at any of them. His mouth hung open and his eyes showed no comprehension. It wasn't until a vibrant explosion shook the ground and a loud boom filled the air that he snapped back into full conscious. His eyes shifted as discrimination and judgment became factors of his awareness again. He looked over at the volcano and squinted. It was spewing out more clouds.

"Amy," he said underneath his voice.

Fear instantly sprung into the pit of his stomach and he began wondering if he would ever see her again. Feelings of guilt tortured his mind. He felt as if he could and should have grabbed her while she was sleeping.

But was that her? he wondered.

He hadn't seen her change into the little boy; he only felt her presence. When he tried to move he became even more frustrated. His body had no energy; it was all being given to his emotions and they were draining him heavily.

"Damn it! Let me up!" he yelled.

He felt it was unfair to have been put into this universe. This was not what he wanted. He knew there was someone controlling or guiding this universe. Everything had an order that could only be controlled by some form of consciousness. And if that were the case, then someone was stopping him, purposely, from moving.

"Can't you just let me up? What the hell did I do to you?" He looked into the three stars thinking they had to be a connection to the creator.

"Answer me!" He could feel the energy drain out of him with each surge of emotional charge.

Alan expected an answer but all he got was silence. "Damn it! What the hell am I supposed to do?" Silence was all that followed.

But then... Alan had an epiphany. *What if this is the answer? If the universe is perfect without strain, if everything in the universe went the way it was supposed to, even in the midst of chaos, then why am I any different? Aren't I a part of the universe?*

This thought brought great inhalation and excitement. He felt the power once surging through him return. The balance within was quickly restoring itself. He closed his eyes and relaxed. The heaviness quickly turned into joy and enthusiasm and a rush of positive energy filled every inch of his body. When Alan opened his eyes he was amazed. His body was glowing and he couldn't help but smile from the intensity of joy he felt at the moment. Without any effort on his part he began floating upward and the same look of astonishment that he had when he first came into this strange universe was back on his face.

Now he was ready to get his friend. At first he questioned which direction to look, but then he closed his eyes and felt within. He knew, he knew exactly where to go and how to get there. He also knew that time was running out. The storm that was looming was no ordinary storm. It was going to change everything and that was something he was afraid of. He didn't let that linger in his mind though. He stayed focused on the task at hand and started running.

At first his speed was limited but then he realized he was running at the pace he *thought* he could run at. He changed his thoughts from the realistic to the impossible and his speed increased to about six thousand RPM's, that's six thousand steps per minute in terms of a human. Alan's power was back!

Chapter 13

The family (Jeff, Joseph, two aunts, one uncle and a grandma) sat at the dinner table waiting to hear some news. The telephone, along with pictures, items of clothing, and just about anything that could be used to help find someone, was spread out on the table. Everyone was frantic and chitchatting away, except for Joseph. He watched everyone lose his or her mind in a relatively calm state.

But then, someone came walking through the door and everyone immediately turned to look… it was cousin Tim. He gave a tired shake letting them know he found nothing. Disappointed, they all quickly returned to the constant chatter.

Jeff mentioned new search areas while others talked about why she would do this or who could have done it. A couple of family members mentioned little Audra and how she just passed away.

"This family is cursed," uncle Bobby said.

Joseph twisted and turned as he listened to little bits of all the conversations. Suddenly, in the background was the sound of a thunderous explosion. The volcano was erupting, spitting more clouds out and increasing the size of the storm. Joseph was amazed that no one talked about it. No one cared. He got up from the table and looked out of the back window. The storm was well over his home and looking nasty. The lightning bolts alone were scary but the hundreds of tornadoes forming in the distance were terrifying!

Little Joseph walked to his grandma hoping she could shed some light on the storm. "Grandma," he asked with his little voice. "What's going to happen when the storm hits?"

"Oh come here now baby. Grandma will protect you," she said.

"But what's going to happen?"

"We don't know. Things will be different I can tell you that sweetie. Now don't worry about such things. Are you worried about your mom?"

"Not really, Grandma. I feel like she's nearby."

Grandma smiled at the confidence of her *grandson*. Moments later they all heard footsteps on the front porch. All of the chatter came to a halt as they waited for the door to open. You could've cut the tension with a knife. Slowly, the door squeaked open... it was Alan! No one spoke. They all just stared with their jaws wide open.

Do they see me or do they see a woman...? He wondered. *I guess I'll know if they charge at me with knives.*

He stood in silence waiting for someone to speak. When he looked into Joseph's eyes he saw a spark, a clear indication that Amy was still in there.

What are you thinking? he wondered as they stared at each other.

"Where on Earth have you been? You have had this family worried sick," Grandma said.

Alan was severely thrown off. Everyone was looking at him as if they knew him. In their eyes they must have seen Sara, everyone except Joseph. Alan knew Amy was looking through those eyes. She might have been confused or out of control but she was in there begging to be released.

"Sara. Are you going to say something? Where were you? I mean what happened? You can't just disappear and return with nothing to say," Jeff scolded.

Alan was desperately searching for Amy through Joseph's eyes. They didn't have much time and Alan didn't want to become Sara again. He stared with intense concentration at Joseph. "Amy," he whispered.

Everyone looked at each other confused.

Jeff was getting angry, fast. He too lost a daughter and he could tell he was losing a wife. He felt as if she was taking things way too far. His eyes squinted and his tone became stern. "Who are you talking to?"

Everyone could see that it was Joseph Alan was looking at. Alan looked around at the family. Their eyes were so judgmental. He started getting really nervous, though he would not leave that house without Amy. He had to try a more direct approach.

He walked up to Joseph and kneeled down in front of him. "Wake up!"

"Sara what are you saying? What the hell is wrong with you?" Jeff was livid.

Grandma wanted answers too, but she couldn't tolerate a bad temper. "Jeff, calm down. All we need to do is settle down here and gather ourselves."

Joseph stared into the eyes of his "mother". He could feel the urge that had bothered him the whole night nudging at him, even harder now. He was so close to finding out what it was.

"Amy, it's you! Snap out of it," Alan whispered.

Joseph felt as if he was a witness at a mob trial. The family was now staring at both of them weirdly. He looked around for some sort of comfort but found a bunch of confused eyes all pointed in his direction.

"It's you Amy. You have to wake up or we'll be stuck here," he was not so quiet this time.

The family stared at them, completely thrown off.

"Sara, do you want to explain what is going on or should I be calling a doctor!" Jeff threatened.

Alan turned to the family. He knew they were going to make it difficult for him to get out of there. "Don't you guys get it? This isn't real. None of this is. All of this is just a dream... kind of."

A couple of the aunts started laughing.

Why does everyone laugh when I say that? Alan pondered.

Joseph looked at Alan and then at the family. He was torn between them. It was in the eyes that he saw the truth however. The eyes of his family members were all droned out and systematic. They didn't seem to really know what was going on, they were acting on a preplanned thought pattern. They were all identified with their personalities and personalities are only surface level and relatively shallow. However, in Alan's eyes there was much more. He was a being that realized he was deeper than what his mind had to offer. That's when Joseph's eyes saw behind the blanket of his thoughts... and found Alan. The image of his mother had faded.

If she wasn't real... then maybe I'm not real either, Joseph thought.

As if enlightened, Joseph smiled at Alan in awe. The shell was cracked and Amy was pushing through. His body began morphing into the shape of a young female's. Amy was back.

Jeff had enough. He didn't see any transformation; he saw his wife going nuts and his son going down with her. He picked up the phone and dialed the police. Sara's *sister* leaned in to feel Alan's forehead.

His temperature was fine so she shrugged her shoulders. "It's not a fever."

Alan looked at the woman like she was insane. *How can they not see this?*

Amy was fascinated by what was going on and in some way she was enjoying it. Her whole body was filled with exaltation and the extreme joy of being. She stared around like a newborn fascinated by the miracle of life itself. However, she was quickly reminded of what was happening and realized the peril of the situation.

Alan was watching the transformation with satisfaction and Amy knew by the look in his eye that he saw everything happen. But when she looked into the eyes of the family she did not see the same excitement. They didn't see a thing, they merely saw little Joseph widen his eyes and look around dumbfounded. She knew they had to do something.

"She's right," Amy said referring to Alan. "You're not real. None of you are."

Grandma fainted after hearing this. The family rushed to check on her while Jeff paused his conversation on the phone.

"Stop this. Just stop it!" He returned to the phone call, furious.

Amy looked at Alan and shrugged her shoulders. Then, they both had an idea. At the same time Alan and Amy looked at each other and then looked at the front door. Their only chance, and they had to take it while everyone was distracted, was to bolt for it passed the family.

Jeff caught the looks and was not about to let it happen. "Come right now!" Jeff said to the other line. He ran around the table to stop anything before it happened. "Oh no you don't." He damn near knocked over Alan to grab Amy by the arm. "You want to drive yourself nuts, do it on your own!" Jeff turned to the family, "Watch her."

Amy was dragged up the stairs and into Joseph's room. "Alan! Help me!"

Jeff was ready to smack the insanity out of "Sara" and hearing those words come from his *son* made him even more upset. "What are you saying? Did your mom tell you to say that?" he threw Amy on the bed and slammed the door. "Listen to me Joe. Your mom is crazy. All of this is real. The only one who is being fake is your mother and believe me when I say I will put an end to her bullshit."

Amy was afraid he was going to hit her or something. The blind fury raging in his eyes was a clear indication that he was pushed to his limits.

The family was completely lost at this point. They were hoping to get Sara back but now they wanted to commit her away. Alan looked upstairs, wondering how the hell he was going to get Amy out. The family blocked him from moving, period, let alone getting upstairs. He figured that at the right time he could make it passed the family and out the front door but he could not do it without Amy. He didn't know her that long but they had grown a bond of some kind, that and the last thing he wanted to do was travel out here alone.

Uncle John put his hand on Alan's shoulder. "Just sit tight. Help is coming."

"I don't need help. What the hell is wrong with you people?"

"It's ok, it's all going to be ok." Aunt Mae said.

Is that all you can say? Alan thought.

Alan looked outside. Another dust storm was moving in. Debris was flying everywhere and not just small stuff. A yard-long piece of white picket fence slammed into the back sliding door. Alan was startled but the others weren't moved.

"Don't you guys see what's happening?"

"What can we do about it?" said the other aunt with absolutely no interest.

These guys are robots, Alan thought.

He sat down, surrendering to the fact that he had to wait. He couldn't help but be afraid that Amy would change back into Joseph up there. Alan would fight his way if he had to, but he was afraid that if he lost his cool he might become identified with Sara once more.

Jeff paced back and forth in the room as Amy sat on the bed, now a little more relaxed. She was devising a plan to get away from the fuming man standing before her. She thought about waiting until they slept but who knew what could be going on at that point. She knew that she would have to sneak passed him or maybe even knock him out.

Ok maybe not knock him out, she thought.

He was quite a bit bigger than she was. However, she was in a world where physics didn't matter. She had seen so many miracles in this strange land and she had no reason to believe the miracles were over.

Jeff instantly turned to talk, scaring her to the back of the bed. "Look son, your mom is going through rough times, we all are. So I need you to stay away from her for a while ok? I'm going to take you out of the house."

This is it, she thought. Amy nodded her head in apparent compliance. *If this guy thinks I'm on his side he'll let his guard down.*

She thought of something clever to say. "No matter what happens everything will be ok."

Jeff chuckled at the maturity of his *son* and returned to his thoughts. He put his head down and closed his eyes. This was it! The moment had come, it was now or never for Amy. With all her might she pushed herself forward and out of the door, closing it in the process. Jeff turned around startled at first and then followed after her.

The family turned their heads upwards to find out where all the commotion was coming from. Alan realized what was going on without having to see it. There was just enough room under the table for him to crawl through and there was no one blocking the other side. While everyone's focus was above, Alan took advantage of the situation and crawled through the tight opening. He prayed desperately for their timing to be right. Uncle Tim caught Alan from the corner of his eye making a move for it. He lunged his heavy-set body forward to stop him but failed. Several other family members turned to try to stop Alan but their attempts were unsuccessful also. With coincidental luck, Alan and Amy met at the landing in unison.

Bursting through the front door and leaping from the top of the stairs, Amy and Alan felt like eagles fleeing a pigeon coop. Unfortunately, however, they left one problem and entered another. A wave of violent tornadoes ravaged the entire area and the sky was a thick reddish black color with lightning spewing out of it in every direction. Since the center of this mess erupted from the volcano, the volcano they came from, their only option was to go in the opposite direction. Their journey was far from over.

Chapter 14

It had been hours since they escaped from the house of insanity. They managed to dodge the tornadoes but the dust storm was still blocking their vision. Thankfully, it was beginning to let up. This gave them the indication that they were going in the right direction. Just about the only thing they could see in this area was those familiar rolling hills and from what they could tell there were no houses nearby. This was both good and bad for them. The last thing they wanted was to repeat the experience they just got out of, but they also didn't want to travel in the middle of nowhere forever.

Alan did his best to cover up Amy from the debris but she wasn't used to chivalry and kind gestures. Most guys, in her experience, were after two things, sex and then sex with someone else. And for the first time in her life she let someone protect her when she was feeling vulnerable.

Alan stopped for a second and covered his eyes. "I can't see a damn thing!" he grumbled in frustration.

"We've been running for at least an hour. This is bullshit!" she added.

It was great that they were finally on the same page but they were also feeding each other's frustrations. It wasn't until they finally saw some light ahead that their frustration eased up a bit. This gave them the motivation to press forward.

After dodging a few large chunks of dirt and nearly toppling over they were able to see clearly. It wasn't that they moved *out* of the storm, it just let up suddenly.

Something's weird, Alan thought.

He turned around and saw the volcano way in the distance. He knew that they hadn't traveled that far in the time they were walking. "I guess distance truly has no meaning out here."

Amy looked around for the housing subdivision. It was nowhere to be found. "You think they're looking for us?" she asked.

"Somehow I get the feeling *they* are as lost as we are," Alan commented. She looked at him waiting for further explanation. "I don't know... They just seemed so... trapped in their heads. Of course, so did we."

Amy couldn't help but wonder how the hell any of this was happening. Her thoughts said it was impossible but she also realized now more than ever that anything can *seem* impossible before it happens. "What is going on?" she asked.

"To be honest, I still don't have a clue. But that guy said this would happen," Alan remembered his conversation with Wu Ming. "That's right! He said stay clear-headed or you'll get lost... or something," he didn't remember the exact quote.

She looked at him curiously. "Who said this would happen?"

"That Wu Ming guy I told you about. He said it would be easy to get lost in my thoughts and become identified with them. I didn't think he meant it literally."

Amy began to wonder who the people she just ran from were or if they were even real. When she thought about the logic of the situation everything seemed so dream like. But as an experience she knew it was real. She went through it, she felt it, and she remembered it. *But how can this be real?* she wondered.

"Do you think those people are real? I mean are they like ghosts?" She felt silly asking the question but she knew Alan was the only person she could ever say it to.

"Who were they? I don't know. What are they? I can't answer that either... Who were *we* is a better question? Did you have any clue as to what you were doing?" Alan asked.

She thought about it. "Yeah, I did. I just, couldn't really..."

"Choose to do what you wanted to do," Alan finished her sentence. "My mind was running without me. I could hear, see and feel everything but it was like all my choices were already made."

She thought about her real life and giggled. "Funny enough that felt familiar."

"What do you mean?"

"I feel that way at home too. Like what I say is ready to come out before it's said. Especially in an argument."

She could feel her inner being wanting to open up to him, and that scared her. Alan looked at her and smiled. At that moment they knew they would not have a tough time trusting each other.

"Yeah. It seems like everyone is like that at home," he said with a smile.

He couldn't do anything but glare at her. He was really appreciating her ability to see the world around her. It was almost sexy.

"What? Why are you looking at me like that?" she said shimmering back at him. She was soaking up every second of his attention.

"I don't know. There's a lot more to you than what I first thought. You're different... I kind of like that."

Amy let out a giddy giggle and immediately retracted. *Am I attracted to him?* she thought with much surprise.

She looked at his face when he wasn't looking and noticed his masculine yet gentle features. His was a very peaceful person and extremely wise for his age, and these were qualities she had never seen in anyone she'd ever dated.

I am attracted to him, she realized.

Alan turned and caught her checking him out. Immediately her teeth glistened as she looked into his dark mysterious eyes. The moment trapped them into a vortex of anticipation. The pull was so strong they were forced to move in closer to one another. And then… they heard the faint sound of trickling water. This was a relief for Amy. She wasn't ready to fall for him even though she wanted to. Amy immediately turned to look for the H2O, though Alan was not as enthused about the water. He knew he was about to get a kiss and he wanted it, badly.

She had to find out where the water was coming from. Amy pulled Alan like a rag doll in search for the source. When they found the source of the water they were amazed. It was a pretty large stream and definitely touched by the hands of intelligent beings. Lining the bed of this little river was the most polished white stone they'd ever seen. Engraved in the stone were symbols of some ancient looking language. The water itself was sparkling and had a strange attraction to it. They both felt a strong urge to touch the water.

Alan stuck his hands in first and couldn't help but smile. There was an intense rush of energy that traveled from his fingertips to his ears. He turned to give Amy a quirky smile and then unexpectedly fell in.

"What are you doing?" She looked at him like he was crazy.

When he resurfaced he had the smile of an adolescent in a carefree environment. She couldn't help but laugh at him.

"Jump in," he said.

She gave him a caustic look. "I don't think so."

"Come *on*," he swam up close to the edge and reached his hand out. "At least help me up."

"Do you realize if you pull me in I will never trust you again?"

Alan grinned. She was on to him. To his luck as she went to help him out she lost her balance and fell without his intervention. Alan started cracking up as he swam over to help her out of the water.

As she burst through the surface and flipped her hair back Alan was mesmerized. The sparkling water gleamed all over her body and her curvaceous figure nearly popped through her soaked clothing as she bounced around.

This is better than an Herbal Essence commercial, he thought.

He was relieved to see a joyful smile on her face; Alan thought she might have been upset about getting her clothes wet or something. But she felt the effects of the water as well. There was definitely more than just hydrogen and oxygen flowing through this stream of bliss.

"Oh my God. It feels great," she felt so intense she had to say something.

"It's like being held by your mother as a baby; total comfort and security," he said.

Alan dove back under. The feeling of being submerged in this water was electrifying but as he swam close to the bottom he noticed something… a current. And a current meant the stream lead somewhere.

Where does it end? he wondered.

When he popped back up Alan stood much closer to Amy. Instantly she felt taken back by his proximity but with this energetic joy flowing through her body she couldn't resist him. Alan could tell she wanted to get close but he also felt the hesitation. Like the gentlemen he was, he backed off for her.

"Come on, it leads somewhere," he said.

Alan enthusiastically swam on while Amy stood still with the butterflies roaming around her stomach. She was surprised, as she actually felt disappointed.

They swam strong for a good mile until the current picked up to a point of raging water. But when they realized the river wasn't calming any it was too late, the current was too strong to swim against.

"Alan!" Amy cried.

Alan fought his hardest and managed to swim next to her. Ahead, about thirty yards, was a waterfall, though there wasn't much they could do except brace for it. The drop wasn't that long, maybe *seven hundred* feet!

"Just hold my hand. We'll be ok. Promise!" he said.

Like a cat being dunked in a pool of water, Amy clinched on to Alan for dear life. She could feel the anticipation and the fear building extreme momentum in her body as she watched the drop off point get closer and closer. And then... they were off!

The feeling of freefalling was one of the most liberating either had ever felt and the smack into he surface below was equally as exciting. The fear of the unknown and then a relief as they realized they were safe were much like the effects of a rollercoaster.

"Alan!" she yelled as she popped above the surface. He was nowhere to be seen... "Ahh!" she screamed as she felt something tug at her leg. It was Alan. He surfaced up laughing his little heart out. "You prick," she said smacking him with a smile on her face.

They looked around to get a good picture of where they landed. A thick forest surrounded the pool of water they were floating in, though this one was more tropical than the last. Amy dreaded heading into another forest. The last one seemed to last forever and that left a bad taste in her mouth for being around trees. But much to their delight, the mysteries of the water continued behind the waterfall!

"Look!" Alan shouted.

Behind the waterfall was a bright and rather large object reflecting light. Alan was helplessly drawn to it and with little choice because the current was pulling them in!

"What should we do?" Amy asked.

"Just go with it."

After being slammed by the pressure of the fall they rose to one of the most divine sights they'd ever seen. Their eyes were popping as they gazed upon an underground sanctuary made entirely of crystal. The whole cave had been hollowed out and sculpted. It was filled with complex tunnels and passageways extending for miles. There was railing on the walkways, cathedral shaped ceilings and staircases leading to other areas, all carved from the purest crystal ever seen by human eyes. On the walls were lighting fixtures, also made of crystal, emitting a blue flame that was cool to the touch.

Ahead of them was a long and dark tunnel. As the water pulled them on, the blue flames ignited, magically lighting their path. The sound of water flow grew heavier as they were taken further into the tunnel, but not only that, they could tell the current was getting stronger. That familiar sound of rushing water was not too far ahead.

"It sounds like another fall. We should we do?" Amy said fearing another drop.

"I don't know if we have a choice."

They didn't have a choice. The water was carrying them and there was nothing they could do about it. There was a point where the crystal cave ended and the lights ceased to light up. This was because they were entering a large opening. Beyond it was total darkness!

As they approached their unknown fate, Amy grabbed Alan and clung to him as tightly as possible. No matter the amount of miracles she'd witnessed she was still afraid.

"Alan!"

"Yeah?"

"I just want to thank you for coming back to get me. I want you to know I…" She didn't finish her sentence. She was feeling too emotional and didn't want to let out too much. "I don't want to die!"

Alan smiled as he held on tightly. Before long they were freefalling again, only this time they couldn't see where to. At first there were the expectations of impact but that moment was taking its time. Twenty seconds went by…thirty seconds…forty…fifty…

Their thoughts were torturous to them. They didn't know what they would hit. Alan felt comfortable after falling for a minute. He didn't know what was going to happen but the fear wore off.

What could really happen? he thought, feeling secure. *But… what if we fall forever? What if there is no landing? What if this is the end of the universe?*

Their fear of falling forever finally came to an end as they plunged into another body of water. Alan began to feel secure again, but the problem now was there was no source of light and they could not see a thing.

"Amy!" he yelled.

She came to the surface and felt around for him. "Alan!"

"I'm right here."

They swam towards the other's voice and met. She was terrified and feeling claustrophobic. Anything could have been down there. They had to be thousands of feet below the surface, and in a semi-alien world. She began fearing spiders and bats; crawling predators with sharp teeth or even worse, water creatures, creatures that lived in the shadows and could see you but you couldn't see them.

"What was that?" she asked terrified, feeling something move passed her leg. It came by again and again as if only brushing against her slightly. "Did you feel that?" She held on to Alan for dear life.

"What is it?" he asked.

"I don't know," she said trembling.

Alan felt the same thing only his mind wasn't quite as active as hers. "I think it's the water current."

"How do you know?"

"I don't."

These words frightened her. She needed security and comfort and the water's supernatural powers weren't strong enough to calm her mind. But when Alan cupped his hand around her soft cheek she instantly felt safer.

"We'll be ok," he said to her softly.

These words were hypnotic to her ears. Beyond the simple vibrations of air that created his voice was the care and tenderness of someone genuine. She quickly forgot her fear of dangerous cave animals as the energy produced by the water intensified his touch, and trapped her within the heat of his passion. Every nerve in her body was lit up like a torch as he caressed her arms. She was powerless against him.

Both of them were nervous, only Alan was not letting go this time. He wrapped his hands around the back of her neck and reeled her in for the most intense and passionate kiss she'd ever endured. She felt like a Popsicle in the middle of the Sahara.

Suddenly, a blue light shined about a mile underneath them! Alan noticed the light while his lips had Amy mesmerized.

"Look!" he said.

The light came up through a long crystal stem and surrounded them in what looked like a giant martini glass. It then became obvious where the current was flowing. The waterfall was pouring into the pool they were floating in and overflowing into the abyss of darkness below. They could see no surface underneath them. The cylindrical crystal stem that was holding them seemed to continue on forever.

The light coming through didn't stop on the rim of the pool, it continued into a crystal staircase that was connected. This staircase led upward to an obtrusive wall surrounded by darkness. In front of this wall was a platform that the stairs connected to. Everything was crystal.

Alan held Amy by the hand and led her up the stairs, both soaking wet. Its transparency was at first frightening but the sight was incredible. As they approached the wall they realized that that's all it was, a wall. The platform neither extended nor wrapped around to anywhere else.

"What now?" Amy asked.

Alan looked strangely at the wall. It was extremely polished and hand carved. "All of this is here for a reason."

He reached his hand out and touched the crystal wall. The individual bulges of crystal instantly melted together and the formation of rock liquefied from the inside out. To their surprise it turned into a wall of what looked like water! Deep into this vertical pool of liquid was a source of light. Alan, like usual, was the first to touch. His arm passed through creating a ripple effect. The first thing he noticed was the texture of the substance.

"It definitely feels like water."

They looked at each other and knew that the only thing they could do was walk on in. With little hesitation they closed their eyes and stepped into the unknown together.

Chapter 15

Incredulous was the best way to describe how both Alan and Amy felt within. They were walking through water, not floating and not swimming; walking. Even more uncanny was their ability to breathe normally in this mystical substance. The liquid surrounded them and they could feel it, but it wasn't getting into their eyes or mouth or any other orifice. They were also able to walk without strain. Usually when underneath water one must use a great deal of strength to move around but not here. It was as if the liquid was there but moved around *them*!

There was still a bright light shining towards them. They couldn't tell what it really was; of course by this time it could have been anything. The light was too bright to come from one of those blue flames and it was definitely too bright to be anything small. The closer to the end they came the more the light seemed like... sunlight!

But we're underground, they both thought.

As they approached the end of this paranormal body of liquid they could only see what appeared to be more water. There were wavy blue reflections everywhere and at every angle. Alan stuck his head out to get a peek.

With great inhalation, shock and disbelief, Alan laid his eyes on what appeared to be a city made entirely of water! He blinked a few times to make sure he wasn't hallucinating, but it was definitely there. He retracted back into the liquid with his jaw hanging low and the curiosity was now probing at Amy's mind. She had to know what the big deal was so she stuck her head out and looked upon the city with the same visage of wonder Alan had.

The city was extraordinary. It had the appearance of a floating saucer and had to have been at least five square miles around. It was fully functional too. There were bridges extending from massive structures that had the appearance of buildings and houses. There were pods of water transporting people from one location to another like flying vehicles. In the center of the city was a giant fountain, thirty stories high. The fountain fed the city its source of constantly flowing crystal clear water. The city itself seemed to be balanced over a circular shaft, one hundred yards in diameter, which led to ocean-like body of water two miles below.

Alan and Amy looked at each other hesitantly. Leading to this city was a thin bridge, also made of water. Alan kneeled down and stuck his hands out. As he touched the bridge he was shocked to find that it was solid. He crawled out on all fours with his eyes closed praying to the high heavens he wouldn't fall through. He was relieved as the water sustained his body. When he looked back he saw that the mountain they were traveling through was made entirely of crystal. Alan mouthed the words "my God" as he gazed from the liquid opening to the top of the mountainside thousands of feet above. When he looked down he was even more dumbfounded. Two miles was a steep drop and with the bridge having the appearance of a nonsolid substance his fear of falling intensified. Strangely, he could feel the water flowing underneath his hands and feet but neither his body nor his clothes absorbed any of it.

Alan reached back in for Amy. She was not ready to take the step however. All she could do was look below at the far, far away ocean. Alan grabbed her hand gently and tugged at it. Like a puppy learning to jump down the stairs, she leaped into the comfort of Alan's thin but strong arms. He slowly set her down to the surface but she refused to open her eyes. She felt great with his arms wrapped around her and she wanted to stay there.

Alan turned towards the city eagerly wanting to move forward. He looked back and watched as the water, or whatever it was they walked through, hardened back into crystal. He set her down and she finally opened her eyes. To help with the fear, Amy focused on the city itself, never once looking below. However, the sight was so fantastic she soon forgot she was miles in the air.

"This has to be a dream," Amy said.

"I know. This is incredible."

It didn't matter if it was some elaborate dream, they were fully aware of it. They were both starting to realize that it is awareness that gives existence purpose not external accomplishments. Alan and Amy were too fascinated to think about anything. They could only feel the wondrous splendor of the sights they were witnessing.

They walked upon a wall about ten feet tall that wrapped around the entire city with no apparent gate or opening. In one smooth motion, Alan reached out to touch the wall and it automatically opened in front of them, or more like the wall fell open. It fell into the floor and continued with the flow of water underneath their feet with absolutely no disruption in the constant flow.

Walking through the gates, they found that the city was far more complex and elaborate than they originally perceived. Thousands of people walked to and fro about their business living somewhat normal lives. Whenever someone wanted to go anywhere the water beneath them would simply form around them and fly off, leaving no trail of water behind. If someone needed a staircase it would simply form in front of him or her as they walked, and the same was true with bridges. Everything was constantly changing but in a manner that suited the needs of the people and visa versa. The people adjusted themselves to the changes of the city with ease.

Alan noticed that *everyone* was smiling or at least had a relaxed look about them. The people of this town seemed so happy and carefree. There were children playing in the streets creating toys and formations, as they wanted. Couples everywhere were holding hands while walking, kissing in the streets and watching the clear sky above. Even the single folks relaxed without a care in the world, they weren't concerned with what they didn't have, they simply enjoyed the time they witnessed.

No one seemed to "work" in this town either. The people did things as they needed to be done and everything they needed was there for them. Everyone was filled with joy and peace.

"Do you feel that?" Amy asked. She was referring to the feeling of bliss running through her body. It was like the feeling they had when they first fell into the river.

"Yeah," Alan said enjoying every second of it. "It feels like before but it's so strong."

Strangely, there were plants everywhere. They grew straight from the water without the need for soil or fertilizer. Alan noticed the roots were visible through the floor. That's when, down the road, he noticed a group of people eating. When they were done they threw their trash on the ground. It took a second but the water absorbed the trash and it was picked up by the current beneath their feet and taken somewhere below. The water flow took care of everything. It supported them in every way by providing the food they ate, grew the materials for their clothes, created the ground on which they stepped, and formed the houses in which they slept.

"How is this possible?" he asked.

Amy didn't care how; she was just enjoying the feeling. "Do you feel the intensity…? My God, this feels great."

They walked through the city amazed at everything and feeling intensely alive. Also present was the intense feeling of passion between them. Amy wanted to jump Alan's bones and he wanted to do the same to her. As they held hands the lust circulated between them like a magnetic substance.

"Are we in heaven?" Amy asked.

Alan stopped walking and pulled her close from the bottom of her lower back. Once again their lips locked and they engaged in a long, slow, enchanting kiss. The bodies they once felt to be their own melded together as one in feeling. And then, their bodies actually started to come together! They started to mold as one in the most euphoric feeling ever felt! Neither of them noticed what was happening. The feeling was so primal and the desire was too strong. The last thing they wanted was to pull apart.

Alan's hands began glowing when he pressed them against her heart. He gently moved his fingers along her collarbone and along the back of her neck and then… his hand became a part of her.

Alan opened his eyes and instantly backed away, separating from her body. "My God! All I want to do is—"

"I know," she finished with a smile. "What now?"

Alan took a second to calm down. He looked around and saw a couple passing by. "Excuse me." The couple stopped and walked towards them, emitting a warm and comfortable presence. "Can you tell us where we are?" Alan asked.

The man looked at Alan strangely. "Why you're here, of course."

"No, no. I mean in relation to some place else."

"Where else do you relate?"

Alan realized he was asking the wrong questions. He thought of something that would be recognizable. "Do you know where the volcano is?"

The couple looked at each other shocked. "Oh," the man said realizing Alan was a foreigner. "You're a traveler," the couple looked at each other and giggled.

"You can say that," Alan said in a confused tone. He didn't see the humor in the situation.

"It's out there somewhere. We've never left the city so we don't really know."

"How can we get home?" Amy asked.

Alan was thrown off. *Why does she want to leave?*

"If we wanted to, that is?" Amy finished.

The couple again looked at them perplexed. "Where else is your home?" the man asked.

"We come from another land. Somewhere far, far away," Alan said.

"Yes I know," the man said with a straight face.

"That land is o-u-r home. We want-to-go-back-there," Amy said slowly as if talking to someone of retardation.

"Is not home where you are?" The man replied. Alan and Amy shook their heads. They knew there wasn't much else they'd be getting from these people.

The man looked at them pleased that he was of help to those in need. "Can I answer anymore questions?" he said with a smile.

"No thanks," Amy quickly replied.

Alan wasn't done though. "How can the water be so solid?"

Again the couple laughed at Alan's ignorance. "See the fountain," the man pointed to the large fountain in the middle of the city, "Its flow keeps the city clean and new. It also produces the energy we need to grow our plants and produce the food we eat. It also disposes of our waste."

"But there's no dirt," Alan added.

"We use energy to feed and sustain everything."

"But how can the water be solid?"

The man and his wife laughed again. "Because of you."

Alan and Amy were thrown off.

Does he mean I created this place? Alan thought.

"If you weren't living on a certain frequency of consciousness you would pass right through the water. It's kind of how we keep out the riff raff."

Amy and Alan didn't really understand that last part mentally but on some level they knew what he meant.

"If we wanted to leave the island and find a way to go back to the land we came from, how would we do that?" Amy asked.

Alan looked at her in shock again. He thought they were done asking questions about their home.

"I don't know how to get back to where you came from other than to find out how you got here. The only way to leave the island is to jump or be sucked into the current below and the only way for that to happen is to lower your frequency."

"How do we *lower* our frequency?" Alan asked.

"I don't know I've never done it. Most people with lower frequencies live on land. They are in constant need to be entertained by useless activities and find drama to be their ultimate driving force. For the most part they find our city unattractive. We in this city like to be free of pressure and unnecessary drama, so we like keeping separated from the land dwellers. But if you wanted to find a way back to the home other than your natural one you might want to look in the mainland city."

This sparked a light within Amy while Alan wasn't as enthused. "How do we find this city?" she asked.

"I don't know that either, but I've heard it's the largest city on the planet. They say you can't mistake it for anything else. But if I were you I'd be careful. There's a storm brewing from the volcano and it's growing fast. Nobody knows how long it'll last but we know it'll change the way people live. It'll probably even destroy half of the planet."

"What will you do here?" Amy asked.

"We have the cave to go to, and besides, our way of life can continue in any form. Those below believe their technology and desires will keep them alive, but I'm afraid there isn't an amount of force or any device strong enough in the universe to protect them from this storm."

There was a moment of silence between the couples. Neither Amy nor Alan could think of anything else to ask them.

"Hey, thanks," Alan said.

The couple bowed and continued on while Alan stood staring at the giant fountain. He particularly paid attention to the process. The water came up from the ocean, shot out of the top, fell into the bottom of the fountain, and from there it dispersed into the city. Everything was self-sustaining. This was his dream home.

"So what do we do?" Amy asked.

Alan woke from his daze and looked at her. "Do you really want to leave?"

She smiled and shrugged her shoulders. He placed his arm around her and she rested her head on his chest.

"Why don't we go relax somewhere? We'll check out the city, see what it has to offer and then make our decision...ok?"

He could tell Amy was really enjoying the city but Alan knew she being tortured within.

"This place is nice but I don't want to stay here forever."

Alan gave her a sarcastic smirk. "I knew you'd say that... We'll get some rest and then figure out how to get home... How's that sound?"

Knowing that Alan understood and complied with her need to return home allowed her to place even more trust in him. His words of care and compassion forced out her pearly whites as she looked into his eyes.

Like magic, the water beneath them formed around them into a pod. Inside, there were seats and even a front window to see where they were going.

"What the hell?" Amy said while laughing.

"I think it's taking us to where we want to go."

That's *exactly* where it was taking them. The pod flew up and navigated through the city automatically. It was the perfect tour for them. They got to see all the different aspects of how these people lived and interacted on a daily basis. They had offices, homes, vacation spots, creative display centers, and so on. There also didn't seem to be a system of currency, everyone's contribution to the enlightenment of the collective was all that they needed. The people carried out the specific functions needed to run the city willingly. Everyone added his or her creative talents in whatever field as it was needed, and since there was no need to gain more, there was no competition or class system. The people were doing as well as they wanted to and it was only they who judged their position.

Though the city was made of water, the buildings were not all transparent. The intensity of the flow varied in the walls as to provide privacy for the individuals. The color of the water varied also. There were no lights like there would be in a normal city but there was the reflection of light that endlessly traveled through the water and into areas needed for illumination, and this too was controlled by the will of the people.

Alan and Amy both got the feeling that crime was virtually nonexistent in this city. Those with the intention do harm or remain stuck in ignorance probably couldn't even find footing on the streets. There were no locks on doors. No security systems or jailhouses, there wasn't even a police force. They might not have been in heaven, but this place was divine.

It was getting close to nighttime as they arrived at a *hotel* of sorts, somewhere near the edge of the city. The view was amazing. Beyond this delicate city was an infinite span of crystal-blue Ocean. It reminded Amy of being on the pacific coast looking out on the pier.

As the pod landed on the ground, it dissipated back into the flow of water. They approached the building wondering how they were supposed to reach the entrance, which was nearly two stories above them. But the answer came in the form of a staircase; it formed in front of them, leading the way inside.

The interior of the building was magnificent. It was reminiscent of a Zen garden with black and white rocks lining the edges of the water walkway and several bamboo-like trees standing tall throughout the lobby. There was no front desk but there were people walking around serving the patrons. A woman in loose fitted clothing walked up to them with a smile on her face. She could recognize a foreigner from a mile away.

"It's so nice to see people from the outside finding their way to our wonderful city," the woman said.

"Excuse me?" Amy asked.

"It's just, the state of the world leaves one to feel hopeless about our civilization as a whole. But every time I see someone from outside this city it lets me know that there is progress somewhere."

"Especially with that storm coming eh?" Alan added.

"Tell me about it," the woman laughed. "Can I help you two find something?"

"We would like a room," Alan replied with a guilty grin.

"Oh ok. Just walk in front of any of our rooms and the ones that aren't occupied will open up to you."

"Thanks," Amy said.

Before heading for rest, they took a stroll through the building simply noticing its structure and operations. With a site so marvelous, one could not help but stop and appreciate everything within view. People were free to come and go as they pleased. Food and service was not only complimentary but given with the most graceful servitude.

As they walked through the hallways, several doors opened while others remained closed, just like the host had said. Alan noticed how thick the water flow was, he couldn't see through any of the doors or walls.

That's so neat, he thought.

They walked by one more room and as the door opened for them they looked into it.

"This is as good as any," Alan said smiling from ear to ear.

They both felt the anticipation flowing through the others' mind. Though, Alan was afraid she wasn't ready for this yet. He didn't want to push or progress their relationship and scare her away. As she approached the back wall, a window-shaped hole opened in front of her. She then thought of a patio and viola, a doorway opened to the outside followed by the formation of a platform and rail.

"Why can't it be like this at home," she said to herself.

Alan walked up behind her and held her shoulders. As they looked out into the city they felt right at home. Everything here felt so perfect for them. Her hair blew in the wind and brushed against his face. He leaned in and brushed his cheek against hers and she tilted her head to look back into his eyes. The urge was back!

He kissed the back of her neck gently while rubbing her shoulders and at that moment he knew she was definitely ready for him to make the next move. She spun around and pushed him back into the room allowing the porch to retract and the door to seal, leaving them in privacy. Alan spun her around and led her to the floor but as they fell, a bed formed from beneath them, catching them in the process. It was surprisingly soft.

"It's a waterbed," Alan joked.

The laughs faded and the passion ensued. Their hands locked together like matching puzzle pieces, as did their lips. Within seconds a soft glow flushed through their *skin* and they began to connect.

"Alan, this is incredible," she moaned, feeling incapacitated by the orgasmic bliss.

The two bodies were no longer distinguishable as within and without they literally became as one!

Chapter 16

Time flew by well into the night as Alan and Amy lay cuddled up in the most literal of waterbeds. Their bodies had separated but within they still felt very much connected. The color of the water in their room changed from light blue to light red as the amount and type of energy released from within them had affected everything in the surrounding area.

There were no thoughts running through their minds at that moment, just feelings of appreciation, satisfaction, and attachment. They both were so grateful to have met each other and they didn't want to let go, not even for a second. Neither wanted to speak and ruin the moment or make a sudden move to alter the comfort... but as time moved along... thoughts once again filtered in, and some of the energy died down. They both knew and dreaded the fact that they would have to move on, more likely sooner than later.

Alan looked at her not sure what to say. "So... how are we going to keep in contact if we find a way back?"

"We'll find a way," Amy said confidently.

"You know how weird this is going to be if we do go back home."

Amy thought for a second. Something in what he said bothered her, but she shrugged it off. "I know. No one will believe any of this."

Alan turned around and stared at the ceiling. He was enthralled by the visibility of the flowing water all around them. *There's nothing stopping it, nothing getting in the way of its path. This city is awesome! This is how life should be,* he thought.

"You know if we do go home it'll be hard to top a date like this."

They both laughed at Alan's joke but Amy was not sincere. This conversation was bothering her. "*If,* huh?"

"What's the matter?" Alan asked. A tear rolled down Amy's cheek and she tried to hide it from him by rolling over. "What's wrong?"

"It's nothing... I was just... I thought about home. The thought made me realize that we might never go back. I might never see my family again."

Alan sighed. The last thing he wanted to do was kill the moment. "Yeah, I guess."

"The thought of never seeing your family and friends doesn't make you sad?"

Alan thought about his home life. He wanted to see his family at some point but he was in no rush. He simply figured one day he'd go back, that was if he *could* go back. "I just hadn't really thought about it till now... but I'm sure we'll find a way back. And until then at least we have each other."

She smiled again and this was a big relief to him. This time a tear of *joy* rolled down her face. He looked at her a little confused. He thought she was feeling better.

"You're so real. I've never met anyone like you... I've never felt this way around anyone before," she said, feeling the attachment intensify.

She was feeling extremely connected to Alan, a connection she never had with any guy. On top of not wanting to let him go, she felt something underneath, something that was unconditional. She knew he would do anything to help her and she would do the same for him. That's when more sad thoughts came into her mind.

Alan hated seeing this. He wanted her to be happy and filled with ecstatic aliveness like he was. "Amy what's up?"

For a few moments she hesitated saying what was on her mind, but she had to give in. She was trying out the whole *opening up thing* and it seemed to be going pretty well. "I don't want to lose you. What if we go back home and we can't find each other?"

Alan thought about it for a minute. "What state do you live in...? That's a start."

"Chicago," she answered. "What about you?"

"Michigan! We're not far from each other. See! This was meant to happen."

She got really excited as she thought about Michigan. She knew it well and traveled there often. "Yeah I have family..." the thoughts of never going home returned, "...there."

The feeling of sadness was like that of a bag of sand dropping into the pit of her stomach. The energy from her emotions sank Alan into a state of depression as well. And as the change in emotions came, the atmosphere around them changed too. The color in the room was fading with their mood, turning everything a grayish blue. And then... a disturbing thought ran through her mind and she quickly stood up to put her clothes on.

"What are you doing?" he asked, shocked.

"We should go. I don't want to get stuck like we did in that neighborhood."

Alan agreed with her on that. He was so wrapped up in the pleasantries of his visit to the city that he almost forgot what had happened not too long before. He remembered identifying in the woman Sara and that was *not* a pleasant experience.

He jumped up and put his clothes on too, though he wasn't ready to leave just yet. Amy on the other hand was getting claustrophobic. She felt as if the longer they stayed the less of a chance they had of returning home. She was getting worried, fast. That's when Amy noticed something different about the floor... It was wet!

Oh no, she thought. She not once felt moisture in this city until now. "Alan," she said with a worried look on her face.

She backed up and tripped on the bed splashing water everywhere. Alan was befuddled. He didn't know how this was happening. Amy felt worse and worse, and as her emotions became more negative, the less solid the surroundings became for her.

"Alan," she called as she slowly melded into the surface.

Alan quickly ran around and tried to pull her out but was unsuccessful. Since the entire city was made of constantly flowing water, everything she touched pulled her into the flow, and the current was strong; its force was far stronger than Alan's. She slipped out of his arms and slapped into the floor.

"Alan, help!"

He quickly wrapped his arms around her but what was solid for him was not solid for her. Alan pulled with every ounce of strength he had. He was terrified of losing her. That's when *his* feet began to get wet! Seconds later he lost his balance and the current got hold of her. Amy fought as hard as she could but her efforts were useless.

She was gone, sucked beneath the building. Alan could only see the colors of her clothing as she faded away. He stood up and sloshed his way through the room. Alan knew that he had to raise his level of consciousness if he were to run through the city. So, he closed his eyes and did his best to relax. Fortunately, some solidity returned, but there were still splashes of water underneath his feet. He walked to the wall and a doorway partially opened to the outside. Instead of a patio there was a pod ready to take him wherever. Alan quickly sat inside and like magic the pod took off.

He knew everything was sucked to the center of the city and that's where he had to look. *I have to reach her before it's too late...! I know I can... Damn it...! I know I can do this... Just don't take her away from me... Please... Just don't take her away!*

A few blocks down he noticed there was a problem with the pod; it wasn't flying right. It was swerving and dipping all over the place. Alan stood up and looked out of the window. As he placed his hand on the sill his hands seeped through the formation.

"Oh shit!"

The pod dive-bombed towards the street and crashed partially into the surface. As the formation of the pod broke away Alan was soaked in water. Bystanders gazed upon the scene in shock. To them, it was like a fatal accident on the freeway. Alan hunched his way forward trying his hardest to reach the fountain.

I have to reach her! I can do it!

He strained and stressed only a few feet more but found himself waist deep in water. Somehow, he managed to pull himself above street level and stand up straight to take another step, but that was it. He stumbled to the surface and put his hands to the street and they went through like quicksand. He moved his elbows trying to gain momentum in one last effort... but there was no chance of rising to the surface again. His thoughts and feelings were so negative he lost the higher frequency. The emotions were like a rollercoaster pulling him along for the ride with little choice of his own. Alan was soon sucked into the current just like Amy.

Everything became blurry. It was like being in a water slide without the plastic tube. He lost his position at first but soon saw the bulk of the water above. He was in the base of the city traveling down to the ocean! At this point he cared little of returning to the city, he only wanted to find Amy.

The long ride down was nerve wrecking. He wondered if he would ever see land again or if the current would even let him back up above water. The plunge into the endless ocean was overwhelming. The current continued to pull him lower and lower... and lower until there was no sight of the surface. Suddenly, he could feel his direction change from vertical to horizontal.

Where the hell is this thing taking me?

It was dark, deep down in the ocean. The little light that managed to creep into the depths of this vast body of water only lit up the shadowy outlines of strange looking animals. Some were as large as whales, others were tiny but in large schools. Luckily, most of the creatures kept away from the current. They were probably afraid of being pulled into it. The animals daring enough to get close were sucked in like a vacuum cleaner and carried along just like Alan.

Everything around the current flew by like it did when he was flying through space. After a while everything turned into a dark blue blur.

No... I've lost her... How did I lose her...? How did I let this happen...? This is bullshit...! I can do whatever I want out here... I can stop this... I should be able to stop...

The resistance within tortured him, as he had absolutely no control over the situation. It wasn't long before he blacked out...

Chapter 17

Repetitious waves and the sound of large and small creatures rustling about crept into the slowly arising awareness that was Alan. There was a stench in the area so foul it actually repulsed the little flying insects searching for food nearby.

Alan opened his eyes to find himself lying in a pile of pure sludge. There were mounds upon mounds of trash and dead animals that spanned for miles along this filthy beachfront. He stood up and cringed at the sight but quickly remembered that he was searching for Amy. Thankfully, she wasn't on the beach mixed in with the horrid filth, so he turned around and walked inland.

He found it hard to walk over the lumps of waste, almost as if he were stepping through a rock quarry, and the foul grin on his face worsened as he got a clear view of just how much waste was in the area and beyond. Not only had the trash extend along the beachfront, it was also being pushed into the marshlands just beyond. The sight was disturbing. Dead bodies of all kinds riddled the floor of this filthy forest, including the bodies of humans. And to top it off, there were toxic wastes and other chemicals mixed into the marsh water emitting a dark colored putrid steam.

The nastiest creatures Alan had ever seen snooped through the waste looking for food. One creature in particular frightened Alan to the bones. It was slimy and dark grey, its skin was similar to that of a pig but its body resembled that of a large lizard, and its teeth were long and sharp enough to pierce the skin of any flesh-bearing mammal! Alan now feared Amy might be among the dead or that she was injured by one of these animals.

That can't happen though...can it?

There was so much to question about this strange world. He didn't really know for sure what could and could not happen. He didn't even know if he was in his body or if he wasn't. He knew he left his body days ago but he definitely could feel the nerve stimulation and senses that were attributed to a physical body. Alan did his best not to trouble his mind with questions he couldn't answer, he just kept looking for Amy. He knew that any current trash would have been dumped in the spot he landed and she was not there.

She must be alive! He looked beneath his feet and sucked in the morbidity. *Or at least I hope she died in the water... What am I saying...? Oh man, please don't be dead... I finally meet a girl like her and I lose her... What kind of luck do I have...? Why the hell does this have to happen to me...? Why can't I just go through something I can enjoy for once...?*

Alan did his best to walk on solid land. He didn't know what was in the marsh water and he didn't really want to find out. He started to notice items that did not appear to come from the city above; large machinery items like drills and saws.

Can all this trash really be from that clean city?

That's when the *Pig Lizard*, as Alan called it, caught wind of Alan's presence. Its tall prickly hairs stood up on its back as a defense signal to warn off predators. Alan figured that any creature that size that throws up a defense that quickly must be harmless. Those were his first thoughts... until the creature snarled and began charging at him!

Alan ran for dear life as the creature jumped, swam and hurdled through the marshes to get to him. Alan was running his fastest but the creature was too agile. He had only seconds before it would get hold of him. He looked back in time to see the creature hurl towards him with incredible agility. Alan turned around while raising his arms to block as the vicious animal tackled him to the ground.

He was pinned and couldn't get away. The creature opened its snout and Alan got a clear view of just how long and how sharp its teeth were. Its four front teeth were larger than his forearm! But... just as the creature prepared to eat dinner... it paused for a second. Alan lay frozen on the ground not really sure why the animal stopped.

Maybe it wants pork chops.

The creature looked up, blinked twice and darted off. Alan didn't really care why, he was just glad the thing was off of him. But all the creatures were running for cover. Something was frightening the life in the area. That's when, in the distance, Alan heard the sound of heavy machinery and the rustling of the plant life. Something was moving through, or more like someone.

Alan ran over the hill just ahead and looked below. There were dozens of men and search vehicles running through the marshland with flashlights and powerful looking weapons. Above the trees there were several hover vehicles with spotlights and infrared sensors; they were searching for something. As Alan looked to his right he saw a shadowy figure hiding behind a pile of trash. Slowly, he moved towards the person hoping they could shed some light on the situation. Just as he reached in the individual crept back slowly, but then... BOOM! A strange pulsating wave of energy hit the person and knocked them to the ground. Instantly, one of the vehicles flew over and shined its light through the trees. It was Amy! Alan ran over to her quickly and picked her up. Luckily, she quickly snapped out of her daze and set her feet down.

"Alan...is that you?"

"Yeah," he responded. Amy realized she was still being chased and took off, yanking Alan with her. "What's going on?" he asked.

"I don't know. Maybe it's our thoughts again," she looked back and could see that the men were fresh on their tail. "I was dropped off at the shore and saw this crazy looking animal so I ran away from it. I didn't want to go too far because I wanted to see if you would come to the shore after me. But, after about twenty minutes those soldier and vehicles came out of nowhere."

The search party was gaining on them. The vehicles above had a hard time searching through the trees but the infantry below could see them just fine. They were only forty yards behind!

"Maybe it's happening because we're getting really negative," Alan said.

"Damn it! Why can't anything stay the same?" Amy yelled.

"We don't know who they are. What are we worried about?"

One of the soldiers fired a shot of that energetic pulse stuff and it flew right over Alan's head.

"Go ahead and find out," Amy said sarcastically.

They ran and ran until reaching a cliff. Alan looked ahead in *amazement* while Amy fearfully looked back at the incoming soldiers. Alan grabbed Amy's attention and pointed towards what seemed like a miracle. About four miles out was the outskirts of a technologically advanced city much like the one that was described to them. The sheer size of the city was awe-inspiring; its radius spanned more than a hundred miles. There also seemed to be a great deal of electricity flowing through the city, a very dangerous amount of electricity. That's when they looked above and saw the storm they'd been running from, it had already reached the center of the city and was causing quite the stir. Nonetheless, they were both filled with jubilation to see this landmark. It represented the way home for them and in the nick of time.

"That's it. That's the city that guy was talking about," Alan said.

"We should head for it."

"We'll never make it with these guys on our tail."

Amy was determined to go home. "Alan, it's in there. Our way home is somewhere in that city! It has to be!"

"We don't know that!"

"We have to search!"

One of the flying vehicles came up to them vigilantly.

"How are we going to get down?" Amy asked.

Alan knew a way but there was only one way to make sure the troops wouldn't follow. "Amy," he said.

"Yeah?"

"I know we haven't known each other for that long but I want you to know that..." he looked away.

"What Alan?" She wondered what the hell he could be talking about.

"I love you!"

She was emotionally rocked by those words but it was at an awkward time. *Why is he saying this right now?*

Alan hugged her and gave her a passionate kiss. She was so taken back as to why he was doing this that she just stood there.

"Make your way to the city and look for the way home! I promise I'll find you in time!"

Before she had the chance to rebuttal Alan pushed her off of the cliff. He looked into her beautiful and confused eyes as she fell down and down until finally being swallowed up by the canopy below...

The spotlights of the flying search crafts shined down on Alan and the infantry finally made it up the hill. All of them aimed their weapons at Alan but this did not frighten him. He was pissed! He didn't know who these guys were or why they were after him but he knew that they had split up him and Amy, again.

"Don't move!" a loud voice said through a megaphone.

Alan didn't care by this point. He was filled with rage and could feel the power surging through his body. It was powered by the negativity all around him. It was coming from the waste, it was coming from the guards, and it was coming from that city. By no choice of his own Alan was becoming deeply entrenched in his thoughts of violence, it was part of the same process that trapped him in sorrow and grief not too long ago. Unfortunately, Alan did not recognize what was happening to him; his concentration was on the bodily dismemberment of those altering his path, and anyone else who'd get in his way. He felt within a new kind of power flowing through his body and knew he had the power to stop these "pathetic fools".

They have no clue about their own reality... They're so blind... An image of violently beating these men flashed through his mind. *...They're so ignorant... They need to be taught a lesson...* Another image flashed by, this time he was jabbing a weapon into one of the men's skulls. *...I'm going to show them how ignorant they are by making them bleed... Yes... I can feel the power... I can **kill** them easily!*

They fired a warning shot towards him. Alan looked at it and laughed... They shot another one, this time a little closer.

"Get on the ground and don't move!" said the voice on megaphone.

Alan was sick of this. He vigorously charged toward the twenty or so men, caring little about the fact that he was vastly outnumbered. They fired several more shots and missed. Alan leaped into the air and tackled one of the men. He turned around and elbowed another trooper sending him flying back several yards. At that point Alan had total confidence in his ability to *ravish* these soldiers.

He took a weapon from the soldier on the ground and inserted it into his stomach. The sight was gruesome but motivating for Alan. Several more soldiers attempted to hold him down, but they were no match for his blind rage. Alan snapped one man's neck with a simple twist. He broke limbs with ease. He felt like he was fighting a group of five year olds. Soldier after soldier they went down like plastic action figures with flimsy articulation. The rage was taking over Alan. His only goal, his only mindset, was to kill, and soon it didn't matter whom, he just wanted to do it.

Several more images flew through his mind. He was seeing himself in alleyways and in the shadows stalking and murdering people. These images put a break in his actions. Alan began to realize that he was consumed by negativity. That's when more men attacked him. A few shots were fired, but that did little to Alan except to fuel his rage... so he continued his rampage. He popped the spine of one soldier out from the man's back, and he gouged the eyeballs from another. As he uppercut into the jaw of the next guy, he shattered the man's teeth like a fine set of China.

A few more images ran through him, this time of a tall man with icy eyes and a deranged look... he was looking at an image of what he was becoming. Alan knew he was beginning to identify once again. He knew the only way to stop it from happening was to get out of there and he knew that he had to do it soon. But before he could make a run for it a soldier from behind grabbed Alan with a chokehold. Two more men came up to him and started beating him. They brutally punched, kicked and choked, but Alan wasn't affected by any of this in a physical way. They simply added to power derived from his ignorant state of being. He was also still getting images of the vicious man committing heinous acts of murder, and worst of all... he was enjoying it!

"No! Get off me. Don't you see what—" Alan was shut up when one of the men cracked him with the butt of their gun.

Alan's consciousness was lessening by the second. His reactions blinded his ability to make a choice in his actions. Alan's once high level of consciousness, that gave him clarity and guidance in the face of turmoil, was quickly covered by raw emotion.

I can't react... I have to stop this...

But it was too late. He reacted a long time ago and he was too caught up in the emotion. He was becoming the emotion. He was becoming the man from the images, the killer from his mind, the one called Crimson. Alan grew an extra foot. His arms thickened by a dozen inches. He couldn't really fight what he was becoming because he *wanted* to fight off the soldiers. That desire to fight was what turned him into the monster.

At last his transformation was complete. The once relatively puny Alan was now Crimson, the large psychopath with a thirst for blood. He grabbed the man in front of him by the head and squeezed.

Crimson's large fingers weren't strong enough to crush his skull but they were strong enough to give the man the worst migraine he'd ever endured. Crimson took the soldier's head and smacked it into the skull of the soldier next to him.

The guy behind him was still trying to hold on. He wasn't really conscious of the fact that Alan had turned into another figure but he was conscious of the fact that he was losing his grip. He was also terribly afraid. With one motion Crimson flipped the soldier over his shoulders and stomped the man till he was a bloody pulp dead on the ground.

The two men on the ground were waking up from the collision but Crimson wasn't finished. He beat them savagely to death and only when there was absolutely no life left in these men did he rise to his feet. His hands, shirt and face were covered in blood. The red contrasted greatly with the pearly whites of his teeth as he smiled. Crimson looked up at the flying vehicles and laughed.

"Is that it?" he yelled.

All of the soldiers were on the ground now, most of them were dead, and the others were severely injured or knocked out. A strange echoing noise was fired in the background. An explosion of light flew into Crimson's back knocking him into a nearby tree. The large man stumbled around as if his legs were made of Jell-O. This still was not enough to stop him but there were more soldiers coming and they had bigger weapons. Three more of these shots were fired. Crimson did his best to dodge them but the impact of the explosions was too much. One knocked him back, the other knocked him forward and the third put him to the ground. Finally, he was running out of energy.

As the soldiers walked up, one of the men put his foot on Crimson's face to move it over. "Is it him?" the man asked.

"Yeah it's him," said another. The soldier looked at Crimson and grinned. "You didn't think you'd get away now did you? You hear me boy?"

"Looks like he was headed for the city."

The soldier looked at Crimson. "You thought you were free," the soldier kneeled down to stare Crimson in the face, "Oh, trust me son. We're going to put you out of your misery."

The sound of heavy winds mixed with the thrusting of the hovercraft engines was helping to calm the mind of Crimson. Something about the wind reminded him of past times, though he could not place his finger on when. However, there was still part of Crimson that wanted to jump up and mutilate these men, but he couldn't... and that pissed him off. There was so much frustration and anguish rolling through his mind, as he lay helpless on the ground. There was also a tiny hint of Alan still in this man.

Can't happen again... Not like last time... Amy... I can't lose Amy... Crimson didn't understand what these jumbled thoughts were about but he knew they were of importance. "No," Crimson said softly.

"What was that boy?" the soldier said in a demeaning manner.

"I'm not who you think I am."

Crimson's face was softening and Alan's eyes were returning! The loss of energy allowed Alan to resurface in the vast sea of Crimson's anger.

"Oh, I know who and what you are and soon you just won't be. We're going to put an end to you," the soldier said as Crimson's body was shrinking back into Alan's. "And when I find that pretty little friend of yours I'm going make sure she forgets all about you."

These words reversed the transformation! Alan's eyes faded away and Crimson's mass quickly returned. This reversal also gave an energy boost to the raging psychopath, enough to cause one more rampage. Crimson stood up quickly and held in his hands the soldier that made the comment about Amy. It would only have taken a second to snap this man's neck but Crimson was enjoying the process of killing him. One of the other soldiers quickly pulled out a weapon and fired a beam of energy throughout Crimson. This time the charge was so strong it knocked him out completely.

Chapter 18

Crimson was transported to a prison located at the top of a tall, cold, snow-covered mountain. Up in this barren harsh land, there were blizzard-like conditions comparable to those in Siberia. The temperature was colder than the North Pole and the wind was strong enough to blow down a house. There was no life anywhere to be found, no plants or animals. Anything left out in the open for long would have frozen solid.

The prison was surrounded by an energy shield strong enough to stop anything, even Crimson. There were also guard towers, automated turret guns and temperatures far below freezing to help keep the prisoners from escaping. Its unique location also made it difficult to escape from. The only other landmarks visible from these high altitudes were more mountains, and far in the distance was the origin of the storm, the volcano! It was still erupting new clouds and was pushing the storm further out by the minute. This storm would soon cover everything!

There were several square facilities that made up the prison. The first building held all of the cells. It was the largest. The second building was for administration and housing for the guards. The third building was the smallest. This building was a gateway to something terrible. Those who received the equivalent to a death sentence were sent here. Once they passed through the doors of this facility they were dropped into an eternity of torture… and no one ever returned.

The aircraft carrying the Crimson landed on top of the prisoner facility where fifteen guards were ready to transport him inside. They were not taking a chance with this one. It wasn't his anger or his size that scared them or even his ability to plow through them like a bulldozer. There was something about this prisoner that was different from the others. Something more. Something they had never seen before. It was the unknown that scared them the most.

Inside, there was at first total darkness. The monotonous sound of water drops echoed in the background along with some ruffling noises, perhaps caused by rats. Other than these faint trickles of noise the area was silent. Moments later a large iron automatic door opened, shedding light into the long corridor. The blizzard vigorously blew in from the outside and the guards did their best to stand strong as the winds nearly knocked them over. Crimson was transported by dolly down the hallway. He was strapped in and guarded like a dangerous animal.

The interior of the holding chambers was not vastly open like a regular prison. It was enclosed and narrow. There were hundreds of floors, each with several rows of cells similar to the catacombs of a beehive. The walls were dark and drab and so was the lighting. It was a very claustrophobic atmosphere. Throughout the catacombs were the screams and tortuous cries of other inmates begging for salvation. Everyone sounded so drab and depressed. Even those being tortured had little flavor in their voice.

The guards finally reached Crimson's cell and tossed him in. Inside of the room was a wooden bench with a blanket, a sink, and one filthy-ass toilet. Still drained, Crimson crawled to the bench and curled up. The soldier that Crimson nearly choked to death was among the guards. His nametag read, *Captain Hess.*

Hess kneeled down to Crimson's level and spat in his face. "I'm gonna be there watching. You think you're afraid now? You'll be begging for mercy," he said deriving pleasure from his captured prize. He looked down upon Crimson like a big game trophy that he could show to his peers. "You're mine now," he laughed.

Hours passed by in the darkness of Crimson's little corner. Not much was visible in this cell at nighttime. Crimson was lucky enough to get a window cell to allow him the pleasure of seeing the white squall outside. All that was visible within the room was the sink, toilet and the silhouette of Crimson curled up in a blanket on the bench. The occasional spotlight shined through the window and lit up Crimson's face for a brief moment. He was dazed and confused. The shock he received did more than temporarily knock him out. It left him in a state of total passivity. The sound of men and women yelling and screaming was also driving him nuts. All he wanted to do was plug his ears up and fade away.

When he finally regained some energy he stood up and walked to the window. He was shocked to see that the storm had now covered the entire mountain and was pressing on to what seemed no end.

Will it cover the entire planet...? What is it going to do...?

The lightning was particularly fascinating to Crimson, so much power in such a thin strike. He was anxious to see what the storm could really do, what power it was waiting to unleash. Everyone knew it was brewing something big but no one knew exactly what. Crimson cared little about the outcome of the land and people; he was simply attracted to the potential of its power. He also wanted the storm to act fast.

Maybe it'll get me out of here.

He knew they were going to sentence him to doom and he knew that doom would lead to an eternity of torture in which he could not control. That was the only thing that scared him, no control. Crimson remembered the good old days of being free and doing what he wanted to. Visions of him strangling his victims raced through his mind, and much to his delight. He particularly loved it when a woman screamed right before he took what was most precious to her.

The blood I've spilled, he boasted within. He thought of how nice it would be to get his hands around Capt. Hess. *Oh, the things I'd do to that man.* Crimson laughed at the thought of the delightful pain he would inflict.

He walked over to the sink and rinsed his face. The water outlined his rough exterior as he took a second and enjoyed the feeling of the formless substance. There was something so blissful about water, something so pure. It reminded him of a great time he had not too long ago.

Oh, I wish we could continue on. Amy and I were in— What...? Not again. He realized his thoughts were off track once more and fought them. *I have to get this shit out of my head.* He opened his eyes and looked in the mirror. Like before, Alan was in the reflection!

"Ahh!" Crimson yelled.

Crimson jumped at the sight of this comparatively puny kid. When he looked back Alan was still there. This sight did not intrigue him it angered him. Some inner part of him felt extremely guilty for letting go of the girl named Amy, and it was the man in the mirror who was responsible. Crimson punched the mirror breaking it into shards. Each falling piece of glass reverberated through Crimson's ears. It was as if pieces of him were falling.

The light from outside shined down on the shattered glass. Crimson looked down at the pieces of the mirror, curious to see if he was still *hallucinating*. Sure enough, in every piece, there was a fraction of Alan staring back at Crimson. To rid Alan from his presence he violently stomped and mashed the glass on the ground while yelling at the reflection. Out in the hallways this was a familiar sound. His voice blended in with the countless other mad screams and yells.

He looked down at the tiny speckles of what was once the mirror. There was no more reflection, to his satisfaction. But then another vision raced through his mind. This one was of Alan breaking free from an enclosed shell. The feeling this vision produced shook the core of Crimson's identity. Crimson grabbed his head and began yelling at the top of his lungs.

"Get out of my fucking head!"

More and more, the images and mental movies of this Alan individual played through his mind. Crimson began banging on the door and on the walls. He was trying anything to stop his mind from making anymore noise, but, like any other human, the harder he fought against his mind the more torturous the thoughts became.

After several hours of banging and screaming Crimson was exhausted. His hands were bloody and his mind was wasted. That same feeling of passivity returned, only this time it hadn't come from an energy-draining weapon. Though by most means incapacitated, Crimson continued to fight against his thoughts and feelings, but there was no energy left, only a splitting headache and some bruised knuckles.

That's when an inner voice spoke softly in his mind, "Don't fight it. Surrender to what is."

These words comforted Crimson. He felt like a lost little boy in need of some parental guidance. He was left with little choice. Crimson relaxed as best he could. He could feel the negativity fleeing his body and it was euphoric. In one rare moment for this identity he was at peace.

Crimson opened his mouth slowly to speak, "What's happening?" These were the words and voice of Alan coming through Crimson's mouth.

Crimson looked shocked. He was frozen. Alan was coming through him and there was little he could do about it.

"Who are you?" Crimson questioned.

"You know who you are."

Crimson was puzzled. He was also becoming increasingly frustrated. "Why can't you just leave me alone?"

"Because… you're not real," Alan replied.

"I'm not real? You're a voice in my head. You are coming through *my* body," Crimson said defensively.

"No. See past the flesh. You are a monster created by my thoughts."

Crimson slammed his hand down on the bench. "Ahh! Stop it!" The migraine strengthened with every burst of negativity. "Just shut up!"

"Do not fight against—"

"Noooo!"

Crimson grabbed the bench and began pounding it into pieces. Throughout the rest of the night he ripped apart, tore up, and pulverized anything he could grab in the room.

Chapter 19

Daylight managed to break through sections of the blizzard outside like light piercing the body of an ocean. The little light that was shining crept into Crimson's dark and isolated cell. He was still sitting in the corner fuming. The entire night he fought against the voices running through his head. One voice was the calm inner voice of Alan; the other was the mad and insane voice of Crimson. He sat like a madman nudging his fingers into his skull to inflict pain. This was the only thing that could stop the conflict. The only feeling that could cease his thoughts.

Then, someone began pounding at the door.

"Get out of my head!" Crimson yelled. But this sound was real.

A couple of guards opened the cell door with their weapons ready to fire. Capt. Hess peeked in and raised an eyebrow. The room was trashed, more so than the usual inmate's room. "You gonna eat or are you going to sit in here all day?"

Crimson slowly removed his hands from his face to look at the troops. His fiery eyes scared Capt. Hess to the inner core. Hess almost forgot what he was dealing with. Crimson stood to his feet towering over Hess and his men.

The best the Captain could do was utter a few words of dominance. "Don't try anything stupid or your death will come sooner than you thought," Hess said with that comforting sense of power over the inmate.

They walked Crimson through the catacombs and into chow hall. This place in itself was a death pit. It looked like a gothic underground party gone wrong. Fat Men in leather masks walked around with butcher knives and bloody aprons, serving up meals while the inmates ran around like wild animals in a cage. Men were attacking women. Women were attacking men. Everyone walked around either preying on someone or afraid they would be attacked. Occasionally, some of the inmates would attack the butchers. The butchers were used to this however. They would simply hack away the individual with their knives and take them to the back room.

One woman jumped like a mountain lion on one of the butcher's backs and tried biting his face through the leather mask. Another butcher came in and helped him out by knocking her unconscious. They grabbed her by the feet and dragged her into the back room. Behind the doors was a tall grim reaper-looking guy, slicing knives, preparing to *prepare* the next meal. She appeared to be it. They slapped her on the table and strapped her down like a turkey and just as the Reaper started prying her flesh open they shut the doors.

Above this room were three walkways. This was the entrance, and in came Crimson and his escorts. The guards brought Crimson to the middle platform and stopped.

"Enjoy your meal," Hess said with a cynical smile on his face.

A large, retractable, three pronged claw came from above and grabbed Crimson. It took him to the bottom of the pit with the rest of the inmates and set him down. The crowd immediately backed away. Everyone feared this man... with the exception of one, a smaller guy sitting at a table off in the corner.

"A! Crimson! Get over here," the guy yelled.

At this table was a group of men and women minding their own business. Their demeanor and sense of calm in their surroundings made it obvious that they were the elders of this facility. Though lost and confused like the other inmates, these individuals had grown used to the system they inhabited and continued on waiting for their deaths with some form of acceptance. Crimson walked over to the table and sat down.

"Stykes," Crimson called the man.

His memories were a little jogged but he remembered a few things. This was his acquaintance. The whole table wanted desperately to be acquainted with Crimson. If they were at least near him they knew their chances of being attacked lessoned because Crimson could pulverize nearly anyone that came his way.

"We heard you was almost free," Stykes said with a bit of excitement.

"Excuse me," Crimson replied.

"I mean free. Like you found a way out of this hell hole... permanently."

Crimson looked at Stykes, extremely confused. He was just starting to remember the more minute details of his existence including who he was and what he was all about. He had been battling with Alan for so long he nearly forgot most of his identity.

"How do you know about that?"

Everyone at the table laughed.

"Everybody knows about that."

"How does it feel man, tell us?" One inmate asked. Several others started asking simultaneously, "Yeah how does it feel...what was it like...how far out did you get?"

Crimson didn't know what to say. He was still confused as to why there was a voice in his mind named Alan. He couldn't remember what happened outside of the prison other than fighting the soldiers that were chasing him.

"You can't hold back on us. We know all about it... You saw the city. You were almost home," Stykes said.

"The city?" Crimson now remembered trying to reach the large city. It was of great importance to him for some reason.

"Come on man, you was almost free. I mean completely free... You don't remember anything?"

"Where was I exactly?"

"Heaven," Stykes laughed. "Any place away from here is heaven in my opinion."

"How do I get back?" Crimson was softening up. These questions were helping him to remember what he was doing.

"I don't know. No one's ever made it that far, other than you. No one from here anyway."

The eyes of Alan were filling in. Crimson's hard shell was loosening. "Where am I now?"

Everyone laughed again.

"Listen to this guy. He's hilarious... You're in hell buddy, or the closest thing to it."

This memory jog was breaking open a path for Alan to resurface. Crimson was remembering things without fighting against them.

"Eh, guys, I think he's got it," Stykes said.

Crimson looked at his hands and chest. *But my memories, what are they... They have to be real... It's what I did... It's who I am... How can I ever be anything different...? No one will ever forgive me...*

Now there was an opening and Alan finally broke through. Crimson's body began changing once again. Everyone at the table watched with a smile on their face.

"That's it man. He's doin it again. He can show us the way out!" Stykes yelled.

They only saw a difference in Crimson's awareness but what a difference it was. He was like a totally different person when he snapped out of his thoughts.

"Give it back!" a voice cried from across the room.

"Try to get it back," another voice threatened.

This sound was all-too familiar for the inmates. "Oh there they go. They're startin up again," Stykes said.

Across the room a large brawl began to brew. What started between two people soon involved everyone in the room. One after the other, inmates were bumped into and accidentally punched, kicked or bitten, and then they reacted. Everyone at Stykes' table remained sitting and did not want to go anywhere near the fight. Crimson/Alan was too caught up in the slow transformation to notice anything around him.

"Eh! Don't kill him yet he owes me money!" one of the inmates at the table yelled.

Alan's eyes were finally through. He could see the world with clarity. There was no anger or negative emotion clouding his vision... until he witnessed the fight. There was a heavy amount of negativity coming from that section of the room and part of him wanted in on it. The negativity was feeding his ego, his desire for action. Alan could feel Crimson wanting to join in and dominate the fight. This was Crimson's chance to come back. The flip-flop nature of Alan's awareness was a danger to his life.

"How can I get out of here?"

"We should be asking you that," Stykes said. Stykes saw that Alan was trying his hardest not to change again. "Eh man, you doin alright over there?"

"No," Alan said with a nauseated visage. "I have to go."

He gripped his stomach and fell to the floor. He was trying so hard not to feel the emotions and feelings. The urge and desires were so conflictive with what he wanted he was weakened in the knees.

The fight made its way towards his table. Now, nearly everyone in the chow hall was fighting or getting beat up. A couple of guys grabbed Stykes and began beating the snot out of him. Alan watched as they pounded the guy senseless.

"Leave him alone!" Alan said with a hint of Crimson in his voice.

One of the guys threw a tray at Alan and this angered him even more and everything began reversing itself at an alarming rate! Soon, Alan's eyes were lost, once again, and Crimson rose to his feet. He grabbed the two men and smashed them together like toys.

"Crimson no!" Stykes yelled.

Three guys jumped on Crimson's from behind and tried to take him down.

"He was almost out you guys, let him go! You're draggin him back down," Stykes said.

Crimson's rage was fully fueled. He beat those men to a bloody pulp and didn't stop there. He ravaged through the men and women like he was chopping weeds down in a field, taking out his aggression and satisfying his urge for more.

"Who else?" Crimson asked while salivating.

To his delight, a gang of people answered his call and charged at him with shanks and other weapons. Crimson loved it; this was pure pleasure for him. He twisted the hands and arms of those coming at him with weapons and then laid them to the ground. Just as he prepared to finish them off, Stykes ran behind him and grabbed him by the shoulder.

"Crimson, you were almost free, man. Don't lose it now."

Crimson picked Stykes up by the neck, pinned him to a table and began choking the life out of him. He didn't care who he was injuring as long as it wasn't breathing when he was done.

"Crim...let me... what... what did I do..." Stykes pleaded with his last few breaths.

But then... something stopped him. Crimson saw something... across the room... something eye-catching enough to make him stop choking Stykes.

"I'm sorry man, I didn't mean to upset you," Stykes said.

Crimson paid no attention to Stykes; he was looking through the crowd.

Stykes started to breathe again and managed to wiggle his way out of Crimson's hands. Crimson's eyes had met with... the Native American's! Crimson knew nothing of the man other than his presence was mesmerizing.

"You're different from the rest of us. You don't belong here, you can get out. That's all I'm saying," Stykes uttered. Crimson looked down sharply at Stykes and he shut up like a dog.

From above came the loudest siren ever heard. All of the inmates knew what this noise meant. The ones that were still conscious from the fight knew to crouch down... except for Crimson, he looked up at the guards carelessly. After the noise ceased, the retractable claw came from the ceiling and aimed at anyone still standing. Crimson made a run for it. He picked up other inmates and *threw* them at the claw hoping it would take them instead, but no, it relentlessly stalked Crimson. As it came within an inch of his face he grabbed one of the talons, but the other two wrapped around him. With all his might he fought the claw but couldn't break free from its grip.

"Let me go!" Crimson said while struggling to break free.

The only other man standing was the Native American. They looked each other in the eyes as Crimson was lifted out of the pit.

"Wake up!" a voice said as if spoken into his ear.

These words were relatively meaningless to Crimson. The small fraction of his consciousness that resonated with the words was buried deep. And though he could feel something pressing at his mind Crimson was easily able to suppress it.

As he reached the top Crimson's attention focused on the guards, particularly Captain Hess. He gazed at him with daggers.

"You just couldn't keep out of trouble could you?" Hess said. The claw brought Crimson in close enough for Hess to feel Crimson's breath. "You think you're invincible do you? You think you can do anything you want?" Hess pulled out a small weapon and charged it. "Take him to the pit."

He put the weapon to Crimson's neck and discharged it and a green flare surged through Crimson's body rendering him unconscious.

"We'll show him who's in control."

The metal claw then took him back down to the floor and released him amongst the other inmates lying on the ground. Four butchers came out of the back room and carried him away on a stretcher.

"That's a damn shame. He was so close," Stykes said.

Crimson was taken to the last building at the opposite end of the prison. In the center of this room was a forty-foot in diameter funnel. Lining the funnel was the most disgusting goop ever seen by the eyes of any living being. It was a mix of rotten human flesh, mucus of all kinds, blood from all creatures and biological waste from unknown sources. This was the gateway, the pit leading to oblivion.

Hess stood with a smile, ready to pass judgment to the cold-blooded Crimson. This part was most entertaining for him.

"What should we do with him?" a guard asked.

"Wake him up," said Hess.

One of the guards waved a bottle filled with pungent fumes beneath Crimson's nostrils. The effect was instantaneous. Crimson lifted his head to find the rest of his body strapped down. At first he fought to be free but he quickly realized that he was at the edge of the funnel!

As if kicking and screaming were going to back him up he pushed at the air around him in a futile effort to move away. "Get me out of here... cut me loose!"

"Not so tough now are you?" Hess said with fulfillment. "You know, no one knows for sure what happens to you when you fall but what I do know is that you won't be coming back."

"You'll all die if I get my hands around you."

"I wouldn't strain too much. You might snap free from the restraints and fall in," Hess flicked out a knife and held it to Crimson's chin. "I hear you're tortured, tortured to the point were you *want* to kill yourself... I might just drop this in there after a while... if you're nice that is."

The other guards watched in amusement. Even the stoic fat butchers were laughing. They too enjoyed the sight of the inmates being tortured.

"You'd better hope I don't get free."

Hess cut one of the straps holding Crimson down and he fell forward partially.

Son-of-a-bitch! Crimson thought. *I have to get out of this. Don't let this happen to me! Get me out!*

"You can beg for mercy you know. I might prolong your death."

Crimson reached out and bit Hess' hand! This really pissed the captain off so he stabbed Crimson in the stomach, leaving the knife inside. This, to the guards, was a tearjerker. Captain Hess and the others were laughing the snot out of their eyes. Crimson was only infuriated by Hess' actions. In an unforeseen action he wiggled free of the straps and managed to grab Hess.

"Captain!" yelled one of the guards.

Unfortunately, they both fell into the funnel.

"Grab him! Quick!"

It was too late. They *both* were spiraling down into the pit of oblivion!

Chapter 20

Crimson and the good Captain fell through a dark tube directly into nowhere! A void of darkness surrounded them in this pit of nothing, darkness and two feet of water. Strangely, there were no lights, yet everything around them in a fifteen-foot radius was dimly lit.

Capt. Hess was nearly knocked out from the fall, and the first thing Crimson did was remove the knife from his stomach. The wound didn't bother him; he was more concerned about killing the Captain. Crimson lifted his hands out of the water and was disgusted by the sludge that came with it. The floor was soft, black and lined with an algae-like substance. The smell wasn't so pleasant either.

Crimson walked over to Hess and lifted him up by the collar. The all-mighty captain snapped out of his daze and nearly pissed in his pants. "No! How did... what are you... please don't," Hess pleaded.

"You squeal now? You pathetic prick. You're not so tough without your *men* are you?"

"I don't..."

Hess wiggled and squirmed but wasn't strong enough to break free from Crimson's grip.

"Let me out of here you son-of-a-bitches! I'll kill him if you don't!" Crimson yelled above.

"They can't hear you."

Crimson looked down at Hess. With great pleasure He began choking the high and mighty Captain Hess and thought, *This place ain't so bad after all.*

"Don't...ehg...we...ahg...can...work...to...gether," Hess begged with the last breaths of his life.

Hess knew by looking into Crimson's eyes that he wasn't going to make it. Crimson was receiving too much pleasure from torturing him.

"Why do you want to go?" said a female voice from somewhere in the shadows.

Hess was grateful to hear this voice because Crimson turned around sharply and loosened his grip on him. Out of the shadows came walking a long pair of *sexy legs* and Crimson's anger softened a little. He gave the woman a tiny smirk as she moved closer to them. She was dressed in his favorite sexy business attire with blonde hair, kitty cat eyes and glasses to top it off. She was perfect for him. His mouth began salivating. Hess, on the other hand, knew otherwise.

"Don't do it," the captain warned.

Crimson looked back at Hess and snarled. He threw the captain like a rag doll and walked towards the woman. "How long have you been down here?" Crimson said to the woman.

She looked at him and smiled. Much to his desire she unbuttoned her blouse and licked her lips. Crimson was in heaven, but not all treats are sweet. His smile quickly faded as her complexion turned a pale blue with maggots eating away at her skin. As if some magical knife ran across her throat, it sliced open and poured out an endless flow of blood!

"What the hell?" Crimson said disgusted.

Hess crawled over to the knife and back away. He didn't want to go too far however, he knew to stay away from the shadows.

"What's wrong? You don't want me anymore?" the woman said to Crimson.

When the woman tried to grab him, Crimson punched her in the face. Much to his detest, her head exploded into a glob of mucus and blood. This did not stop her however. She continued to crawl towards him as the maggots came crawling out of her head!

"We have to stick together," Hess pleaded.

"How do we get back up?"

"I don't know."

The hand of a man whose nails were cracked and yellow and whose flesh was eaten off and peeled back, reached out and grabbed Crimson's foot. Crimson desperately kicked the hand away but this wasn't enough. Several more hands popped out of the ground.

"I know them. I sent them to death," Hess said while trembling.

What? It can't be… no… he's right.

These were the men and women, inmates and citizens that Crimson and Hess killed or had killed in their lives.

"I killed you a long time ago!" Crimson yelled. The woman with the maggots crawling from her neck tackled Crimson to the ground. "Get off me!"

Hess tried stabbing her in an attempt to stop her but found it hard to kill a headless woman. "She won't die!" he screamed.

From underneath, one of the hands reached out and grabbed Hess by the arm. Another grabbed his foot. Arm after arm reached around him and slowly pulled him under the surface. He suffered the most agonizing pain each step of the way down, and below his torture would continue. Before long the good Captain was gone.

Crimson punched, kicked, an elbowed the zombies. He was able to fight off the first twenty but was over powered by the countless others coming out of the ground and shadows. The headless maggot woman climbed, once again, on top of Crimson and began stripping. He fought hard as she undid his pants in an effort to *rape him*!

"What's wrong? Not in the mood?"

Crimson screamed helplessly as the zombies took control, "Just kill me and get it over with!"

He managed to kick off the headless rapist but another grabbed his leg from below... and then another... and another. Somehow, Crimson rose to his knees but the arms beneath were too strong for him. He looked around and saw hundreds of walking dead coming from the shadows to feast upon him. And then, the zombies holding his leg were able to pull it beneath the surface.

"Aaahhhh!" Crimson cried in agony.

He managed to pull his leg out of the sludge and found that his foot was eaten off! His victims were having their sweet revenge it seemed. Crimson closed his eyes and awaited his doom.

"I just want to die!" Crimson cried as the dead victims tortured and mutilated his body.

"You beg to die yet you've never lived," a calm voice said.

Crimson opened his eyes wondering which zombie spoke to him. "Just end it! Kill me!"

"Your fear will keep you stuck in torture. Your anger will only feed your ignorance," the voice said.

The voice was so loud and clear. *Who is it coming from?* he wondered.

He opened his eyes again and viola! There was no one anywhere. The zombies were all gone!

What?

He was confused and still shaken up, but much to his relief, his foot was back and his scars were gone. He searched through the ground and found nothing with the exception of the disgusting goop beneath the water.

"Where are you?"

"Everywhere," the voice echoed all around him.

Crimson stood up and looked around. There was nothing and no one to be found.

"Is this another trick?" he said to himself. "How long? Huh. How long do I have to go through this? What do you want from me?"

"Death will not put your mind to rest," the voice was spoken as if it were next to him this time.

This was familiar… out of the shadows emerged the Native American!

Crimson looked at the man startled. "I know you."

"But you don't know who you are."

"What are you talking about?"

"You are lost Alan. Anger has clouded your vision."

Crimson looked at him even more strangely. *He called me Alan.*

"If you are not careful you will be trapped by your mind's torture forever. And I don't mean in this pit of illusion."

Crimson's defenses were up. He didn't know what else this pit had in store for him. "What do you want?" Crimson asked suspiciously.

"Tame the mind by realizing what it is. Do not fight against it."

Crimson charged the man and tried to grab him, but The Native American simply raised his hands and lifted Crimson effortlessly into mid air without laying a finger on him.

"How are you doing this?"

"Listen to me. You have not lost her but she is lost."

"Who?"

"You know who."

Crimson was frustrated. This man was talking in jumbles. "What are you talking about?"

The Native American moved in close. "If you don't wake up now I don't know if she'll make it. She needs your guidance. It's why you two were brought together."

"Would you make some sense? Who are you talking about?"

Crimson knew. He knew deep within who and what this mysterious man was speaking of. He could feel Alan rising up from within and that angered him. He would die before losing his identity to Alan. That's when more zombies came from the shadows, lots more. Their distorted faces and deranged eyes made Crimson realize that it was time to make a choice.

"If you do not wake up you will be stuck here forever. Go into the darkness of your mind, rise to the surface and be free. You no longer have to swim in ignorance Alan."

"What the hell do you mean by wake up?"

Crimson looked around frantically. He did not want to be free of his identity; it was all he had. *Who would I be without it?* he thought. *I wouldn't know what to do.*

"You've lived your entire life in fear. It's stopped you from truly living, from truly seeing. But you have nothing to fear anymore. To see the truth you need only be aware, and more importantly be aware of what's going on inside of you."

"But I can't..." Crimson wanted to resist so badly. He didn't want to release control.

The Native American put his hands on Crimson's shoulders. "Remember when you first came out here? You felt incredible. You could do whatever you wanted without restraint. It was because you wanted nothing. You feared nothing. Your mind was at ease. Everything you witnessed and interacted with was observed with absolute clarity. You *can* go back to that state of being... but you must make the choice."

These words rang loudly with Crimson and he realized something. He realized that he was fighting with himself.

How? he wondered.

The voices of Alan and Crimson spoke together in unison, "I am only one. How can I fight with myself? Which of me is real?"

"If you look beyond your mind you will see beyond the fragmented universe it created. Then you can see clearly the world, not without but beyond thoughts. And at that moment you will know that you are much more than what your thoughts can imagine."

The battle within was over. The identity of Crimson was not destroyed but shown for what it was, and the fear within Alan that brought about the change of identity was lessening. He was realizing that if he simply remained aware he would always have the ability to go beyond the confusion.

"Don't let your ego consume your reality. There is so much more out there."

Alan's body had almost returned to normal. He looked at it astonished as that glow from within was shining brightly, without any effort from him at all.

I've been so consumed by my negativity and emotions. I never took a second to relax and see what was going on within me. He was left to ask the obvious, "Will this keep happening to me?"

"If your thoughts are in control. If you believe that you are what your thoughts say you are, than you will always become a reflection of your thoughts."

"If I'm not my thoughts… than what am I?"

"You are the consciousness that *gives* existence to this world. And so is everybody else. We are all connected. We are all one with everyone and everything."

"But what about my mind? I can't live without it."

"You must restore the balance that is lost within you. A balance that was lost in humans eons ago. You must see your mind as the powerful tool it is. Let it do its work. It does not need to be controlled. Neither does the world around you."

"How can I stay like this?"

"Continue to wake up every time you fall asleep. Every time you become aware you regain power. When you are aware of what your mind is doing your mind will no longer control what happens to you… Stop the inner dialogue!"

Alan's confidence wasn't impenetrable but it was strong. He would only need to experience what was being said on his own to know it within.

"Searching for freedom outside of yourself will keep you stuck. You are already free; you simply need to realize it."

The Native American pointed behind Alan. When he looked there was nothing. "How can I find Amy?" When he turned around the Native American was gone. "How do I get out of here?" he yelled into the vast emptiness.

There was no reply. But somewhere in that silence was Alan's answer.

How the hell do I get out of here?

Alan felt within and knew that he had the power to leave if he truly wanted. For a second he thought about exploring the shadows but then realized that he was tired of being in the darkness. He stood in the center of the light and closed his eyes. The water began to rumble, the black sludge began to clear, and a cyclone of water billowed around him in a brilliant dance of wave formations. Finally, the water concentrated beneath him and shot Alan upwards. As Alan flew back through the tunnel he illuminated the darkness!

Chapter 21

Around the funnel were four guards and a couple butchers. Out in the mountains, in this morbid facility, they'd all seen some crazy things. None of them had ever seen anyone come back from the pit. The guards were the first to notice the rumbling of the room. Then came the sound of rushing water. One of them walked to the edge and tried to look below. They were all baffled by this strange noise.

Like a hot water spring, thousands of gallons of water burst out of the funnel and Alan was thrown into the air. With out any strain or effort he landed on the edge of the funnel. Also to his luck, was the water knocking out most of the men in the room and sending one of the butchers into the funnel while anyone else was slammed against machinery.

"He got out!" the one remaining butcher cried with his raspy deep tone.

The butcher's first instinct was to chase down the loose inmate but when he looked into the eyes of Alan he saw something frightening. There was no fear in Alan's eyes and no anger either. The butcher saw something way beyond his comprehension and it scared him.

Once regaining his balance, Alan calmly walked to the door and exited the room. He was free within but when he heard the alarm go off he did feel a bit of fear rise within him. He knew it was time to find a way out. Unfortunately, there wasn't anyone there to guide him.

But then, he felt something, something puling him in a certain direction. At first he wasn't sure were he was being directed, but then it became clear, the inner impulse was guiding him to the catacombs.

Can Amy be in here too? he wondered.

Somehow, through the hallways of this enclosed hellhole, Alan managed to dodge the guards as they relentlessly searched for him.

"There he is!" yelled one of the guards.

Alan's only choice was to take off down the nearest corridor. But to his misfortune there was another batch of guards searching for him at the end of that hallway too. He searched frantically for a way out or for some sort of hiding place. As if something were tugging on his leg, Alan mysteriously looked to his right... a door! He sighed with relief as he went to open it... the door was locked. But then, he felt heat coming from below... a ventilation shaft! With only one choice Alan crawled into it.

Where the hell am I going? he thought.

Alan had no clue, or better put, his mind had no clue as to where or what he was going to do. All he could do was trust his instincts and go the way that felt to be right.

After about twenty minutes Alan's ego started gaining strength. Thoughts of confusion and being lost were becoming more potent and so was the fear of being stuck in *this miserable prison.*

I can't get stuck again. Amy needs me. Alan noticed that his thoughts were bringing up a lot of negative emotion. *I have to relax. I have to...*

Alan realized that he had to slow down his thoughts by realizing that most of them were random and useless. That's when the floor beneath him collapsed and he fell into a hallway. He just so happened to fall right in front of Stykes' cell!

Stykes saw his buddy free and got excited. "Hey!" Alan ran up to his cell now feeling a chance for survival. "You're free this time, baby," Stykes yelled.

"How did I get out of here before?"

"I don't know man. But you were like this."

Alan looked down the hallway and saw a control panel.

"Where you going?" Stykes yelled.

Alan didn't know what to do so he pressed all of the release buttons. Every inmate on the block was free. They all slowly exited their cells and looked around.

"What's going on...yeah, who let us out?" said a few inmates.

That's when the alarm in that sector went off. Alan knew the entire building was on alert now. He also knew he'd have a much better chance of escaping if there were tons of inmates on the loose.

"Stykes!" Alan yelled. "Come with me!"

He and Stykes ran through several floors of the catacombs, opening doors and letting loose the inmates. The whole place was running amuck.

"Where's the entrance?" Alan asked.

"I don't know but do you really need it?"

Alan thought about it. He realized that he was always looking for a way out but it was almost always in front of him. He looked into one of the cells and stared at the window.

"This place can't hold you back anymore. This time you're free. I can tell." Stykes said.

Alan closed his eyes and visualized an opening coming to him. Moments later, a bright luminescent light filled the room and a gaping whole opened in the wall. Alan could feel the power flowing throughout his body. There was a realization within him that had never been there before. He was starting to see that perhaps the goal wasn't being free of thought, but rather reaching a higher level of it, a level of pure consciousness without the internal and *repetitious* dialogue!

I can do whatever I truly want, he thought with an inner smile.

The blizzard outside was atrocious. The winds immediately flew throughout that sector of the catacombs knocking over Stykes in the process. He crawled over and sat back in the corner unsure of what Alan planned to do. Alan was standing in the newly created hole and staring out into the white squall unsure if this were the way, but once again, he realized that the way was everywhere.

"Come with me. You can leave too," Alan said.

"Na I can't. I wouldn't know what to do."

"You've got to give it a shot. You can't just stay here."

Alan reached his hand out and Stykes took it. He was feeling some of the energy emanating from Alan and for once in his life Stykes felt some clarity.

"What's the plan?"

Alan was familiar with these situations. He knew exactly what to do.

"Trust me!"

Alan jumped out into the white squall, pulling Stykes with him, without knowing what would happen.

"What the hell are you doing?" Stykes yelled in terror.

Alan simply closed his eyes and relaxed. The wind of the storm carried them down to the bottom of the facility without a scratch! When Stykes saw the outside world he freaked. He hadn't seen anything beyond the window view in decades. For him, this was the most liberating feeling ever. However, they still had an entire mountain to climb down and on top of that they couldn't see what direction to go in.

"Man! The storm has reached this far out," Stykes said with a surprised look on his face. "This thing is bigger than anybody thought."

"I need to reach the city. Do you know which way?" Alan asked.

"No. I can't really tell from here but if you get me to the bottom I can take you there."

A bright spotlight shined down on them followed by a loud and irritating siren.

"Damn! What do we do?" Stykes asked.

Several shots were fired at the ground beneath their feet.

"I don't want to die! Let's just give our selves in."

Alan paid little attention to Stykes' fear. He simply continued to feel within and trusted the feelings he had.

I have to keep going. I know I can make it.

As if fate spoke to him, a large gust of wind came in and the radars on the turret guns found it impossible to lock onto their targets.

Alan looked at Stykes and smiled. *Trust me.*

Alan and Stykes ran for it. The guards in the towers took aim and shot blindly towards the suspected escapees and guards from all corners of the prison came swarming out in unison like bees stalking a predator. They too did not hesitate to open fire. Bright flares of energetic gunfire whizzed by Alan and Stykes' heads, but that wasn't the worst of it. In front of them was the giant electric shield surrounding the prison and that thing wasn't letting anything through.

"We're dead," Stykes said in disparity.

Alan looked into the night sky. All that was visible were thick patches of snow and beyond that the clouds of the storm. When they looked back they saw hundreds of guards headed their way.

"Well, it was a worthy effort I guess," Stykes muttered with trembling lips.

Alan closed his eyes trying his hardest to concentrate. He was trying to bring in a clear visualization of the men being taken down but for some reason it wasn't working.

Maybe I'm not conscious enough.

The guards raised their weapons to fire. They aimed their sights on the targets and... BOOM! Another strange coincidence struck...

literally. A bolt of lightning came down and caused an explosion near the guards sending them all face down to the ground. This was followed by several more lightning strikes that hit the building simultaneously. The effect was miraculous. All the power was shut down including to the shield!

Stykes looked in disbelief as he saw the guards, lights and fence down and out. "There's no way."

"Have faith my friend," Alan said with a smile.

Alan and Stykes quickly moved off the perimeter and began their trek down the mountain.

Chapter 22

The way down was, by normal circumstances, horrendous. The blizzard winds were frigid, they couldn't see a thing, and it was hard getting a stable foot on the ground. However, Alan didn't feel the effects of the weather like Stykes did. He was on a different level. Alan could feel the power surging within him as if he were connected to a constantly flowing source.

After several hours Stykes nearly froze to death. But to his luck, the temperature was finally beginning to rise. It had stopped snowing also, and they could finally see the forest that lay at the bottom of the mountain. They couldn't really see far into the distance due to the heavy layer of fog about five miles out.

Something told Alan that this was his destination; something also told him that he must make haste to this land. He noticed that the storm covered the *entire* sky now. He could feel within that it would soon release what it was holding within. However, Alan had confidence that he and Amy would be safe, that they would find their way home before it was too late.

After several more grueling hours the two escapees reached the bottom of the mountain and entered the forest. Stykes had to take a second to catch his breath.

"So where are we headed?" Stykes asked.

"The city."

"I know you're determined and all but are you sure you really want to go there?"

"I need to find someone and I *know* she's in there."

Stykes raised his eyebrows. "You might want to rethink that. That ain't exactly the place to go when you don't know where you are."

"Wait a minute," Alan was thrown off. "You were all excited about me going to this city at first but now you say I shouldn't?"

"That was until I saw the storm. It's a lot worse than I thought."

"Listen. I have to go there. If you think you might know the way I am *begging* you to take me, if not I understand… but I must go now."

"Alright." Stykes raised his shoulders and led the way.

They ran through miles of tropical forest, dodging small and large animals, ferocious plant life, and rugged land obstacles until finally reaching a small path. It was dark and narrow but it was definitely a path to somewhere. Alan excitedly ran forward but soon noticed he was alone. When he looked back he saw Stykes waiting at the edge of the path. Alan threw his hands up and ran back.

"What are you doing? Let's go."

"Are you crazy? I'm not going in there."

"Why not?"

"That place is going to hell. Or more like hell is going there." Stykes pointed to the sky. Above them were swirling dark clouds filled with lighting bolts and ferocious winds. Even worse, the storm seemed to get nastier from there on out. "That city was already tearing itself apart. After this storm hits nothing will be the same."

"I don't get it, it's just a storm."

"No, it's more than just a storm. It's a reality check. The people think their money and technology can give them everything they need. They think they can outsmart the planet but this storm is more powerful than anything anyone's ever seen. Everybody knows it and they don't know what to do. The fear is making everyone lose their mind."

Lightning struck a nearby tree scaring the crap out of them.

"Holy shit!" Stykes yelled as he jumped back.

Then, the winds increased to nearly unbearable speeds. Leaves and branches fell off of trees, dust and debris kicked up from the ground. The area was so atrocious that they had to yell at each other just to hear one another.

"I wouldn't go there if I was you. You won't last. If the storm doesn't kill you first the citizens will. There are some crazies living in there."

"I have to go. There is no other option!"

"Well… good luck to ya!" Stykes thought about everything Alan did for him. "You showed me the way out. I don't know how long I'll last but it's the greatest thing anyone could have done for me. Thanks!"

Alan reached his arm out one last time for Stykes and they shook hands. "No problem"

"Just remember to stay on the path and don't get off… I hope you'll find what you're looking for."

Stykes took off running in the opposite direction. Alan watched him as he ran off into the shadows. The feelings of isolation in a dangerous area soon began settling in. There was uncertainty all around him. Every step forward moved Alan into the unknown. Behind the leaves, underneath the bushes could have been…

What?

Alan looked sharply as something ran passed him! He didn't know what the hell it was, he only knew it was quick and possibly deadly. Seconds later, it did it again, only this time *behind* him!

Oh shit.

He looked down the dark path and timidly started walking. For standing still was the worst thing to do.

What happened to my confidence?

The path was long, dark, and unpredictable. There were sounds of creatures coming from all directions. Some sounded large and some sounded small but the sound that really frightened Alan was the disturbing yelp of an animal being attacked by a predator. There was at first the rustling of dirt and debris and then a sudden end of movement. He knew at that point whatever creature being stalked was dead! Alan wondered if there was anything large enough to hunt him.

In any case he had to keep going. To keep his mind clear and free of torture he focused on the middle of his chest. This seemed to divert the attention away from his thoughts and into his body, which in turn, raised his level of consciousness. The thoughts that did pop into his mind were of Amy. He thought about finding her and returning home. He fantasized about the good times they would have and the life they could develop together.

But, as time teetered on, he began to lose hope in the path. He had been walking for a long time and feared that the landscaping was changing as it had done so many times before. The darkness crept into his body and he began slowing down at every movement he thought he heard next to him. His mind was playing tricks on him.

Alan was somewhat relieved when he approached the wall of fog he'd seen way up on the mountainside. This was a sign of that he was headed in the right direction.

The city can't be too far off...I hope.

There was then the faint smell of something burning. He wondered if it was the forest burning but he didn't see any fire. His concern for the smell was soon forgotten as he saw, not far in the distance, the low illumination of steady light.

They look like streetlights!

This meant there was civilization near by! He could see that the source of the light was coming from over the hill. This gave Alan the motivation to run for it. He trudged his way to the top and peered beyond the forest. Though, the excitement faded as he had indeed reached the city. At the bottom of the hill was one of the worst neighborhoods he'd ever laid eyes upon. The smell of smoke was coming from random fires lit throughout the neighborhood! Cars, homes, and random objects left lying around were set ablaze. There were people running around destroying and vandalizing property. Others were chased and killed like lions on gazelles. Throughout the city vigilant civilians protected and fought back against the predators running amuck through the neighborhood. They took shots at anyone who seemed to be a threat.

There was that familiar sound of screams and yells of torture that Alan heard from the prison only it was not so drab. These were people that wanted to live. Alan's guts sank as the voices came in from all directions.

These people are worse than the prisoners.

To make matters even worse, he looked beyond the neighborhood. Miles down the road was the city of hell! Above the center of the city was a swirling red cloud that seemed to be pulling in the storm and concentrating it directly above. Something told him that the power of the storm would have its most profound effects there. Electrical currents surround the buildings, transferred between them, and shot out into the sky. The sight was an amazing spectacle as there was lightning coming from above and below! It looked like a huge conductor.

There were fires twice the size of the ones in the surrounding neighborhoods set ablaze in that hellish downtown. The entire city looked like the devils riot ran through and left a trademark. That's when Alan realized that the wall of fog above was smoke!

Holy shit!

This was all a bit of an overload for him. He had no clue how he was going to make it through the streets, let alone find Amy in the midst of it. Just as Alan prepared to walk down the hill and into hell he saw several funnel clouds above. All around the city and all at once, random *stationary* tornadoes sprung their way down. Their force drew in objects but they didn't move. The lightning strikes began occurring more and more and with freakish intensity. More and more they struck around the city setting something else ablaze. It was happening. The power was slowly unleashing.

Chapter 23

Wind kicked up dust and debris all over the place. This only added to layer of pollution already plaguing the air and the ground. There was trash and biochemical smells everywhere. Alan thought back to the beach where he was dumped off, and realized that nearly all of the pollution came from this city.

It's no wonder this place is going to be destroyed. The planet probably can't take anymore.

The street he was on was poorly lit and every street he passed was about the same with the exception of one, and it wasn't that bright. Still, it was the best choice for him in this unfamiliar town. Nearly every house was broken down, boarded up or on fire. The people who lived in these homes either were evacuated, evacuating or looting from the former. Random people were running through town with televisions, couches and other odd items while families packed up and prepared to search for cover. The best description of the area was that of a town preparing for a hurricane, while enduring one of the worst riots it had ever seen. Alan gazed at all of this and wondered where they were all headed.

Amy could be anywhere in this mess, he thought with disparity.

He walked along the sidewalk feeling clueless and out of place. Alan could tell by the looks he was receiving that the people in this town could smell his fear. These people were of a different breed. Their culture was used to a way of life much different from Alan's. It was somewhat similar to the differences in the prison, only Alan hadn't been conscious through that experience. This time he would have to go through the experience fully aware, there was no turning back for him.

That's when a dreadful thought entered his mind, *Is Amy lost in the identity of an inmate... what if I left her back there and didn't know it... what if she was within the mind of Stykes and we broke out together for a reason?*

No matter what *could* have been, he had to keep going. He could not afford to go back and search for Stykes because if she was in the city he had to get her now or it would be too late. At a nearby house there was a group of individuals drinking and loudly yapping away on their porch. They had weapons and barricades set up in front of their house in case they were attacked.

What the hell are they preparing for? It looks like a damn war zone out here.

The people seemed like they were used to these conditions. He now realized that the city was in chaos long before the storm arrived, just as Stykes had said. Alan walked passed the house trying not to look. The last thing he wanted was to attract attention to him. He could feel the eyes staring him down as their laughter and conversation came to a halt. They watched this innocent loner travel by in silence and with caution. He could feel the eyes on his him like crawling insects on his skin. He only hoped they would view him as harmless and leave him alone.

"He's gonna get eaten up," one of the men on the porch said.

"Hell yeah he is," replied another.

Alan knew by these words that they were not a threat to him and out came a sigh of relief. His attention was so focused ahead that he didn't notice the psycho ride up behind him on a bicycle.

Alan jumped back ready to swing. "Jesus," he said beneath his breath.

"Get the hell out my way!" the man mumbled as he rode by.

Alan was on edge. His defenses were on high alert. The faint crackle of a fart would send him jumping into the air right now.

He noticed the sound of wood cracking and soon spotted that familiar reddish-orange glow behind a few houses. His eyes locked onto a disturbing sight as he walked around the corner. There was a house on fire, but the worse of this situation was on the front porch. Two older males drank and laughed as they watched a woman burn to death. The woman's son screamed in horror as he watched his mom sizzle in agony. The mother flipped off of the porch, onto the front lawn and began melting away like a wax figure. The two men, still drinking and having a good time, walked off the porch and began laughing hysterically the woman. The kid was left on the porch surrounded by flames, screaming for the safety of his mother and praying for his own life.

Alan felt the need to step in so he cautiously walked closer to the home. When he got a closer look at the men, their demonic faces sent Alan three steps backward. Their eyes were black with a yellowish glow around them. Their skin was disfigured and rotten. Instead of hands the men had what appeared to be claws. Their fingers were a good ten inches and their nails were razor sharp.

Alan looked at the woman melting and then at the kid trapped in the fire. He wanted desperately to help them but he wasn't so sure he could take the two freaks standing in the way.

Oh Shit! he thought. They now took an interest in him!

He knew that on some level he could be injured out here but he didn't want to see how badly. Alan was of some use however. Out of the corner of his eye he noticed the little boy on the porch pass through the fire and sneak off. He would give the boy a few seconds to run before taking off himself. The poor woman was left to die unfortunately. She melted down into the front lawn as if she were an ice cube set on a grill.

Alan couldn't wait any longer, he ran for it while he still had a chance. The demons took a quick glance back and noticed the kid was gone. It took them approximately two seconds to decide to let the kid go and hunt down Alan. They moved with the agility of a spider and they ran like lions, occasionally stepping on all fours. Alan turned corners and jumped hurdles as fast as he could. His speed, too, was extraordinary, but his fear, once again, restrained him from his full potential.

Alan ran down a street that happened to be under battle. A dozen demons were attacking a young man. And out of a boarded up house came seven citizens to his rescue. They shot and beat the demons repeatedly but it took a direct shot to take them down and these things were quick and hard to hit. They dodged the gunshots with ease. Alan didn't know who the defenders were but he knew they had guns and he knew they were normal… on some level anyway.

Just as one of the demons jumped to tackle Alan it was shot back by one of the citizens. With few other options Alan continued on to the pack of vigilantes. He didn't have a gun but Alan picked up a stick and helped to fight off the attacking demons. Eventually they managed to force all of the demons to retreat. They didn't have much time however. Alan helped in dragging the injured boy to cover.

"You alright?" one of the vigilantes said to the injured young man.
"Yeah."

A middle-aged woman looked at Alan surprised. She could tell from his demeanor that he wasn't from around here. "Who are you?" The woman asked.

"I'm lost," Alan replied.

A big man, in his early forties, looked at Alan and laughed. "No shit. Looks like you're in the wrong neck of the woods son."

"I'm trying to get downtown. Is there an easier way?"

The big man looked at Alan, surprised. "You can't get into downtown from here, it's been blocked off for years."

"Why the hell do you want to get down there anyway? You're trying to steal some shit ain't-cha!" the woman added. She'd seen enough looters in her time.

"No. I'm looking for a friend."

There was a thump up on the roof of a nearby house. Everyone got quiet and looked around.

"Got dam it! Where the hell is Tubbs?" the big man yelled.

Several more thumps came about on all of the surrounding houses. The first thing to be seen was their glowing yellow eyes and then their sharp and deadly claws. The demons crept slowly to the peak of the roofs and waited.

"What are they waiting for?" Alan asked. The civilians were ambushed from all angles and there were more of the demons coming, lots more. "Is there any way whatsoever to get down there?"

"Son, this whole city, shit the whole planet, is about to undergo the most profound change it's ever seen. You want to be deep underground, trust me," the big man said.

The demons simultaneously jumped from the roofs in attack formation and more came from the side yards of the homes. Everyone instantly began shooting at anything that moved. The resistance managed to hold back the first wave of demons but there were too many of them. A young guy in his thirties was above Alan shooting away as one of the demons tackled him to the ground and savagely mauled his neck.

"Start shootin boy!" the big man yelled to Alan as he blew the demon away.

Alan grabbed the gun from the fallen man and started shooting demons. Another man was taken down. Alan turned around and shot that demon, he was getting the hang of this. Sadly, the vigilantes were outnumbered by about fifty. Out of what seemed sheer luck, a large bus-sized hovercraft came flooring down the street. This was in the nick of time as it distracted the demons and gave the resistance an edge.

Several of the windows on the craft rolled down and out came gunfire. The demons pulled back but they weren't finished. The gunfire did, however, buy the group enough time to get into the vehicle. The man driving was an older black man named Tubbs. As the group dragged in the wounded, Tubbs gave Alan, who was outside contemplating, a strange look.

"Boy, get in here!"

Alan looked at Tubbs and then at the predators. He did not want to get sidetracked and he had no clue as to the destination of this vehicle.

"You goan die if you just sit there. Na come own!" Tubbs yelled.

Alan reluctantly jumped into the vehicle. The demons quickly charged it once the gunfire slowed. With luck and a little skill they managed to fight them off.

Alan looked around and saw that there were families, couples and friends packed tightly within. "Where are you headed?"

"We got to get underground." Tubbs replied. He looked at Alan who was tense and uncertain. "Have a seat na, I know you're scared."

Alan sat down on the floor feeling lost once again. He felt betrayed by his feelings. He thought that he would be able to go downtown from the direction he took and somehow be led to Amy in a short amount of time. Something had pulled him in that direction and he trusted those feelings.

It's too late. I know it, he thought.

Alan looked out of the window with much disparity. Just as he was told, there was a large forty-foot steel wall separating the outer neighborhoods from the inner city.

"You ok there son? You look confused," Tubbs asked.

"I don't know. I thought... I felt as if I would find what I was looking for but..." Alan got quiet. He didn't know how to explain what he wanted to say.

"Boy you just in the wrong neighborhood that's all. What the hell you doin out here any way?"

"I'm looking for somebody. A friend of mine."

"Well what the hell are they doin out here?"

Alan wasn't too sure how to explain the situation. "We're kind of lost."

"Well that's obvious. You damn travelers is always get'n lost out here."

Alan wondered if he could get a more defined answer of where he was from this guy. "Where exactly is here?"

"Son, haven't you learned anything yet? *Here* is where you are. It's not in relation to, in the proximity of, or nearby. You're just here. If you'd come to accept that in the first place you wouldn't even be here."

What? Does this man know what I'm going through? How could he? Everyone else seems oblivious to it.

"Do people like me get lost out here often?"

"We're all *like* you. Some are just more lost than others. Quite often you travelers come out here and get caught up in the mix of thangs."

Suddenly, several demons started banging on the windows of the vehicle. Whenever the men went to shoot the demons they would simply go back on top of the roof.

"Hang on everybody!" Tubbs yelled.

Tubbs swerved the vehicle and ran over a dismantled car on the sidewalk. This sent the bus-like hovercraft about fifteen feet into the air. When it came down the hovercraft bottomed out on the street, but they quickly regained speed, and much to their luck, the demons were shaken off. Alan looked back as the demons smacked into the pavement and then instantly got back up.

"What about them?" he asked.

"They're lost too. Only they're stuck. I would say forever but there's always a chance for freedom. Even in the most ignorant of people."

"They're people?"

Tubbs gave Alan the *silly little boy* expression. "Like I said, we're all the same on some level. See, a while back those in charge of the city felt as if our *sector* was too much to handle, so they blocked it off. Completely. There was no food, no water, and no medical assistance given. We were all left to take care of ourselves. A lot of the people were very angry, naturally of course. Only *they* got so wrapped in their anger that they became what you just saw."

This concept was easy for Alan to grasp as it had just happened to him. He too became a monster in some ways, just like the ones attacking the civilians in this city.

"How do you guys live like this?"

"Well at first it wasn't so bad, there were only a few of them. But as this storm approached everyone started going nuts... but anyway... I just take life day to day. Your mind will accept its environment. You get used to it. And besides there's nowhere else to go."

"But there's plenty of other places."

Tubbs chuckled, "I've lived here my whole life. I could run and find a place that'll take care of me but would that really be better? You got to make real choices in life, you can't just run for safety all the time."

Alan looked around at the situation. "But I thought that's what we're all doing."

Tubbs squinted his eyes and shook his head at Alan, the *smart ass*.

"You need to stop thinking about everything and open your eyes a bit more. I'm not running, I'm shuttling. These families need to get to cover and so do you."

"I can't. I have to at least try to find Amy."

"She must be somethin' special... sounds like love to me. Mmmm hmm... the lovin' of a good woman. Cain't go wrong with that. If you do find her, make sure you appreciate her for who she is. The last thing you want is to ignore a girl who truly loves you."

Alan thought about her, the love he felt in her presence, the soft touch of her cheek pressed against his, the smell of her hair, her gorgeous smile, even her sassy attitude she had at times. All of this brought a smile to his face.

"Yeah. She's definitely worth it."

A bolt of lighting struck down in front of the vehicle forcing Tubbs to swerve once again.

"Sorry folks. Hang on!"

Everyone was bounced around but then quickly resettled.

"What's with all the lightning?" Alan asked.

"It's that damn city. We got these annoying absorption devises that pull in the energy from storms and such to keep the city running. But, those dumb bastards made it so that the city sucked in everythang. So na, the very thing used to help the city will also be the city's downfall."

"What, no one thought about this?"

"Normally the city could absorb a storm passing through, but the amount of energy coming through this particular storm is too much. The city's tryin' to absorb it all but can't handle it. If it weren't for the total consumption of energy it would not have overloaded in the first place. My guess is that nature's tryin' to readjust the balance that's been lost for years."

They finally reached their destination; it was Tubbs' house. The people with guns got off first and cleared the path for the unarmed. Tubbs ran up and opened his front door. Alan looked at this commendable character and felt a sense appreciation.

This place isn't filled with all nut jobs after all, he thought.

A couple of vigilantes guarding the back of the craft saw, in the distance, a massive group of demons headed their way.

"They must have caught on," a vigilante remarked.

The demons did catch on and they were headed for a feast. There was about forty people waiting to be taken underground and they all had to go through Tubbs' narrow home. Everyone nearly stumbled over one another rushing to get into safety.

"Got damn it! Back off!" Tubbs yelled.

Like a herd of sheep they managed to squeeze everyone in and shut the door before the demons arrived.

"What now?" a woman cried.

Boom! Boom! One by one the demons were attacking the house. Eventually the place was covered with them.

"Can they get in here?" Alan asked with a worried look.

"They don't want to."

Tubbs opened a cabinet and pulled out the good old automatic weapons and passed them out to the willing. Alan dropped his weapon a while back and didn't really want another one. He knew there was another way to take care these guys, he just didn't know how.

"Everyone follow me." Tubbs led the way to the basement.

The demons were centralizing their efforts on one spot, the front door. Wood and a few sheets of metal blocked it but the door itself was made of glass. It only took a few minutes before the demons broke through. At first it was only the hands of the demons but they managed to open a hole large enough to fit through. One by one they poured in through the window. A few brave men stayed above to fight them off while the rest went below for cover.

Tubbs lit a dim light and guided the group through his basement. It was narrow, dark, and moist. At the end of the basement was a small room with a small door. Tubbs went in and pulled out the carpeting. Beneath it laid a hatch in the floor.

"Now once you're down here we can't help you, and I'm sure there's more of 'em," Tubbs announced to the group.

He opened the hatch revealing a staircase leading down into darkness.

"You're staying here?" a little girl asked.

"Oh yeah. Someone's got to do it sweetie."

There were several shots above, and they were close to the basement door. This was a clear indication for the group to get moving.

"Now remember folks, just hang in there. This storm will be over and everything will be different. If you stay together you'll stay alive and that's what matters right now." Tubbs looked at Alan and spoke to him directly, "Take the path to the right. It'll take ya downtown. If ya make it above, I wish ya luck in finding your friend."

"If?"

"Ya never know what'll happen. Jus follow ya intuition and ya might just make it."

Alan thought for a second. He realized that his feelings hadn't let him down after all. He had in fact been shown the only way to get downtown. His confidence was restored.

"Hey, thanks," Alan said.

Tubbs gave him a smile and began ushering people down the stairs. Alan was the last to enter. As he descended down the staircase he turned to look at Tubbs. When the hatch was shut the group was left in darkness.

No one wanted to move. Everyone remained against the side of the staircase, petrified.

"Mommy. What if the stairs don't go all the way down?" a little girl asked.

Alan walked to the front of the line. He too, didn't know what was ahead on the path, but he knew within that this was the way. Meeting Tubbs was a sign that his doubt was just a lack of understanding and a feeble attempt to control the situation.

"You don't have to see the whole staircase, you just have to take the next step," Alan said with a certain tone of leadership in his voice. He said that for the little girl but the whole group took comfort in those words.

Alan could feel that sense of omnipotent divinity within and began to glow a soft blue. The little girl behind him was fascinated at first but everyone else soon saw the miracle unfold before their eyes.

"He's an angel," a woman in the back uttered.

This gave motivation for the entire group to get up and follow Alan. The people needed guidance and he was there for them. As they traveled down the stairs they all traveled as one.

Chapter 24

The staircase was about eighty flights leading deep down to the underground. For the longest time there was only the sound of water drips and the wispy breeze of the wind. After a long haul down they finally saw a faint source of light other than Alan. This was good and bad, good for the group because they were underground, away from the storm, and bad for Alan because he would have to separate from the group soon.

Something walked by the bottom of the stairs, freaking Alan out and turning off his blue luminosity. His pacing quickly changed from steady to cautious. A sense of calm arrived, however, once he heard the disjointed grumbling of human chatter.

Down to the left of the tunnel, where Alan *wasn't* heading, were bums, citizens from above, and more bums. They made themselves a little village. There were makeshift houses created out of bed sheets, newspaper, boxes, and old clothes. Their source of heat came from the fires burning in the empty trashcans; each one had at least five individuals gathered around it. There were thousands of evacuees down there; they were mixed in with the poor people, who already lived in these tunnels. Ironically, the tunnels were the only protection they could afford at one point and now it was the only protection available.

This is it. Time to go off alone again, Alan thought with a hint of sadness.

As the people trickled down into the tunnel Alan looked at them wishing he was going in their direction. One of the mothers walked up to Alan and shook his hand.

"Take care," she said.

Another man walked up to and did the same. "Good luck son."

After several more goodbyes and good lucks Alan was left to move on with his journey. He noticed that the side of the tunnel made for the pedestrians was decently lit and had a certain level of security. The direction in which he had to walk was dark and wet. Not far down the path it curved, leading to more darkness. Alan was unsure of what he would encounter down that way, but he had to do what he had to do. Alan set off for the dark path. Some of the poor folk noticed this loner traveling alone down the dark path and raised an eyebrow. They knew something he didn't.

As Alan pressed on through the tunnel the amount of people occupying the wall space was thinning.

I wonder why no one is coming down this way.

He saw ahead in the shadows a drop off point. As he ran for it he soon noticed the sound of running water coming from below. Sure enough, there was a steady flow running through a sewer system.

This must be the sewage for the city. That means the inner city can't be that far.

The problem was that there were very few lights down there. But the determined Alan bravely climbed down the ladder and submerged into the shadows of his destiny. He could barely see a thing.

Alan paid attention to the heavy flow of water in an attempt to find the exit. He was so occupied with listening to the water that he didn't hear the footsteps creeping towards him! From around the corner came a desperate looking fellow dressed in ripped clothing accompanied by a foul stench. He approached Alan and flashed his multi colored teeth while extending his grimy hand.

"Ehe man can yuu get me some change. I sho could uuze sum food?" the man asked.

The puzzled yet startled look on Alan's face didn't seem to faze the vagabond. Alan twitched around when another hobo grabbed his shoulder from behind!

"Whatchu doin down here? Don't chu realize this place ain't safe for lost little boys?"

"How do I get out of here?" Alan said in a panic. He wasn't sure how to respond. His only thoughts were leaving, quick.

"You caint! You stuck na!"

These guys were toying with him. Several other drifters saw the situation and got excited. They wanted in on the fun.

"Letz get some munee off of em."

The first two bums sandwiched him in so he couldn't leave. Two more arrived, and that's when Alan got physical. He shoved the guy in front of him to the ground, and looked down the tunnel. He thought of running but for some reason felt as if he should stand strong. Then, two more tyrants walked up to the circle of intimidation.

"Just tell me—"

The beggar cut him off, "Oh you los now boy. You los na!"

"Please, I just want to—"

One of the bums grabbed his clothes and felt it for quality. "Dis good. I sholl like to have dis own my back."

"Yes sir! Nice shoes too," said another vagrant. The bums were grabbing him and shouting in his face, they were having so much fun scaring this lost soul.

Alan felt trapped, but he was tired of running away. He closed his eyes and meditated within the center of his chest, with as little thought as possible. He did not want to react and he didn't want to run in fear, he knew this situation could be taken care of. He imagined an explosion from within his body and… BOOM! A wave of energy expanded from within, shoving back all the hobos.

"Tell me where I'm going!"

The beggars now looked at him with fear. Their game was over.

"I don't know. Man he crazy!"

"How do I get downtown?" Alan asked.

"Whatchu want to go downtown fo? The storm's runnin through."

"I have to go… Now please," his tone softened and he slowed his speech to a calm, "Tell me how to get downtown."

"Maannn just tell him. I don' want em down hea."

"You go dat way, bout a mile," one of them pointed the direction.

Alan relaxed and straightened out his shirt. "Thank you."

"Be caefu now boy. Dem Crazies down there. You see them yella eyes you start runnin."

Alan gave them a nod "thanks" and continued on with his destiny.

"That foo is crazy himself."

"Dey show gone teah em up."

They all watched curiously as the lone traveler walked down his path.

When Alan felt a breeze swoop into the tunnel he knew he was headed in the right direction.

It has to be coming from outside!

Along the walls were hobos here and there, lying down. These guys were like the cockroaches of the society, most hated them but they would probably survive the longest down here. Some gathered in small groups around the few remaining trashcan fires, while others simply curled into a ball and slept. The few that were down here gave Alan a glance, but it must have been his new demeanor that made them leave him alone.

The water in the middle of the sewer was slowing down as Alan walked along his allotted path. Most the water Alan had encountered on this journey was clean and revitalizing but this stuff was ripe with the waste of a society that had no appreciation for life. In fact everything about the city, so far, was life draining. He could only imagine what the downtown was like. Unfortunately, all of the collective negativity kept his mind going at full speeds, although he was able to at least monitor it. That was a small step in the journey to be able to choose to stop thinking.

I wonder if I can stop whenever I want... There are so many thoughts up here... Damn it...! That was a thought... Oh shit, so was that...! Damn it...!

The *idea* of stopping thought kept him thinking. That's when he realized something. *Maybe it's not about stopping thought all together, but thinking with clarity... Without the constant involuntary mental chatter... My thoughts are part of a process in which I am the beginning... And if I am the beginning then... ... ...*

And then it happened. There were no more thoughts! It felt like an empty stadium and he was standing directly in the middle of it. He had felt this clarity before but this was the first time he was consciously aware of what was going on.

I could get used to this.

The incredible feelings of divinity came back within him. It was mind blowing. He knew from that point on that he could choose to feel this way and that he didn't have to wait for something to happen.

That's when he heard something move in the distance. A group of hobos warming themselves up heard the same noise and looked ahead. They knew what it was and they were afraid. Two of them instantly ran away, the other two gave Alan a fearful look as if they were waiting to see what he would do. After a few seconds one of them decided to join his friends in the run to safety while the other tried waking his friend on the ground.

Alan could feel fear rising within him. But this was a different type of fear. It was more primal. It was more of a natural protection system than a fear created by his ego.

I can still feel within. And there's still clarity, but my senses are on high alert.

The drifter lying down finally woke up and scurried to his feet in a panic. He tried gathering everything he owned in his arms but he didn't have time. Three pairs of glowing yellow eyes crept out of the darkness, and like jackals, they leaped out from the shadows and attacked the bums, sinking their claws into them like animals.

Alan watched this primal act unsure of what to do. He wished to run but he feared his movement would get their attention. Unfortunately, one of the demonic thugs turned their attention to Alan before he could make a decision. As their prey died the other demons looked to Alan for their next meal.

Alan's bolted for it! But their run was so animalistic and agile. One of them jumped on and off the side of the tunnel walls like it was all a game while the others spread to each side of his shoulders. Alan tried his hardest to outrun the demons but the harder he tried the slower he moved. His running quickly slowed down to a jog. It was happening again.

"Damn it!" he yelled. *Why can't I do what I want?*

He realized at that moment that it was *his* thoughts he was running away from; it was the fear. In a twist of alignment, Alan stopped with his eyes closed. The predators circled around him in attack formation but didn't attack just yet. They were curious as to why he stopped moving. And then… he did something shocking! Alan turned around with a smile on his face, and the three demons looked at him more puzzled.

Alan looked into their glowing yellow eyes and chuckled! "You guys."

The demons didn't return words, they just looked at him funny. As a dog would react to a strange noise, one of the demons cocked his head and aggressively moved forward with his teeth snarling. Alan looked beyond the aggression for the first time and saw in those eyes… pure ignorance. It was fear they fed off of and they couldn't take it, it could only be given. And Alan was through feeding them.

In one last attempt to scare him, the approaching demon jumped at Alan. Alan simply looked into his glowing eyes and peered through layers of anger, hatred, and foolishness. The demon stared back and saw infinite wisdom within Alan's eyes and something happened in those few seconds between them. The demon dropped to the ground as if suddenly weighted with a thousand pounds, and looked up to Alan, as a scorned student would do to his teacher.

The demon's face softened, and his eyes ceased to glow. The claws this individual once used to kill were now, in the presence of purity, harmless. He was changing just as Alan had changed. Beneath this demonic figure was just a scared young man with nothing else to do but dominate those he could control. He felt so lost and now more than ever, stupid. The boy realized that for so long he was doing what he saw others do and fell into the same pattern. For once he questioned why and how he became so lost.

"I'm sorry," the boy apologized.

The two other demons were flabbergasted. They didn't know what the hell was going on. In a moment of fear they ran away. Alan reached his hand out to help the boy rise to his feet. The boy saw in Alan's eyes not a man, but a divine spirit. Alan smiled, bowed humbly and walked on in peace. The boy stood in the shadows for once with the ability to make a choice as to what he would do.

Chapter 25

Finally, there was light at the end of the tunnel. Alan was feeling great. He knew he had just helped out a lost soul and above that, he faced his fears. There was the feeling of inner security and he regained full confidence in finding Amy. Just around the bend was, much to Alan's delight, a source of artificial lighting.

Finally, the end is near, he thought.

Around the bend came walking a squad of policemen. They didn't see him at first but when they did they freaked out.

"Don't move!" yelled the Sergeant as he aimed his pistol at Alan.

Alan froze and put his hands in the air. They had weapons and they seemed ready to use them.

"I don't think he's one of 'em Sarge," said a policeman.

Alan approached the squad with his hands still up. The last thing he wanted was to get shot after he heroically faced the thugs from hell.

"Where are you coming from son?" Sarge asked.

"I'm trying to get downtown."

"You are downtown. Why are you coming from the outskirts?"

"I can't really answer that officer."

"Well you better find an excuse," the Sarge scorned.

"Look, a friend and I were traveling through the city and we got split up. I think she's somewhere up there."

"Not up there, she ain't. That place is empty."

"I don't expect you to understand, but I have to look for her and I will find her regardless of your permission."

The Sarge and his troops were surprised at Alan's matter-of-fact tone and the two deputies sarcastically giggled at him.

"Come with me," Sarge said. He took Alan forward while the squad of deputies continued to clear the path Alan just came from.

As they walked back Alan could hear thousands of voices coming through. That's because there *were* thousands of people being herded into the tunnel from above. For a second he feared Amy could be lost somewhere among all these faces. But there was something poking at him, Alan felt as if she were above. He didn't know why, he just did, and he had come to trust what was felt within.

"If your friend was in the city she's down here now. There's no one left on the streets," Sarge said.

"I still have to look. I'm sure she's up there."

"I can't let you go up there. You won't make it through the storm."

Alan looked at the masses of helpless people. He wondered if maybe, just maybe, she could be down here. Yet within all the faces he could and couldn't see, there just wasn't that spark.

I have to trust this feeling. It is, after all, the same intuition that got me to the city. "Something tells me to look above. I have to go," Alan demanded.

"Son, the whole city has been ordered to go below. This storm is going to change everything. We can't let you back up there."

"But she could die up there. You've got to let me go."

Sarge gave the signal to have Alan forced into the crowd. One of the hundreds of cops grabbed Alan by the arm and forced him into the herd of people.

"What are you, crazy, kid? All structures are unstable up there. It's nice and solid down here. You'll be safer," the cop said.

Alan walked though looking at the many faces. These were not bums; they were wealthy citizens with lives that had been interrupted by nature.

"Can't they just stop it like usual? We have more important things to attend to," Alan heard a posh man in his fifties say.

"I don't get it. They've always done it before," said another. "I heard there's nothing wrong with the system. That it's all scam."

"I say we demand to be let back up!" the man proclaimed.

Alan gave them a disgusted look as he made his way through the mass crowd of people. He felt like he was in a factory farm full of animals waiting to meet the butcher. Everyone seemed so fake and materialistic, so blind to what was happening. Almost everyone snubbed their noses and grumbled about the *inconvenience* of the storm. Their clothes were stylish and flashy as if they were waiting to attend a ballroom dance. The women checked their makeup and did their hair while looking around to see if anyone noticed them. The men wore impressionable formalwear as to keep up the image of respectability.

This is ridiculous, Alan thought. *A life-threatening storm is getting ready to strike and you guys are worried about makeup.* Alan felt disgusted. The scene reminded him of home.

He pushed and pushed through the lame mass of people until he finally reached the entrance. As he peered out beyond the doorway he saw something shocking; there wasn't just a couple thousand people, there was hundreds of thousands of people, probably close to a million. They were lined throughout the entire freeway system. Literally everyone who lived in the city was headed down into this tunnel. The people in the city waited till the last second to decide to evacuate.

They must have truly thought their technology would be enough to stop nature.

Alan had to admit that he felt a little safe down in this ditch. It was brightly lit and made of the thickest metal. Its rectangular shape was also meant to provide security in such a situation. The high winds and electrical storms were guided around and above while the people in the freeway were untouched.

The only problem was that Alan was trying to get out. There were hundreds of staircases leading to the above streets but all of them were jam packed with people coming down for safety, and on top of that, there were police regulating the traffic.

Alan took a second to notice the city. It was huge and technologically advanced. The place looked like Tokyo on speed! Holographic billboards were on every corner flashing bright eye popping colors and catchy slogans. One of the holographic commercials flashing against a skyscraper read:

If you want it, we've got it!

This seemed to be true because every corner seemed to have the same stores with different logos. There was an endless repeat of fashion store/restaurant/furniture store/bank, all one-stop-shops for the same products. No one seemed to do anything for themselves in the city either. All of the vehicles were driven on a magnetic strip for automatic driving. There were thousands of monorail trams lining the city at every twenty feet. There was literally a transportation unit to take anyone anywhere they wanted to go. These people were used to controlling everything with the push of a button.

There weren't, really, any natural aspects of the city left for Mother Nature to take care of. The trees were synthetically grown. A control switch adjusted the lawns. And their source of water... they could *produce* the best-*looking* water anybody ever laid eyes upon. Who needed a storm?

The storm appeared to have already done a number on the city. The system had overloaded causing power-outages, fires, and the strange phenomena of electricity flowing around the buildings. There was so much energy coming down that the storage systems began releasing it everywhere. The entire city looked like one of those magical orbs that, when touched, the electricity would centralize to your fingertips, only it was on a massive scale and the finger tips were giant sky scrapers! And to put the cherry on top, there were the enigmatic tornadoes that came down and stayed in one position. They were throwing concrete, glass and everything else, in all directions. This was the oddest storm Alan had ever seen!

Gawking time was over however. Alan figured if he didn't push his way up the stairs he would never make it. So he nonchalantly pushed, slithered and dodged his way between people and started heading upwards. One of the policemen spotted Alan trying to go up the stairs and stopped him.

"Kid, where do you think you're going?"

"Up," Alan answered in his nonchalant tone.

The cop looked at him funny and shook his head. "No. You're not." He grabbed Alan and shoved him towards the tunnel.

Alan didn't want to get into confrontation in front of all these people. There was only one thing worse than an ignorant person and that was a lot of ignorant people over-stressed and in a crowd. Alan's only hope was to find another way up, so he ran down the freeway against the masses.

Damn! I was almost up there.

Then, the storm let out another taste of its power. Everyone watched in fear as several lightning tangents struck the city causing power surges and power overloads in the many electrically run systems. The wind began picking up and tossing around objects as large as cars! Several more stationary tornadoes sprung down from the skies causing all of the loose debris to be sucked into the funnels.

Is this it?

Below, in the freeway, it was hard to feel the effects but Alan could see the damage above. For a second he thought the people of this city just might make it. But when he looked into the sky and saw that swirling red cloud he knew the storm still hadn't released its fury.

No one else seemed to be concerned. Everyone was still carrying that same visage of boredom, and arrogance… that was until one of the tornadoes sprouted down directly into the freeway! It began sucking up hundreds of helpless people from all directions into its funnel and somewhere above the clouds. Alan ran for dear life with thousands of others. People were tramped, stomped, and mashed by the stampede of frightened citizens.

This was his chance. While everyone was preoccupied, he ran up a staircase that wasn't packed with people. A cop looked at him for a brief moment but didn't stop Alan; his attention was on the twister like everyone else's. Alan looked back for a second and was sadly relieved. If he had gone up the stairs he would have be sucked into that tornado.

Poor bastards.

For a second he felt bad. Alan knew that there was the only one entrance into the tunnel and now no one had a chance of getting to it. But his concern was light, as he had finally gotten above!

Now to find Amy!

Once Alan saw the center of the city he knew that she was somewhere down there. The only thing stopping him now was the electricity, tornadoes, fire and ferocious winds. Not much at all.

Chapter 26

The wind knocked Alan around like a ping-pong ball. It also knocked debris *into* him. The amount of dust in the sky was filling in by the second and soon blocked the view of the skyscrapers. Alan's only means for cover was to run close to one of the buildings.

Suddenly, a strike of lightning zapped in front of his face and connected with an adjacent building. He could feel the cells in his body cook, as he was only feet away from it. Alan quickly decided it would be best to hang low, and this was in his best interest because a car was thrown over his head seconds later!

These were near unbearable conditions for anybody to travel in. He was beginning to wonder if anyone was left out here. In that instant a bolt of lightning struck the building behind him. The surge of power was so great it shattered every window of the building and sent millions of shards headed for the ground. Alan barely dodged the falling razor sharp slits as they smashed into the street behind him.

Alan desperately needed more cover. His only option was to run into a nearby alley. He felt so confused and helpless. *How am I supposed to find anybody in this?*

But there was still that urge; that tug, pulling him towards the center of the city. In a moment of clarity he walked to the end of the alley and gazed out towards the center. Coincidentally the winds calmed a little and cleared a visual path for Alan to see.

That's it!

He was staring at the top of the tallest building, which also happened to be the center building. That's where he was being pulled. Somewhere on the top floor of that large, black, cylindrical, man-made construction was Amy, and his way out. He could feel it with every ounce of energy that made up his body.

Alan gathered the strength to move on. There was a fire blocking his direct path so he had to make a slight detour of several blocks. He looked around the city and had an epiphany. *This is probably the calmest this city has ever been.*

Strangely it was. There were cars thrown into buildings, windows smashed and chunks of the buildings tossed everywhere, but there wasn't the busy flow of human activity and now the city's power was out, or better said, out of control.

Alan walked along with his eyes open. Still, he held reservations that Amy might not be in the city. This was because there was no one out in this barren wasteland. Those were his thoughts until he heard the faint murmur of a group of people not far from his position. Alan darted around the corner to find a group of twenty elderly folks making haste. Behind this group were two men struggling to pull a stubborn old woman.

"Ma'am there's nothing more I can do. Now you have to come with us or you'll die," said one of the young men whose nametag read *Tim.*

"No! I want to stay. All of my stuff is up there," the woman yelled. She was referring to the senior home they just left.

"Sally, just come on!" One of the elderly yelled back.

The group was moving towards the freeway but Sally didn't want to leave her things behind.

Roy, the other assistant, was also trying to get Sally to move forward. "I'm sorry but there is no other option!"

Sally smacked Roy in the face while Tim tried to restrain her.

"Old senile bat! Do you want to die?" Roy asked.

Sally dropped to the ground like a spoiled brat who wasn't getting her way with her parents. The two men tried to pick her up but she was too much for them.

"Leave me alone," she pouted.

The two caretakers let her go. When she fell back to the ground she was surprised.

"That's no way to treat a lady," Sally scolded them.

"Forget her. It'll be too late by the time we drag her down there," said one of the elderly men in the group.

"We can't just leave her behind," Sally's friend pleaded. "Sally stop fighting. Come on with us."

Out of the corner of their eyes they saw the silhouette of a figure walk out of the fiery smoke. It was Alan!

"What are you doing out here?" asked Roy.

"I'm looking for someone. A young girl with dark hair, about yea tall," he leveled her height with his hand, "and soft features."

"I doubt anyone is out here except for us."

Alan looked at the old folks. *Maybe she's within one of these people,* he thought. "She had on a brown sweater and black pants. She's got dark brown eyes with fair skin…"

"I did see a girl like that a couple of days ago but she's probably in the tunnel now."

Alan's face lit up. *Maybe she was down there after all.* "Where did you see her?"

"I don't remember. She might have been in the building looking for shelter," Roy said.

Alan immediately looked towards the center of the city.

"It's useless. You'll both be dead if you don't leave now!" Tim added.

"Well the freeway is blocked by a tornado if that's where you guys were headed. I wouldn't try to find shelter down there," Alan remarked.

The group became distressed after hearing this comment.

"Where are we supposed to go?" asked one of the elderly women.

"They just forget about us like we're dogs, and now we're stuck out in the middle of this storm. We get no respect," grumbled one of the seniors.

Tim and Roy didn't know what to do. They were the only ones taking care of this group. Everyone else abandoned them.

"Are you sure about this?" asked Roy.

"That's where I just came from."

"Where are we going to go now?" asked one of the seniors.

Roy looked around. He and Tim were clueless. They all knew that their building was too dangerous to return to and they couldn't think of anywhere else they could run for cover. Alan looked into the center of the red swirl. It was quickly expanding and spinning like a whirlpool. The sound this swirl emitted was a loud and deep groan, the type of sound you'd hear just before an implosion. The group was terrified. There was no hope left in their minds.

Alan looked at the center building and pointed. "What's up there?"

"It's the City Center building. There's tons of stuff."

"Would there be people up there?"

Tim thought about it and something sparked within him. "Yeah, now that you mention it. There are holding cells up there. They keep people in cells who've broken into the city. If they caught your friend and she didn't have a city permit it's likely they took her up there."

"Would she still be up there?"

"It's definitely possible."

"Maybe we can find cover in that building. It is the strongest of the city," one of the old men added.

208

Roy looked to the group and announced where they were headed. All that was left was convincing Sally to go with them. Tim and Roy tried picking her up again but she was too resistant.

"I don't want to go. Leave me alone."

Alan saw that this was not a woman to be taken by force. She needed to be courted like a debutant.

He walked up to her with a smile. "We are headed for the City Center. It's probably the best place for everyone and it's not far from your home," Alan said with the politest of manners.

"What's it to you kid?" Sally the smart ass remarked.

"I'm looking for a friend."

"Well she obviously ain't here now, is she?"

"No, but she might be up there. And it might provide cover for us all."

Alan held his hand out for the stubborn woman. She looked at him surprised. He held his kindness after a rude gesture.

"Now this is a gentleman," Sally proclaimed to the faces of Roy and Tim.

"Help me find my friend and I'll take you where ever you want to go. I promise."

"Well I'm no psychic kid. What do you want me to do?"

"Just come with us. Get yourself out of danger."

"Ooh, my valiant white knight has come," Sally said with playful sarcasm.

Their little break from turmoil was over however. From the center of the red swirl came thousands of horizontal bolts of lightning. They spread through the sky like a sheet of ice breaking from too much pressure. This was followed by a crackle of thunder so loud it shattered windows on several of the buildings. The group quickly picked up the pace and hurried to their destination.

Chapter 27

The journey was rough but, they were now approaching the center of the city. The group had to form a human chain just to make it through the wind. Above, the swirling red clouds had spread to the furthest reaches of the city. It formed a funnel but, strangely, it went up towards space.

That is so weird, Alan thought.

Lightning struck the City Center and sent one of those familiar surges through it, only this time the release of power was so strong it popped out a chunk of the building and sent it hurling towards Alan and the group.

"Look out!" Alan cried.

But it was too late. The group scattered but the large chunk of steel and concrete slammed into two senior citizens. The sight was morbid.

"Keep moving!" Roy called out.

The three youthful men, Roy, Tim and Alan, ran to help up the scattered elderly. Sally, who was in front of the group, took the lead and pushed on forward.

"Keep moving you lazy bones. We're almost there," she demanded.

The wind basically threw them into the lobby of the building. The youngsters fought hard to close the doors only to have their efforts defeated when the wind shattered the glass that made up the doors. Everyone covered up as the sharp shards flew into the lobby. They desperately needed to move on but if anyone had gotten up they would have been sliced. Alan laid low to the ground and gave inspiration for the group to crawl on inward. The only problem was that large glass windows surrounded the entire lobby and it was only a matter of time before those shattered.

"How do we get up?" Alan asked.

"Hold your horses kid, we just got inside," Sally reprimanded.

"Please! I need to find her now. How do we go up?"

"Usually the pods will take you but I doubt they're working now," Roy said referring to the elevator pods.

"Are you sure they aren't working?"

Roy looked frustrated. "If they are you don't want to take them. We have to get underground. Your friend might even be down there."

This notion was a possibility, Alan realized, so the group moved on to the staircase. It was dark, cold, and silent in this creepy shaft. Alan felt like he was stepping into a grave. The more they descended down the staircase the more Alan felt that this was the wrong direction, and not just wrong, but deadly. When they reached the bottom he really felt his stomach plummet.

"I have a bad feeling about this."

An old snobbish man spoke down to Alan, "Well the chance of survival is minimal if it is to be subject to your feelings, now, isn't it?"

Roy looked at the group. "This is the safest place, people. We'll hold up here."

The group felt comfortable with Roy's decision. They opened the maintenance door and …nothing. It was empty and calm. This was surprising to Alan because he could feel certain doom just beyond that door, but it looked safe inside.

"Is there anyone willing to help me?" Alan asked.

"You're crazy, you young vagabond. How did your filth get into our city anyway?" the old snob asked.

"Keep your decrepit mouth shut you old fart," Sally scolded the snob. She turned to Alan and decided to stick it out with him. "I'll help you. I don't want to be stuck with these rotting corpses anyway."

"But Sal you might not make it," Sally's friend begged.

"Don't worry hun. I'll be fine." She pointed to Tim. "You! You're coming with us."

"Why am I going?" Tim asked.

"Don't be a wuss," Sally egged. "Come on. Lets hurry up."

"Thank you guys so much," Alan said.

As they walked out of the room Roy closed the door and locked it, being extra precautious. Alan looked up the seemingly endless flight of stairs and felt overwhelmed.

"Can we try to take the pods?"

Tim shook his head, truly wishing he hadn't gone with them. "If you want to check fine, but I doubt they're working."

The three of them made it back up to the lobby and into the pod station. It looked like a mini movie theater. And more importantly, the lights were on!

"Everything looks secure," Alan said.

"Well…The auxiliary power is working," Tim said. "But that doesn't mean it's safe." He didn't want to go in this thing at all.

Alan and Sally sat inside and strapped themselves down while Tim reluctantly followed. On the side of the seats was a remote control to operate the pod. They all pressed the same floor and like clockwork the pod activated.

A calm female electronic voice spoke through the speaker system, "Welcome to the City Center. You have entered the Elepod, one of the fastest and safest modes of transportation available. Please fasten your seat belts and enjoy the ride."

The pod took off slowly but then shot up like a bullet. It was actually a surprisingly smooth ride.

Outside things were boiling. The red swirl had *finally* reached its breaking point! The first reaction came from far, far away in the volcano and spread through the clouds in the form of electromagnetic light beams. The light spread through the cracks of the clouds and shined down its rays in an instant. The planet's entire sky lit up like a Christmas tree.

Once the power reached the swirl it shot down in one massive strike, illuminating the entire city. Every billboard and every electronically powered piece of equipment was activated. This effect only lasted for a few seconds however. The surge ignited everything and blew off the outer shell of every building and facility in the city, glass or concrete. The center building had glass surrounding every inch. When it blew, the shards from its windows covered a good mile around.

The power surge infested its way into the building and shut off everything, including the auxiliary power. Alan, Sally and Tim were stuck in the dark.

"Oh shit," Tim said, freaking out. "I knew it. Why did I come with you guys?"

"Oh shut up!" Sally shouted.

Tim desperately tried to activate the pod again by mashing every button on the control panel. "I knew this was a stupid idea," Tim mumbled.

Alan calmly got up and looked around. Like every elevator he'd ever seen, there was an escape hatch above them. With no other option left, he climbed out and helped to pull Sally up while Tim pushed from underneath.

"There's a door right here," Alan said while looking at the half opened door just above his head.

Unfortunately, the door wouldn't open.

Chapter 28

The problem outside was escalating in the harshest of ways. The large funnel above the City Center inverted downwards and began the second reaction of the storm. It came down in the form of a tornado, the largest one yet! Its massive size covered the City Center building entirely! But this was no ordinary tornado; it was a vortex of destruction.

First, a wave of black smog loomed from the giant twister and seeped into every crevice and every corner of the city. The people on the freeway watched in horror as the black smog smothered the city and continued outward. An eerie calm immediately followed the smog and all of the isolated tornadoes and lighting tangents ceased after the smog had passed.

Second, came a wave of devastation. Everything outside of the tornado fell subject to the wrath of this cyclone's destructive power. It ravaged everything in its path! Entire buildings were shredded into tiny particles within seconds. Landscapes were reshaped instantly. The people watching didn't even know what was coming until it was over them, and like that... they were no more. The fog and its wave of apparent annihilation spread far beyond the city, to what seemed no end. The trek of this brutality led back to the volcano where the storm originated, and changed everything in its path just as predicted!

The tornado shook the City Center vigorously, but it did not destroy it. This was about the only thing left relatively untouched by the cyclone's burst of destruction... for now at least. Alan, Tim, and Sally were still trying to get out of the elevator shaft when the second reaction hit. Thankfully, wires didn't hold the elevator pod; it was floating on a propulsion system. Also to their luck, the power being cut didn't affect the elevator pod... however, the vigorous shaking did. The building shook so hard that the pod actually cracked, damaging the propulsion jets beneath it.

"Got it!" Alan yelled in the nick of time.

He climbed through the door and turned around to help the others... but he only had Sally by the arm when the pod fell beneath them. Tim tried desperately to hold on to something, but inevitably free fell into the darkness... and to his death below.

"Give it up kid. I'm not worth it. Go find your friend," Sally cried as she dangled by the arm.

Alan, of course, didn't listen to this nonsense; he pulled her up with every morsel of strength left within him. She was amazed.

"Thanks kid. You got spirit, I'll give you that."

Alan feared the worse for the people below. There was within him a strange sense of doom for anyone away from his position. They were midway up and the building wouldn't last much longer. What he didn't know was this was the only thing left on the planet!

He remembered the words of the man in the city of water, *"The way out is probably somewhere in the city."* Alan of course was not leaving until he found Amy.

"What the hell happened?" Sally asked.

"I'm not sure," Alan replied with a now curious look on his face.

They traveled over to the outer rooms of the building and opened a door. They were both shocked to find the entire outer rim of the building gone, torn off in the initial strike. Even worse was the black swirling tornado surrounding the building. Alan managed to pull Sally back just before the door was yanked off its hatches and sucked into the tornado. The winds were atrocious, but somehow they managed to get away. They ran quickly to the staircase realizing the severity of the situation.

Alan looked below and saw a strange looming black smog reeking havoc on the building one floor at a time. He then knew that he had made the right decision.

All of those people, he thought.

He looked above and saw that he had a good hundred flights left to go. "Come on," he said to Sally with determination.

Alan was forced to move slowly due to Sally's health condition and she was about as fast as a horse with three legs.

"Why don't you just go without me, son."

"I'm not leaving you behind no matter what you say, so you better just get used to me helping you out," Alan said putting a smile on Sally's face.

The way up the stairs was long and tedious. Both of them felt the end in some shape or form inevitably coming. The only question now was how and with whom.

"Why don't you tell me about this girlfriend of yours," Sally said trying to calm her mind.

Alan smiled at the sound of the word *girlfriend*. He didn't know what to call Amy, other than someone he genuinely loved, but girlfriend would suffice.

"She has dark hair, she's fairly tall, and very pretty. She has the most graceful smile. Her eyes could melt the North Pole… she really hates to be helped, kind of like you." Something clicked in Alan and within Sally.

"Sounds like me when I was younger," Sally said as she thought about her youth.

Alan was starting to see it. *It has to be her*, he thought. "Her name is Amy. Does that name do anything for you?"

"The name no, but what you described sounds a lot like me when I was a young woman. I was so beautiful… Oh, the places I've seen, the people I've met. You would have loved me then. I had guys all over me when I was your age. You couldn't have resisted I know… I know… but now… now I'm just old and wrinkled."

This is definitely her, Alan thought. "So have you seen who I'm looking for?" Alan said trying to bring out the inner Amy.

Sally rambled on, "I haven't had someone looking for me in a while. I think they all forgot. Oh, who blames them? I wouldn't come looking for me either."

She was going on a tangent in her mind.

What the hell is she talking about? he wondered. "I'm sorry but—"

She began crying from the feelings of abandonment. "Oh, it's ok. I understand. Everybody leaves me."

"We don't have much time. Amy is that you?"

"Amy? Who the hell are you talking to?"

"Amy, if it's you snap out of it!"

He grabbed her by the shoulders vigorously, trying to bring Amy out, and Sally smacked Alan right in the cheek.

"Have you lost your mind son? Obviously I'm not who you're looking for."

"I'm sorry. I thought… You really wouldn't understand."

Alan was semi confident that this woman was the outer shell of Amy. But he was *not* positive however. They continued up the stairs, but when Alan had an idea they suddenly stopped moving.

"Why did you stop?" Sally asked.

"Maybe think about the description I gave you. Close your eyes and see the image of the girl I described."

"Boy, have you lost your damn mind?"

"Please… this," he thought of something clever, "… this might help you to remember."

Sally closed her eyes and visualized. Alan looked at her intensely waiting for something to happen but they only had minutes before the deadly smog below reached them.

"See if you can remember being in a few places like a neighborhood or a city made of water. Remember when you first woke up in the forest with me stand—"

She opened her eyes sharply. Something sparked within her.

"Oh, wait a second. I remember now," Sally said exciting Alan. "I saw that girl here yesterday."

He was shocked. *How can she have...?* "You mean you're not..."

"She was upstairs looking for a way out," Sally continued. "I forgot to tell you, I work in this building. I see most everybody that comes through here."

Sally began coughing viciously.

"Are you ok?"

She raised a hand while continuing hacking a lung up. "I'm sorry," she let out a few more hacks, "I'm sorry, I'm not doing too good anymore." She lifted her head up and nearly fell over from the dizziness. "Uh. Uuhh. I feel horrible. I'd better go lay down."

"No!" He realized how loud he shouted, "No please. Just tell me where I can find her. Please."

Without her Alan had no clue how to find Amy.

"I think she's still up there. They probably locked her in a room and forgot about her when they evacuated."

At that moment another wave of vigorous shaking vibrated the building and knocked them to their knees. Alan peered over the rail and saw the black fog only a few floors below.

"Come on!"

Alan lifted her back up and hoisted her on his shoulders. His determination was set and no storm would stop him from reaching Amy.

"Calm down boy, you're so anxious all the time."

"Sally, we don't have any more time."

"You're always worried about time. You need to relax a bit."

"I don't think you understand. This whole town is being ripped apart."

"This town needed to be torn apart years ago. All of the people are so fake and trapped in their own little world. Frankly, I'm glad it's all over."

These words were frustrating Alan. It was like she wanted to just give up and keel over.

"Why are you so anxious to die?"

"No reason to live anymore. Everything that I owned was in my apartment. I lost my life when I left there."

"Life is much more than a few things. What good are they if you're not alive anyway?"

Sally looked at Alan and realized that he was right. Something she rarely did.

Chapter 29

Miraculously, Alan's grim determination gave them a few minutes ahead of the black smog. After traveling more than one hundred flights of stairs they finally reached the floor used to house temporary prisoners. He kicked in the door and looked around like a crazed maniac. Sally was running out of energy however. She stumbled to the ground coughing and wheezing. She was dying.

"Sally! There's no time! Please try."

She laid on the ground in misery. "She'd be... in the back," Sally said with a raspy voice.

Alan ran as hard and as fast as he could to the back rooms. There were so many narrow hallways and doors. He had only the option of checking them all!

"Damn it!"

Room after room, door after door, Alan relentlessly searched for Amy, but nothing turned up, no trace of anybody.

"Come on! She has to be in here somewhere!"

He ran to one last and final room, thinking that this one had to be it, and opened the door... it was, of course, empty. He knew in his mind that he should start figuring a way out but the emotional pull was too strong for him to feel motivated. Everything he felt had led him up here, but there was nothing to be found. Alan felt so confused, and once again, lost.

"What?" Alan asked under his breath. "*What* am I supposed to do?" He was feeling angry now, angry and betrayed by his own feelings. With every ounce of that anger he punched a hole in the door and began shedding tears. "Where is my answer now?" he shouted. "If everything happens for a reason, then why am I here?"

There was no answer, simply silence. The building shook a few more times but this didn't faze Alan. He was prepared to go down with it all.

What did I do wrong...? What was I supposed to see...? I felt as if I was supposed to come up here... I did what I felt I should do... Why am I not seeing what I should see...?

From behind, Alan heard a loud thump, and for a second he thought that it was Amy, but to his dismay, it was Sally.

"The...dust..." she tried getting out. Alan grabbed Sally and held her up. "Did you... find her...?" She nearly passed out.

There was something about seeing this old woman dying in his arms that reminded him that this journey was not about getting what he wanted, it was about seeing the truth of what came to him. He thought about her life and how the things she'd accumulated consumed her. Alan knew that that wasn't what life was about.

If I know that, then how can I give up now?

This thought gave Alan the motivation to press on to the very top; it was all that was left.

"Come on Sal, wake up. Wake up please!"

"You have to... go without me."

"Come on! Please give it a try. It's worth it, trust me."

"No... it's not worth it... I'm useless... my life was... lived a long time ago."

"Life is here, now. It's not some image of having a *life*. You are life!"

Sally took these words to heart and managed to squeeze an ounce of health back into her bones.

"If only I," she let out another coughing tangent. "...had met you before," she said feeling a little better.

Alan grabbed her from underneath her shoulders and carried her the rest of the way.

"You're coming with me!"

"Well! You don't give up do you?"

They scurried to the staircase only to be met with the black smog.

"You've done good trying to help me, but it doesn't look like there's anywhere left to go." Her violent coughing erupted once again and her body didn't have any more reserves of preservation. "I'm sorry... about your... your friend. I... I thought she was still up here."

Sally dropped to the ground and began losing consciousness.

"Amy. Is it you?" he spoke softly in Sally's ears.

Alan was hoping with one last chance that Amy would come out of this old woman.

"No kid... I'm sor... sorry." These were Sally's last words. She died in Alan's arms.

"Damn it," he said while tears came flowing out of his eyes.

The tears weren't really because he didn't find Amy, they were because he genuinely cared for the woman in his arms. At that moment, Alan noticed that something changed within him. He, for the first time, saw someone from this world as more than just an obstacle in his path. When he first started this journey he didn't really view these people as much. There was only he and Amy traveling in the land of lost souls, but now he saw something in these individuals. There was more than the superficial exterior they thought themselves to be. Even more, he saw within, how even he, with his disdain for society and its fakeness, had identified with *not* identifying. Even more humbling was the fact that, despite all of the realizations and all of the awakenings, he was still the same as everyone else, in most respects. With that realization came complete understanding of the cycle of life, and more important, acceptance.

Alan didn't know what to do by this point. So he decided to carry Sally's body with him to the top floor. By now the black smog covered him completely, leaving him to feel his way to the top. He could feel the smog eating away at everything around him, the rails, the walls, and even the remnants of Sally. He was so concentrated on getting out that he didn't feel the body in his arms get lighter. When he kicked down the door to the roof, a cloud of the black smog billowed out before him.

The first thing he noticed was that he was inside of a monstrous sized tornado surrounding the entire building; it was both a splendorous and terrifying sight. The second thing he saw was the clear skies above. It was actually daytime. And last but not least… he was delighted… to find Amy, not Sally, lying unconscious in his arms. He looked at her so confused yet so grateful, everything he was looking for and needed was with him the whole time. For a second he felt silly.

How many times do I need to have this happen before I realize I'll always be ok? he thought with a tear of joy rolling down his cheek. "Wake up! Amy!"

With only seconds before the storm collapsed and devoured them and the rest of the building, Alan covered Amy and cleared his thoughts. He felt within his body from head to toe, feeling the energy of life within. His tears fell softly upon Amy's gentle face and he leaned in to kiss her, as if for the last time.

From somewhere deep inside she could feel his presence and woke up to the most pleasant of feelings. She opened her eyes with a blissful look and kissed back with equal intensity. Immediately, a wave of light illuminated, from them on out, the entire city in a bright splendorous light! In the passion of the moment and the joy of being, she wrapped her arms around him.

It turned out that the storm was not destructive, only manipulative. The inhabitants, for once in their existence on this strange planet, saw their surroundings in its true form, unstable and constantly changing. And for the first time, the people were able to see beyond the concepts they had been trapped by for so long. Some of them halfway expected this to happen, while the others were completely dazzled and forced to evolve!

Alan and Amy seemed to be floating on a large bed of light. Above them, they could see the sky open up as the clouds from the storm dissipated. Alan looked up at the three suns that were coincidentally centered directly above! In that instant their luminosity lit a thousand fold, only the light shined in the form of a perfect triangle!

Everything around Alan and Amy became light as well. It was much like when Alan first explored beyond the regions of his known universe. The area seemed to shrink and expand infinitely at the same time. They were soon surrounded in the comfort of pure light. It became apparent that they were no longer standing on solid ground; they were floating. They could not help but laugh and cry simultaneously. The joy of the experience was too intense to hold in.

"What is happening?" Amy asked.

"I don't know."

Alan laughed as he remembered this being one of their first conversations together. He also remembered feeling this way many times through this strange journey and wondered if that was the point of the journey in the first place.

"Why? Why do we feel this good right now?" Amy asked with a blissful smile on her face.

"I don't know. Does it matter?"

This time the feeling was not intensified by the power of an outward flow of energy; it all came from within. They felt great to be alive. Alan thought about where he was and remembered going through this once before. He stuck his hands out like he did at the beginning of the journey and ran his hands across a familiar surface. It was, of course, a door leading to the blue room. Alan gladly pressed against the door and they both stepped beyond the light.

Chapter 30

The blue room was the same as it had been when Alan first arrived. People were still walking around amazed and in wonder. The guides were talking to first-time travelers as they searched for some answers. There was still the endless library on one end, a large golden door at the other and many small doors along the edges of the room, one of which Alan and Amy were walking through.

Alan noticed that they did warp back to the center of the room and he found this perplexing. The whole time he thought that the three suns where a symbolic representation of the triangle in the center of this room. *Maybe they were.*

"What is this place?" Amy asked, awestruck.

"The beginning," Alan replied with a fair amount of uncertainty.

He really didn't know what this room was, all he knew was that it led you to where ever and whenever you wanted to go. Alan noticed a woman stepping into the center triangle and activating the outer pillars of light. He wondered if this woman would go to the same place he went to or if she would be taken some place else.

"Looks like somebody had some fun," said a familiar voice from behind.

They turned around to find a face that Alan was very happy to see, Wu Ming's. This man was the only person Alan had met in this experience who knew some answers and he knew how to take Alan home, a place Alan now wanted to go back to.

"I don't really understand," Alan said. Wu Ming simply smiled at Alan. He knew what Alan was going to say before the words came out of his mouth. "Was what I went through real?"

Wu turned to Amy who was barely paying attention to the conversation. When she caught all eyes on her she snapped out of the wonder.

"What?" she asked without a clue.

Alan knew what Wu Ming referring to; the experience had to have been real on some level because Amy had come back with him, but then there was the next question Alan was prone to ask.

"Is this real now?"

Wu Ming responded at first with laughter. "That's up to you."

Amy was lost. She had no clue as to what they were talking about. The entire experience was unreal in her opinion, only now had she truly given it some thought to if it were real on some level.

"What is going on? Where are we?" she asked.

Alan laughed as he heard the familiar question he once asked not too long ago.

Just as Wu Ming prepared to speak, Alan answered for him, "This was all meant for us. We've been in the same spot the whole time. We've just been looking outside for answers. All we ever had to do was look within."

"But why? Why am I even out here and how do we get home?"

Amy was concerned with returning, though she felt on some level much more relaxed and not quite so anxious to return.

Wu Ming smiled and chuckled a bit. "It looks like you've found your way home."

At first Amy didn't get it. She looked around wondering what the hell he was talking about, but then it clicked, she realized he was referring to within. Once before, she would have laughed at all of this *philosophical nonsense* but now these words of wisdom had some meaning for her.

"I wonder why you don't remember coming to this room," Alan said to Amy.

Wu Ming knew why and placed a gentle hand on Amy's shoulder. "Like I said to you Alan, it takes a certain level of awareness to make it this far. This one just needed to be shown the way," Wu Ming referred to Amy.

"What about when we go home? Our physical homes I mean. Has time changed?"

Amy thought about Alan's question and something deep within her triggered, she didn't know what, but there was something speaking from within her.

"Time is an observation. At this level of consciousness there is no difference from what is to what will be. It's all right now. This applies to the world you're used to more than anything," Wu Ming said.

Amy was still feeling lost among other things. "But… what was the need to see all of this? Couldn't there have been an easier way to go through it?"

"That depended on you. Does life need a point to exist?"

That's a good question, she thought.

She realized that questioning *why* really just led to another question. The truth was always in front of them, they simply needed to *open their eyes*, so to speak.

Alan looked around at the doors, the dome, and the triangle. So many directions and so many possibilities, it didn't seem to matter what way he took in the first place. "How do we get home? I mean our… you know what I mean."

Wu Ming laughed and walked them over to the large golden door at the end of the room. Alan and Amy looked at it amazed by its magnificent design and craftsmanship. It seemed to be made of solid gold and polished to a mirror shine. Strangely, the reflection of the door was not that of Amy, Alan, or Wu Ming, it was a movie of someone's life. The film first started at birth and then moved through the individual's childhood.

"That's me!" Amy shouted.

They were watching Amy's life from her first steps all the way to her first days of school, and beyond. Alan was enjoying this footage; even the embarrassing moments that Amy wished had not been played. The voice inside of her began nudging again; it was trying to tell her something. Alan turned to her and noticed that she was deep in thought.

"You ok?"

"Yeah, there's just something bothering me and I can't think of what."

"Well… I guess all that's left is remembering your address. I mean me remembering *your* address."

They both smiled and once again entangled for long a passionate kiss, but the inner nudging was bothering her even more now.

"There's something…" she mumbled.

She looked at the movie within the door, which was in her middle school years, and reached out to touch the surface. Her hand passed through it like so many of the reflections they had encountered. The urge to press on was intense and Amy obeyed the feeling.

"Amy, don't!" Alan yelled.

But it was too late. She was gone. The last thing Alan wanted to do was become entangled in another journey but he had once gone to the edge of existence to reach Amy and he was not about to lose her now, not when they were so close to going home and living out their normal lives. Alan looked at Wu Ming who was simply watching the movie. He was waiting for Wu to say something, but the guide simply looked at Alan, waiting for him to make his own decision. Alan hesitated for only a second more before running through the door to retrieve his love.

Chapter 31

At first, there was only a dark blur with some muffled sound, but light soon shed upon the scene. He was at Amy's fourteenth birthday party. There were about twenty girls sitting around eating pizza and yapping away about boys. Amy was in the center fantasizing about calling up a young man she had a crush on for years.

"Amy," Alan said.

No one could see nor hear him. He had no clue as to how he was going to find the real Amy so he simply walked around the house. When he passed through rooms he was transported to another time in Amy's life. This time he was in the middle of an argument Amy and her mother were having. It was about Amy's grades in school and whether she was doing good enough to get into college. She was eighteen at the time.

When Alan walked out of that room he was taken to a party at some frat house. There he saw Amy in present form drinking with some guy. She had the same clothes, the same hair, and the same snappy facial expressions.

Alan tried getting her attention but she could not see him. Amy and the intoxicated drone she was speaking to walked upstairs and into one of the dorm rooms. Alan feared the worse but by this point he figured he would wait to see what happened before jumping to conclusions. So he ran up behind them to find out what would happen.

They entered a bedroom, with no one else inside of it, and sat on the bed. The frat boy took the drink from Amy's hands and set it down on the table. There he began *putting the moves* on her. But she was not going for it. After a few pathetic attempts of the *jerk* trying to take her shirt off, Amy left the boy pissed off on the bed. Alan followed her as she stumbled her way out of the house, but when he passed through the front door he was transported to another scene.

Before his eyes was a winding road covered in snow. There wasn't much out in these parts other than ice, trees, and more ice. Alan could only think of what he was going to see next but then… a deer crossed in front of him. Oddly, the animal was able to *see* Alan. He walked up to the kind creature and went to pet it, that's when the deer took off forward. It was as if it were leading him somewhere. They ran around the curved road for more than a hundred yards until finally the deer stopped.

What now?

The deer took off into the woods to the right.

O-K.

But then, Alan noticed something ahead, on the road. There was a fresh path in the snow made by a vehicle. When Alan saw the tire tracks leading off of the road and into the lake his stomach fell beneath his knees. But he was quickly uplifted as he saw Amy standing by the side of the lake watching her car sink into the water.

"Thank God," he said to himself.

She turned around when she heard his voice.

"Alan!" she said in a panic.

Alan was a little thrown off by the fact that she could see him, but he was simply happy to see that she was still alive.

"My God, I thought you…"

That's when it hit him. If she could see him that meant this was the real Amy… and the past Amy was probably somewhere in the vehicle. Amy stood watching her car sink into the lake while remembering what happened that night. She clung to Alan's arm as she shrieked from the scene. Alan was too devastated to watch the rest.

"Don't look. Just don't look," he said in a futile attempt to comfort her.

To the right was a wall of light leading back to the blue room. They both sadly entered. Alan gave Wu Ming a depressed nod and then hung his head again.

"Wait a minute! If I go back now I can call an ambulance," Alan said in the heat of excitement.

She was at first enthused about the idea but she then remembered he lived in Michigan.

"You can't do that. You're hundreds of miles away."

"No. All I have to do is call an ambulance. They can find you no matter what state *I'm* in. I just have to go home and call!"

This gave her hope. Some part of her mind believed it could work.

"You know, that's probably why I didn't remember coming out here. We have to do it quick though. The water is freezing and I probably won't last that long."

That's when something clicked in Alan. Something about her entire life movie had bothered him; something about the way it felt. There were some things that just didn't fit, like a cassette tape she received as a present on her fourteenth birthday party; it was a *New Kids on the Block* album. Though it was only a small detail, he knew that the group had long since been gone by *his* fourteenth birthday, and he and Amy were roughly the same age… he thought.

"What year is it?" Alan asked with a depressing suspicion.

"Ninety-nine, why?" she asked with no clue as to what he was getting at.

Amy had just confirmed his worst fear. Alan stood frozen, unable to even blink.

"What year is it for you?" she reluctantly asked.

"Two-thousand and six."

Alan was speechless. He didn't know what to say. Amy was at a loss for words as well. She turned to Wu Ming who looked at her with the most comforting eyes.

"But that doesn't mean you're dead... Does it?" Alan was reaching for hope.

They both knew what had happened and they both knew that the only thing they could do was accept the reality. Alan held Amy's hand, desperately wishing that it was all just an illusion, but it wasn't. All that was left between them was the background noise of the room and an odd feeling of loss.

"I don't want to lose you," Alan said, being the first to break the awkward silence.

"I'm so sorry Alan. I forgot all about that night. Everything was a blur and it all happened so quickly. The last thing I remembered was the night before and after falling asleep I woke up next to you."

"You didn't do anything wrong." Alan was calming down from the initial shock. He knew on some inner level that this too was ok.

"Death is not the end of life. It simply opens a gateway into a whole new experience," Wu Ming said.

These words were now obvious truths to Alan and especially to Amy. Knowing that her body was gone and she was still, in all essentials, *her*, calmed her mind down. She felt relaxed and free of all the burdens her life pressed upon her. She still missed her family, but something within her let her know she would always be close to them. She noticed within her a split. There was her mind, which wanted to be sad and fearful for all the loss it believed to have sustained, and then there was the ever-growing presence, the rising consciousness. This presence was intrinsically connected to the power that created the universe and everything beyond it. She also strangely noticed that she was not burdened by the weight and heaviness of a body. It was as if a simple realization changed everything about her. The form she always knew to be her now felt like a pale reflection of collected memories. Instantly her face began glowing her hands were as soft as a feather. Alan looked at her and knew that she was changing into a formless being. The feelings of loss within him began thickening again.

"Everything is ok. You've helped me to see far beyond anything I ever could've seen, even with physical eyes," Amy said, for once trying to ease his mind.

The three of them chuckled at the joke but Alan could not help but shed tears.

"You were the main reason I wanted to return home," he said.

"I know. I wanted the same, but this is the reality. Most people will never have a chance to see life beyond their concept of it. You have to guide others as you have guided me. Help them to 'die' before they are dead... Help them let go."

Alan knew that this was his outer purpose in life and now he felt equipped to do the job.

"I wonder if I'll ever see you again," Alan said.

"I'm sure we'll find each other. One way or another."

Alan was pleased to hear the confidence in her voice. She turned to Wu Ming, who was calmly waiting for her to ask a question he most frequently was asked when someone left the physical realm.

"What do I do now?" she asked right on time.

"Like I said, death is an opening to a gateway. You must choose to walk through it."

He opened the large golden door and that luminous blinding light shined in once again. This light captured the entire room.

"Where will this take me?"

"Where ever you want to go, if you're ready," Wu Ming replied.

She nodded her head and smiled at the calm guide. Amy turned to Alan and embraced him one last time. They both felt the warmth of love transferred between them as if it were a tangible substance. Alan brushed his cheek against hers for the last time and stared her in the eyes. There was so much said between them without words. The moment seemed to last forever.

But after a few minutes they both felt as if it were time. Even as they separated Alan could feel her next to him. Amy turned towards the source of the light and continued her journey... into the purest state of consciousness. Alan watched with a smile on his face and tears rolling from his eyes. After a few moments Wu Ming closed the door and the room returned to normal.

Alan took a second to collect within, and then finally turned to Wu Ming. "So, where's my door."

"This way."

They walked across the room and looked into the ceiling, which was filled with total darkness. Alan was shocked.

"I thought..." he didn't finish the sentence.

Wu Ming was raising his eyebrow waiting to see if Alan understood what he was *saying*, and he did.

"Are you sure you're ready to return?"

Alan looked into the darkness with a look of concern. "There's nothing there."

"Oh there's plenty there. You just have to let it unfold."

These words of wisdom put a smile on Alan's face. He remembered a wise man he met on his path telling him to enter the darkness and wondered if this was what he spoke of all along.

"What happens when I go home? What should do?"

Wu Ming gave him a smile followed by silence and Alan completely understood once again. He looked at Wu and reached out for a handshake. Wu Ming gratefully complied. Alan took one more look at the Akashic Library and wondered if he should leave it behind just yet.

"Can I return to this place?" Alan asked.

"I'm sure you'll find a way back sooner or later," Wu said with a smile.

Alan slowly stepped onto the triangle and was once again beamed into the darkness. Wu Ming, with a joyful smile on his face, watched as Alan dissipated into nothing.

Chapter 32

A low frequency vibration sent ripples of energy through Alan. He didn't know where he was but he felt, now more than ever, close to home. The vibrations riveted through him, increasing in strength, until finally his body was at a constant state of energy flow. He felt that incredible feeling of vibrant aliveness and infinite energy.

Alan reached his hands out, wondering if he'd touch another door but there was nothing. It wasn't until Alan felt something beneath him, pulling him in, that he realized he was headed somewhere. Alan looked below and found a thin silver cord connecting him to something too far away to be seen. The darkness had depth after all. Alan pulled at the cord and was sent into hyper drive towards its other end. In the blink of an eye he found himself floating nearly two hundred feet above his home.

Alan thought about his body and this thought carried him the rest of the way. Everything happened on autopilot. He passed through the roof, entered his room and twisted around and settled his way back to the physical reflection of himself. His vision matched the position of where his physical eyes were located and Alan noticed something strange. He was seeing through two sets of eyes. One set of eyes was closed while the other was open. When Alan felt reconnected with his body he decided to open his physical eyes. When he did everything was realigned. He tried closing his eyes to see if he still had double vision but that phenomenon had passed.

That sucks, he thought jokingly.

Things felt different. He didn't really appreciate the lack of true body weight until he was back in his physical body. He felt sluggish and far more confined, but with a stretch and a yawn he was on his way to readjusting. It had, after all, been quite some time since he'd been in control of his physical body.

He wondered if time in this realm had passed since he left, so he checked out the clock; it was four-o-five in the morning. He remembered the last time he looked at the clock it had just turned three.

Not much has changed here it seems.

He took notice to the window, which was still open, and a slight chill ran through his body. As he got up to shut the window he paused, wondering if he was really experiencing what he was experiencing. As he turned to look at his bed he felt satisfied with the apparent answer. The sheets were moved and there was no body lying down.

Epilogue

A couple of weeks had passed since Alan's initial out-of-body experience. Since then he experienced five more, but never traveling to alternate universes; he kept it local. Along with his newfound hobby, it turned out that Alan had an exceptional gift for communicating with others and showing them how to see beyond their mind-made problems.

He saw everything in a new light, even the ignorance in the people around him. He always knew that they were part of a large system, blindly living through their lives, but what he now saw was that he too, in some way, was part of the same process. He finally realized that the only way to make a real difference was not to fight against, but to help those who were lost within the ego of human thinking.

His stroll through downtown was no longer filled with the constant judgments and analytical mental remarks he once was forced to think about. He was now a free man in so many words. He felt this freedom all the way to Doc's office with an inner smile. As he walked in, the young receptionist barely paid attention to him, she simply waved her hand for him to keep going into the office. Alan noticed that this girl was having a particularly bad day. There was tissue everywhere and her eyes were glassy from the overflow of tears. In previous visits their communication was pretty shallow and always brief. Alan was there to talk about his problems and she was there to talk on the phone and get paid. She was one of those popular girls Alan was attracted to and hated at the same time. This time, however, he figured he'd take the extra step to talk to her, to try really communicating.

"How are you?" Alan asked.

The girl didn't notice that Alan was talking to her. Alan walked to the counter and waited calmly for her to answer. She looked at him surprised.

"I'm sorry, were you talking to me?" she asked with a surprised look on her face.

"Yeah," he answered simply.

She cleaned off the collection of tear rags and tossed them into the trashcan, while wiping her face off.

"I'm good. I'm ok... I guess... Why?" she asked wondering why he had interest.

Alan thought about saying something smooth to her for a quick second but realized that *acting* was useless. He would try a different approach.

"I've been coming here for about a year and we've never really said more than five words at a time to each other. That's kind of sad," Alan said. She was at first thrown off by his frankness but it made her laugh. "Are you ok?" he asked.

She looked around and realized that he knew she was crying. "Oh yeah. It's just some dumb boy. You know, girl stuff."

"Don't hate the guy. We're all a little ignorant at times."

They didn't really know what to say after that so Alan bowed his head and continued on to his meeting. The girl watched him walk away and thought, *How strange... cute though.*

The first thing Alan did when he walked into Doc's office was set the book Doc gave him down on the table.

Doc looked at Alan a little taken back. "You didn't like the book?"

Alan laughed. "The book was *really* interesting, but I don't think I'll need it anymore."

Doc raised his eyebrows in shock. It was only a little bit ago when he first gave the book to Alan. "Well I guess I can't force you to read it," Doc said with a quirky smile.

"No, no, I don't think I'm going to have any troubles with the…" Alan thought about a clever way to insinuate his experience, "…techniques."

Doc knew at that moment that Alan had experienced something last night, something that changed him. He could see the change in Alan's eyes.

"So, you want to tell me what happened?"

"Not today. I want to take some time and…reflect upon what happened… I think I'm going to take a break from therapy. Actually I think this might be the last session. I feel like I'm done talking about my problems. I'd like to try something else."

Doc could see the change in this young man, much the same change that once happened to him a long time ago. "I'll tell you what… I'd like to continue our conversations. How about we meet every week and talk about *experiences* not problems, free of charge. I'm curious to hear where you've gone."

The smile on Doc's face indicated to Alan that he knew exactly what he just went through.

"I'd like that a lot," Alan said feeling a sense of male bonding between them.

As Alan left the office he nodded to the receptionist and exchanged smiles before he walked out. The little conversation they had was the most sincere she'd had in a long time… and she wanted more.

"Excuse me!" she said, instantly feeling the fear of making an ass out of herself.

Alan was surprised to hear her voice calling him back. He strolled backward and looked at her without anticipation and truly wanted to hear what she had to say.

"I was just thinking, I mean it's just a thought, but, you think, maybe, you'd like to... grab a bite to eat...? Some time, it doesn't have to be now, I mean... uh... yeah," she said, feeling extremely embarrassed for asking a guy out.

Alan's eyes comforted her. They made her feel as if it's ok to express herself even without him saying anything. Alan was at first reluctant to say yes. He had, after all, just lost someone close to him, but there was an inner nudge telling him to say yes. He looked within and then looked at the receptionist.

"I'd like that," he said feeling extremely good about his decision.

Alan accepted her number gracefully and then looked at her strangely. There was something familiar about this girl. "What's your name?" he asked.

"Sheri," she said with a smile.

Alan thought about the feeling for a second and then decided that he should not analyze what he felt. "I'm Alan. I'll give you a call," he said, returning a smile as he walked out.

As he made his way home Alan kept getting a strange feeling about the receptionist. There was something about her that he just could not place. He did what he could to not think about it, in hopes that an answer would come in his clarity, but nothing came.

The late hours of the morning pushed on to the afternoon and Alan felt an urge to meet Kyle at the library. So, acting on impulse, he put on a light jacket and headed out for his destination.

His parents were out in the garage cleaning, and in the midst of an argument. It was the same old fight, one person did this, the other did that, this person should feel bad for what they did, and that person should feel even worse for the things they'd done before that. It was an endless cycle of blaming and accusing; one Alan wanted no part of. As he walked into the garage they quieted down, like usual, and pretended nothing was wrong.

"Hey, hey, look who decided to come help us out," his dad said.

"Actually dad, I'm going to the library."

"What a coincidence," his mother said with much sarcasm.

Alan looked at them feeling the negativity floating in the air.

"I just wanted to thank you guys."

"Why?" his mom asked.

"I know you don't understand or agree with what I'm doing but you do allow me a certain amount of space and I want you to know how much I appreciate it."

Alan smiled with integrity and continued walking out. His parents were thrown off; their negativity was cut from its roots. They didn't know how to respond other than with smiles. His dad's smile was at first genuine but was soon covered with a *manly* sense of sarcasm in the face of sentiment.

Making his way through the mess in the garage, Alan accidentally knocked over a shoebox set on top of an old dresser. As it splattered onto the ground hundreds of pictures fell out and spread everywhere.

"Still groggy eh?" his dad said jokingly.

Alan started to pick up the pictures with the help of his parents. One picture in particular caught his eye. His jaw dropped and his eyes bulged as he looked at a very old picture of… the *Native American*. He was dressed in full headgear and native clothing.

"Who is this?"

"That's your great, great, maybe another great uncle. He was a medicine man for his tribe."

"He was also a shaman. He helped guide lost spirits to the path of freedom," his mom added.

Alan's dad sighed, as he did not believe in any of that "spirit stuff". Alan was shocked in disbelief and amazement.

"What's the matter?" his mom asked.

Alan simply shook his head. "Can I copy this?" he asked.

"Sure," his mom said.

Alan walked away shaking his head and chanting, "I can't believe it, I just can't believe it."

Alan's parents watched him as he walked away, wondering what the hell was so incredible.

Later on in the day, Alan was sitting down in the library researching old car accidents when Kyle met up with him. The bags in Kyle's eyes along with the pale face and smelly breath were indicators that Kyle had a horrible hangover. He really looked like shit.

"Dude. Don't ever start drinking."

"What happened to you last night?"

"I don't know. I went to this after-hours party and got trashed. When I woke up this morning I was naked next to what I think was a girl."

The girl at the computer next to them overheard the conversation and began giggling.

"Sounds like fun," Alan casually remarked.

"What did you end up doing? Were you banging your gurl-friend?" Kyle said in the most obnoxious tone.

Alan did not answer; he simply continued his search on the computer. He pulled up several archived newspaper articles on the archive files about car accidents that happened in 1999.

"What are you looking for?" Kyle asked.

"An old friend."

But then, he pulled up an old picture of a girl who froze to death somewhere in a suburb of Chicago.

"Is that her?"

Alan studied the picture with excitement. But for some reason he couldn't remember exactly what Amy looked like. "I don't think this is her."

"It's a shame she died. That chick was hot."

Alan paid little attention to his friend's ignorance and pulled out a picture of Sheri. Kyle felt foolish when his friend didn't react to his comment.

"Who is that?" Kyle asked.

"A friend."

He studied the pictures together but they looked nothing alike. The girl who died had features close to those of Amy's, but Alan didn't feel as if it were her. Sheri, on the other hand, looked nothing like Amy, but Alan still had a feeling there was more to Sheri than meets the eye.

"Dude, does what you're doing matter all that much?"

Alan looked at Kyle and laughed. He realized that he was right, though in a different sense than intended.

"You're a genius," Alan said as he closed down the computer.

"What do you mean?" Kyle asked.

"It doesn't matter who I think she is. She is who she is period... right?"

Kyle was confused. "I guess."

They walked out of the library and stood out front to finish up their conversation. Alan immediately took notice to the beauty of the sky while taking in a clean breath of fresh air.

"Dude, man. What is up with you?" Kyle asked. Alan simply looked at him with question in his eyes. "You're like... different. What you need is to come out with me and get laid by one of these sorority chicks."

Alan laughed, "I'm good."

"Really, check this out. I met these girls at the party last night. They were hot! Trust me. I told them I had a friend and they said they'd be down for hanging out tonight."

Alan laughed at the offer. He thought about how he would have taken his friend up on this not so long ago, but now he just simply didn't want to.

"Dude I'm telling you. You could get lucky tonight man, by some hot piece of—"

"I'm gonna pass. Thanks for considering though."

Kyle was in total shock. "What? Are you crazy? I mean they're hot dude! Hotter than those skanks you talked to at the coffee shop that one day, and they're easy too."

"Enjoy yourself."

"Cm-on. What are you doing today?"

Alan thought about his day. "I don't know." He knew absolutely nothing about it and loved every second of it.

Kyle looked at Alan stunned. "You aren't whipped already are you...? Come on you wuss... Dude it'll suck without you... Come on... Please." Kyle eventually stopped, realizing that he would not convince his old friend to go along.

Alan walked down the road and into the sunset knowing that for the rest of his life he would have the ability to make a choice on his path. More importantly, he was enjoying every step of the way!

Author Biography

A native of Detroit, Michigan, Marquis White was a young man looking for answers when he met a friend that introduced him to the possibility of leaving his body. One night, after months of studying out-of-body experiences, Marquis got up from his bed and noticed a strange feeling, like he was free and clear from the confines of what he considered reality. That's when he turned around and saw *his body* lying beneath him. Though the experience was fascinating and awe inspiring, Marquis came to the realization that no matter how far he could travel beyond his normal world, he would always have to return to deal with his personal life.

He spent years investigating and searching for the answers of the universe until finally realizing that all of the answers have always been and always will be within. He currently lives in Michigan with his wife Brittany.

Acknowledgments

In a world filled with chaos and ignorance it is a blessing to know that there are people out there who are taking the steps necessary to bring about change in the consciousness of the human mind.

Pam, once again, the help you've given me during the creation of this book and beyond was and is incredible. I can never thank you enough. I would like to thank John White, for your skill and creativity as an artist and for being one of the best uncles a nephew could have. I would also like to thank John Magnus, for taking the time to read my book and for giving some of the most insightful advice I could have received. And to the pioneers who travel into the unknown and unorthodox, because of people like you we are able to move past our conceptualized living and dare to live in a world that is blessed with uncertainty.

I would also like to give thanks to my friends and family: Grandma, Martha, Steven, Kelly, Esther, Jennifer (one and two), Mark, Mathew, Harry, Stuart, Sam K, David (Double D), Brian (Milky White), Ricky Mum, Terrance C, Mr. Farah, Mr. Rivetto, Mr. Russell, and countless others, you all have been a great help! And to the people who helped to make the O.B.E. demo. Your efforts will not be forgotten!

In loving memory of
Donald Todd
June 10, 1943 - Nov 20, 2006